Acclaim for Nathan Leslie's

A Cold Glass of Milk

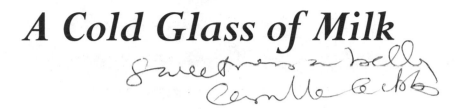

Deft and sly and subtle with woe, these are stories about a world gone loose and runny at the edge, a world as much of high hope as of low life, a world inhabited by the aggrieved, the mystified, and the needy. Mr. Leslie has the sensibility of a poet, keen to note the large in the slight, mindful of the power of the right word at the right time. Here's a collection that gets under the skin quickly and works its way inexorably toward the cockles of your heart. Read 'em, as the man says, and weep.

Lee K. Abbott

Leslie brings us many intriguing people in his quick and deep stories. Through layers of concrete and the uniformity of small town America old histories of immigrant ancestors lurk, and an irrepressible eros springs up to create a breathtaking view of various alienated characters. I have thoroughly enjoyed these exciting stories.

Josip Novakovic

Nathan Leslie is a most gifted writer, and A Cold Glass of Milk *is an impressive effort—original, inventive, and rich in tales that amuse, delight, and move.*

Jay Neugeboren

Published by

UCCELLI PRESS

PO Box 85394
Seattle, WA 98145-1394
Toll Free: (866) 206-2311
Email: pub@uccellipress.com
Website: www.uccellipress.com

Book Design: Toni La Ree Bennett

Cover Photograph: Toni La Ree Bennett

Author Photograph: Julie Newell

First Uccelli Press Printing, 2003
Printed in the United States of America.

ISBN: 0-9723231-1-2
Library of Congress Control Number: 2003112307

A COLD GLASS OF MILK

In addition to being nominated for a Pushcart Prize, Nathan Leslie's fiction and poetry have appeared in over eighty-five publications. He was the winner of the 1994 Chandler award for fiction, and the 2000 Katherine Anne Porter prize for fiction. *A Cold Glass of Milk* is Mr. Leslie's second book of short fiction. His first book of short stories, *Rants & Raves*, was published in January 2003.

Dedication

*This book is dedicated to the memory of
Ann Leslie and William Pfefferkorn.*

Acknowledgements

I'd like to thank the folks at The Writer's Center in Bethesda, and The MFA Program at The University of Maryland for their advice and support. I'd also like to especially thank Julie Newell and Matt Katz.

The stories in this volume originally appeared
in the following publications:

"A Cold Glass of Milk" in *Barkeater*, "Paige: The King of Taco Makers" in *Mystic River Review*, "Saving the Tree" in *Ranchmart*, "WAC: The Art of" in *Timber Creek Review*, "Yesterday was Rivet" in *Deeply Shallow*, "Amanita and Bolete" in *The Brown Dog Review*, "My April" in *Scribble*, "And Then We Can Decide" in *Fodderwing*, "Brown Datsun" in *Crab Creek Review*, "Beige is Nice and Regular" in *George and Mertie's Place*, "Bloodworms" in *Higginsville Reader*, "Sons and Daughters of Apostates" in *Madison Review*, "We're All From West Virginia Sometime" in *Unlikely Stories*, and "The Tender" in *Sulphur River Literary Review*.

Table of Contents

A COLD GLASS OF MILK

I don't know if this story is one you want to hear, but it's the only one I can think about right now. It was when I found out Henry Weis is one man I respect, and that's saying a lot.

My name's Phil Ames, and I'm thirty-two.

See, nothing seemed to be going right for me. My wife Greta and me, well, we'd been on the skids for half our lives. Most of it on me. That and we weren't even into middle age yet according to the numbers. One morning she got a fire under her, boy, cussing up a storm for all the things I didn't do. I mean, she had a point, but she could have waited till after my coffee and Raisin Bran. Damn woman.

"Phil, do the pipe would you?" she said.

"I'm going to do the pipe," I said into my cereal bowl.

She went to the fridge and got herself one of them big old oranges. Didn't get me one, you know. It was maybe ten in the morning and mist was rising up from the grass like we lived in goddamn England, and there she was, peeling that orange so the pulp sprayed into the air, smelling the place up.

"I've been asking you to do it for how long now?"

"What did I say? I'm going to do it." We were playing our usual chicken.

"You're all talk," she said. "'I'll do it honey. I'll do it this weekend, promise.' Then you're off to Bilbo's drinking and tossing them darts." Few months before I got myself some of them tournament quality darts, the kind you got to assemble the aluminum feathers into.

"Jesus, I can't do everything," I said. She had her back to me, not listening.

"Either that or you're up at the Y. Try using some of those fancy muscles you got there."

"Right," I said.

"That's right, that's right," she said. She had a point in there, but she couldn't just leave it at that.

"I know, I'm sorry," I said, but I was thinking *Boy, you're whipped*.

"Go ahead and think of yourself. Think of yourself."

"I'm going to do it," I said. Then I went to put a cap on, got a pair of work gloves. I was out there in a pissy mood when she left for work with her iced coffee and her fruit in a brown plastic bag.

Dig a garden out front, construct a walk through the garden, dig a drainage pipe so the garden don't float away. That woman's thumb was so green it was spreading to her brain. Anyhow, Greta was the one who was all talk. Five one and a half, cute little upturned nose, sandy hair, and lips puffy up front—there are reasons I ended up with her. But unfortunately them lips don't stop at puckering up; they also nag like no tomorrow.

See, I was out there digging because Greta had one on me: I had a thing with one of her friends a year or so back— this short woman named Gina with hair as long as her body— so there I was still paying my penance in hard labor. I get this way, guilty about things even if I don't want to. I can't help it: I have a woman problem, I guess. The way I saw it then, a man's got to have space to roam, and I guess I resented being chained up to a ring.

Anyhow, I did it again a few months before I was out there at the ditch trying to make amends. I was out at the Y with Greg one night hitting the weights when I saw this woman named Nell. Real bountiful, with nice dark hair, thin and wiry down past her shoulder blades. She was peddling on the exercise bike with them slippery black tights under her gray sweat shorts, forearms cocked on the handles, pressing the buttons, no ring.

"Look at those legs, man," Greg said. "It's like they're about to burst." Greg's a plumber buddy of mine. I was staring when we went walking through to the free weights. I'm telling you, the woman's legs were some rippling and muscular things, like them Clydesdales you see on the ads. This is my way: I find one thing in a woman I like and concentrate on it.

So we were doing curls, bench presses, and after a few rounds Greg hustled me up to her and asked her to come get with us after working out. She jumped for it, boy. Well, to make a long story short we were into each other real hot. Only I had no idea Nell was Greta's boss up at the *Times*, where Greta was doing hourly secretarial work at the time. I knew Nell worked up there 'cause she had a parking sticker on her bumper, but work didn't even come up with Nelly until the end. Anyhow, I had no idea. If I knew then what I know now I wouldn't have done nothing—I wasn't out to ruin things with my wife or nothing.

Me and Nell, we'd meet up in her place in Westminster. I'd stay an hour most, then shower and drive home with the windows open, chewing Twizzlers with the jungle music from Baltimore pumping. Well, all that lasted only a couple months. I ended things when I started getting bored, plus Nell had this damn skinny white cat that would jump up on the bed during our rumbling. She wouldn't let me lock the runt in the bathroom even if I'm allergic to them animals. When it was good, though, Nell and me hit it off good, real good. She had this smell to her I liked—pine trees or spruce or something—and her skin was darkish white like the color of that oatmeal soap Greta gave me last Easter instead of jellybeans. Nell was always playing the do-gooder, volunteering Saturdays for the damn crack-head shelter, all that.

But this story ain't about these women. It's about Mr. Weis and me, about how I left Finksburg and came down to West Friendship right across the Carroll border. I don't know; I guess I'm a no-good buffoon when it comes down to it, probably a bastard on top of all that, but at least I got some temporary relief.

So as I said, I got Greta fired when Nell and her put their pretty heads together one day; Nell didn't want no problems so that was bye-bye for Greta. Well, a week later my wife took up the distinguished profession of haircutting up at this Westminster joint, Dell's Cuttery. But before that we had it out, boy. She was out that Saturday organizing files and labeling for overtime. I was still busy out back digging her daggone drainage ditch when she came home. Slipping in that twenty feet of five-inch PVC, and covering it up with the dirt I dug—it was a drag. At five the next morning in the dew, I re-sodded the whole nine yards before she woke up. Couldn't leave a project hanging, even if Bill Phelps owned the property.

Anyhow, that afternoon Greta came home fired-up; I mean, besides the way she slammed the car door out front, I could just hear it in the way she walked. Thump. Thump. Thump.

"Asshole!" She chucked her red plastic Thermos at me, missed, then flipped her shoes off, threw them at me too, missing again. "Asshole!" She was kicking up my project with her bare feet like a pissed-off baseball manager, even if it was her idea. Dirt was flying up into the grass, and her hair was covered in it.

"Hey, hold on. What are you doing?"

"Screwing it up! Screwing up your hole," she said.

"Hey—" I walked up to her and reached for her hand slow, but she swung it away.

"Shut up!"

"It's your garden, man."

She stopped and looked at her feet all brown, then kept on kicking and screaming for a few minutes until she tired out and stood there staring at me dry-eyed and piercing. Then she dropped her arms straight to her waist, and fisted the fabric of her dress in and out of her hands.

"You got me fired. Now what? Now what are we going to do?" And at that she plopped down in the grass, brushing the hair off her face, and shaking the dirt out of her hair, crossing her legs with her chin poking into her chest like some little hippie girl. She had one of her few nice skirts on, this blue and black flowered thing which draped over her little legs and made her look so cute I wanted to hug her until my arms hurt. But nobody said nothing or even moved. She still wasn't crying, right. My wife ain't no sissy or nothing. Greta fought her way up from scratch. Alky parents had to give her up for adoption when she was eleven, and twenty years later she was still struggling with things of the past. Plus we had this whole issue of should we adopt or keep working at kids, never mind what Dr. Breen said about the likelihood of it all. I tried to support Greta, but sometimes I guess I let her down.

"Why did you do it?" she asked.

"I don't know what to—"

"Just don't. Okay? Jesus I can't believe it. I can't believe you," she said.

"Look—"

"I want to know why, of all the ones—"

"I didn't know—"

"Yeah right," she said.

"I swear, I didn't know where she worked." I was trying hard to look at her. But it was hard.

"Man, I'm really, really trying to make it," she said. I looked up and she was looking right at me, and it was then I realized I messed up in a way I couldn't take back. I felt real bad then, like I did it on purpose, like I cut her down because she was used to it.

"I'm sorry, I'm real sorry, Gret."

"Yeah." That was all she could say. "Yeah."

"That's all I can say, I'm sorry. I don't know." Long wait, then she spoke.

"'I didn't know where she worked.' God, Phil."

"I'm sorry." I didn't know what to say except that.

"I don't know," she said. "What now?"

It guess it really got to me. I felt about the lowest piece of crap on earth. So next morning after wrapping up the project, I picked up my box of music, tools, and a bag of clothes and went looking for a place with my $2,000 of savings, leaving her ten hundreds to cover the rent and things for a month until she got it settled. Don't trust them banks as far as I can throw them.

See, I was laid off a month prior. I had worked twelve years for that rotten potato chip factory up in Hanover; got to be a day shift foreman after three years. But they were letting folks go since the big boys announced the damn merger with that other company. Got to be really settled, renting that rancher in Finksburg, commuting up to Hanover like them people in Montgomery do down to D.C. I felt real nice, comfortable like a sitcom family or something, even if it was a potato-chip eating one. Then these things happened, which made me think of this story my mother used to read me when

I was a kid. It was about a reed and an oak tree, only the reed was the stronger one 'cause it could adjust. Well, I guess I was an oak then.

Driving south about an hour, I was looking for work. Didn't turn up much. First I drove to shopping centers off Routes 26 and 40, looking for colorful flyers taped up to store windows, or on them green community bulletin boards, but I didn't find nothing. I almost brought myself to use the classifieds at High's, but somehow it reminded me too much of what I did, so I kept on driving.

Then off 32 there was a road called Weis Road. I liked the name, so I turned off there just driving, looking. I kept thinking, God, I love this land. That morning I went rolling over the hills through the sun and I could smell the fresh-turned soil, manure and grass clippings, and looking at the land two-months seeded brought my mind back to when I was a kid living in Lewistown. My grandfather owned a little farm out that way, and me and the family would go and visit and do a little farming on the side, and one summer we had a plot out back with beans and cherry tomatoes, but it's something I didn't know much about. He's gone now and my own parents too, five years back. My damn Uncle James got the farm if you can believe it.

So back a few miles the road dead-ended right at this big old white farm house newly painted with red window sills, plus there was some cars and pickups parked out front, and a sheep dog wandered around the porch. The address was 7970 in red hanging over the porch on a curved wood plank, and right on the door was *WELCOME* painted with each letter in a different color, like a kid's kindergarten rainbow. After all I'd been through it made me smile, boy, so I did something I wouldn't do normally—I parked in the gravel driveway, and walked on up and knocked on the door. I was thinking maybe they know of some work or a place to park myself for a few months.

I waited for a long time, not hearing nothing, then knocked again. Then I heard feet on the wood floor, and the voice told me to hold on. The door opened. Well, it was a female, as if I didn't have enough of them things. The girl was maybe twenty, curly blondish hair pulled back in a pink band, and big floppy eyes cute as a button. She was a little chunky up front with a short neck and a man's shoulders, but with a smile that exploded on her face, and arms that seemed to have no hair or nothing.

"Hello," she said.

"Hi. I'm looking for some work, if you know of any."

"Right. Mr. Weis is who you're looking for," she said. "He's out with the goats."

"You got some goats?"

"Well he does. I'm just, like, a tenant," she said. "My name is Mara, nice to meet you." She stuck out her hand and I took it, shaking my head inside.

"Yeah, hi," I said. "Does Mr. Weis have a road named after him?"

"Hey why not?" That's when that smile really lit up. I think she was laughing at me, or at what I didn't know. That's when I was sure I'd have to see what made this place tick. "Hey, let me take you to him," she said. I said okay, and we walked around the side past more cars with hoods open, and a guy working on one. The dog followed us. We walk right on past the man, and she told me later that's Vernon who helps Mr. Weis in town and also likes working on old cars. He didn't look up or nothing.

"You'll like it here. You can't beat it," she said to me, like she believed it too much. That's when I decided to let them do all the talking, and allow my presence do the rest.

Well, we walked down a hill and up another, and up at the top of it I could see two men down in a marshy pasture surrounded by about forty-five, fifty brown and white goats spread out around tussocks the size of tree stumps. The dog went running down the hill like he just remembered what he was supposed to do. This was mid-spring, May Day actually. I stopped there up top and turned to the girl.

"Which one is Mr. Weis?"

The girl pointed to the man on the right who was wearing a suit and tie with a baseball cap and black boots under his dark pants. Well, both men watched me come up to them, and as I got closer I could see who was in front of me. The one man who wasn't Mr. Weis was tall and thin with a mustache and sagging eyes that looked like they had seen better days. He wasn't wearing a cap, just jeans and a dirty green T-shirt with a faded design reading "Charm City."

Mr. Weis was the kind of man I would imagine would have a road named after him. He was short and stocky, with big shoulders and a hunched look to his back, big floppy ears sticking out the sides of his head with hair springing out of them. But it was the big brown beard he had which threw me, plus the glasses and formal dress. It was like the man had them things on but could whip them off, like you could if they were fake. It was strange, boy.

"Hello," I said. They both nodded.

"I hear you have work," I said. I watched a brown goat off to the side stand on its hind legs munching leaves from a sapling.

"Yes I do." Mr. Weis looked at me long, his eyes scouring me up and down, making me feel them. He just stood there watching me. "You're hired," he said. "We need another keeper. Get some boots on." I was wearing my tennis shoes, but I thought he was joking so I pulled a quick laugh. But when the other man started asking me real soft about the weather, and how nice the spring is considering the free fodder for the goats, I knew Mr. Weis wasn't shitting me.

"Plus the rain last night," the other man said. "It's a break."

"Yeah, right," I said. I nodded to show I was up for anything for some cash.

"Normally we wouldn't let them graze down here with this standing water," the tall man said. "But since it just rained last night, we knew it wouldn't be too bad. Plus these does got to get a break from all that winter bran and corn silage sitting in them. If we're going to get any decent milk this year." He wasn't saying it like he knew I understood what he was saying, he was announcing for all present. I looked at all them brown and white things chomping on that grass like there was no tomorrow, and those two men standing right in the middle of all of them, and I thought, *what the hell am I doing?*

"Wait. I'm not sure if I, I mean, if I know much," I said to Mr. Weis. "You don't know who I am," I said.

"You don't have boots?" he said.

"No," I said, "I don't." That's when I thought he'd call the whole thing off, but he didn't.

"Mara, could you please get this gentleman a pair of my work boots from the barn," Mr. Weis said. The girl was still at the top of the hill, with her legs crossed like she had to go, but the way she drooped her shoulders, she looked sad and lonely up there watching. She waved circular-like, and disappeared under the green.

"I wear size ten," he said. That was fine with me, and I nodded to him it was. I wear size eleven, but I could put up with a little pinch for an easy in. Mr. Weis turned to the other man and asked him to take me up to the sheds for some work, then he turned sideways and looked out at them goats clumped in the weeds.

"Saanen Twenty-six has mastitis. Milk her every hour on the hour," he said. "Put the hot towels on her caked udders after that, then do it again. Toggenburg Nine has foot rot, plus the new Saanen kid is ten days. Get them first—we've waited long enough. Wendell will show you the process." It was then I figured he was talking to me, not the other guy. "But give love to Twenty-six. She's a queen. She produced seventeen times her weight last year."

I had no idea what he was talking about, so I asked him if he had a place to stay, and if he needed me to fill out any forms.

"What's the point? $400 per month. You can have the attic, no charge. Move in this evening if you want."

Mr. Weis then turned his head to his grazing herd. You could hear the grinding chew if you listened to them, and you could tell Mr. Weis loved them animals from listening to the way his voice sounded in ordering. Then Mr. Weis turned back to Wendell and just nodded. Wendell started walking up the hill, not saying nothing, and I followed.

"Oh," Mr. Weis shouted at Wendell once me and him were halfway up the hill. "Don't forget the chevron."

So we had our tasks laid out for us, and this was a time when I had to do a good job at something to prove I could. I was thinking it sounded like something new anyway, why not? At any rate, I felt good being out in the sun. As we were walking up to the sheds in back of the house, I started asking Wendell about the place. He told me it's a tenant house and Mr. Weis owned other houses in Ellicott City and Columbia and other places, plus both him and Mr. Weis are from Howard County and have lived there nearly all their lives. Wendell lived in that house himself, in Room Two next to the girl. About the goats, all I wanted to know is what I do with them, but Wendell said I'll show you, and wouldn't add to that until we got to the buck shed.

The boots were sitting on the front porch when I got up there, caked mud and shit on the soles, but not too tight, nice and worn-in on the insoles. I sat on the edge of the porch and put them on while Wendell watched.

"Hey, you smoke?" I said.

"No," he said.

"You mind if I smoke?"

"There's work to do," he said. Then he loped off towards the sheds. I didn't get a bud all that day, which about drove me crazy by the end of it.

Out back were three large sheds, one red, one yellow and a smaller white one which looked more like a chicken coop to my eyes. Wendell led me to the red one.

"This is the buck shed," he said. I could smell the piss in it from about twenty feet away. "We have to clean a couple up," he said. Then we walked in. Got hit in the face by the smell then crawled through it, pretending to be used to it. Boy, I thought I was going to die from breathing that goat stench in, and I started coughing anyway. Wendell walked me down the long aisle of empty stalls to Toggenburg Nine, which wasn't empty.

"That's why we keep the bucks here away from the does," he said, brushing his hands towards the bucks in there. "You don't want this man-smell in your milk. Beet pulp and turnips are bad enough."

We got to Number Nine and Wendell took out a paring knife from his back pocket and handed it to me. He pointed at the buck. He was a brown goat with white stripes, limping around in the stall. He had little notches in both his deer-looking ears, and his front right foot looked bigger than the others.

"See that foot," my co-worker said.

"Yeah."

"Trim it. I'll be right back."

"Where are you going?" I said. I probably sounded as nervous as I felt.

"Stay put, I have to get some supplies from the milking shed." As Wendell was doing his business, I stared at that daggone buck and didn't do nothing. It creeped me out, boy, him sizing me up. I looked into the buck's eyes, and it was like I could see a grown man's eyes in a goat's body. There was a brain in that thing's body. I could tell that.

"How are you doing?" I said to the animal. He was bleating and carrying on, looking at me like he was trying to figure out what I was thinking—weird animals. I couldn't even open the gate.

"We're going to do two things here," Wendell said, walking back down the aisle towards me. "I'll walk you through them." He was carrying a big sack, which read *copper sulphate*, and also an aluminum pail full of water, and an unmarked brown medicine bottle with a little yellow smiley-face sticker on the cap.

"What's that for?" I said, pointing to the smiley-face. For a second I thought it had some sick meaning—maybe poison disguised. Wendell looked down at it and grinned.

"He likes to mark things, I guess. He don't like confusion. Just to let you know, we keep some things right here in the shed. Fever thermometer, gauze pads, pine tar, and ointment. Some needles. Some oak bark powder when they got the runs," he said. "But I got to go the barn for the serious stuff."

"Oh," I said.

"He is a good man," Wendell said. "He helped me out a lot."

I thought, good enough to give us the dirty work while he stood in the field admiring his herd. I was thinking, the man don't even have the courtesy to shake my hand in the bargain, too trusting. But by the end of things that day, I think I got it.

"So how about that foot?" Wendell asked me, like I had to prove myself to him.

"Right." I opened the gate, and got down on my knees with the knife. I started to cut, but the goat shifted, then bucked, and I tried to grab at his legs.

"Pet him on the side," Wendell said. So I did. I couldn't believe how soft it was, like petting a damn mink coat. Or just about.

"Okay," I said. With my left hand I kept on petting him on the side, and with my right I curled the knife between his white legs and lifted up, trying to cut the swollen hoof. It took maybe ten minutes 'cause the goat still moved some, but finally I did it, and I admired the shavings on the hay. Wendell bent down and looked at the hoof, then stood up.

"Good," he said. I stood up.

"Thank you. I don't know if I did a good job."

"What's your name?"

"I'm Phil."

"Good to meet you, Phil," he said, then shook my hand.

He handed me something he called Detoll solution and I applied it on the hoof I scraped, then on the other three. Then he took the copper sulphate bag and reached in to spoon some into the pail full of water while shaking it, and we stuck the goat's foot in the pail, then the other hooves one by one. After about ten minutes, we took Nine's foot back out and dumped the brown water outside the shed, and I felt better.

"Let's go castrate that kid," he said, walking away.

"What's that?" I said.

It didn't help that Mara came out to watch or that I got to dab up the wound with disinfectant afterwards. I caught up to Wendell when he stopped at a stall with them three white baby goats in it.

"Wait a minute, I ain't never done this," I said.

"It's easy," he said. "I'll walk you through it."

That's when Mara came bouncing out with that smile going ballistic, boy, like she could smell the operation from inside the house.

"Hey guys, you got one?" Boy, she looked good too.

"Yeah," Wendell said, "He wants this one done seeing that Mom was inbred, and Dad was too. Mr. Weis accidentally linebred them, and you know," Wendell said. "He wants it done in case. Even he makes mistakes sometimes."

"Like all the time," the girl said. "I mean. He does."

"Or maybe it's just the goats," Wendell said.

"It's life that, like, gets to him," she said, snapping her head to me still grinning. "Have you ever done this before?"

"No." I was sweating like a dog. It was hot in there, and I didn't like the idea of cutting into no goat's manhood.

"Oh my God, it's so easy. It's therapeutic too, especially if you've had the hombres I've had." She hopped up on one of the stall rails, and straddled the post, her legs wrapped around them. She had a black dress on, with a green T-shirt underneath, and the wood was rubbing her thighs pink around the edges. Man, she kept touching my shoulder with her palms too—she was all over me.

"I love doing it," she said. "My first castration, I sliced and, like, kind of closed my eyes, then opened them and I mean, when I opened them I could feel the warm things in my hands! It's, like, so exhilarating, that blood gushing out the balls and everything! What a trip!"

Boy, it was strange 'cause I felt like I wanted to jump her right then in that stall, but same time I didn't even feel like I had nothing down there to jump with really. Wendell grinned and smiled, joking with Mara about the pincer method—which sounded just as bad. He grabbed the other two kids and put them in the next stall temporarily.

"Mara's his daughter," Wendell said.

"Got you," I said. She was playing games. She was playing all kinds of them.

So I bent down to do it, and I felt like throwing up. It took me almost five minutes to grab them things, which were really nothing now that I think about it—the little white Saanen kid was only about the size of a tall white mutt, with an orange tag in its ear. I grabbed the little white scrotum in between my fingers and bent real close to focus. Then with them two laughing and telling me I ain't never going to be able to get it up again, I took the razor blade and sliced right where Mara said to, right across the bottom of the sack, and blood did come squirting out like out of a water gun.

"Yank it man! Yank it!" Mara was shouting. So squinting and tugging, I yanked the string of spermatic cord out with a jerk, and slowly started to dab with the cotton balls.

"Hey, *bueno*, whoooooo" Mara shouted and clapped, and I sat there dabbing them little balls with a blood line down my elbow into the dirt.

It was only after the three of us quick friends went inside the house to that big old yellow kitchen, getting orange juice, that Mr. Weis came in with his hands clasped together at the palms. We knew he was coming, leading all them goats to their stalls with only the dog.

"Wendell, you castrated the wrong kid," he said real calm like he was telling him the farm needed more feed. I almost said that I did it, but decided not to since it was Wendell who pointed out which one it was.

"I thought it was the little Saanen orange-tag," Wendell said.

"That was the purebred. It was the yellow-tagged kid."

"Oh no. Oh. I'm...oh. I'm sorry sir," he said.

"Yes, I know. Could you please tend to the cottage cheese, and the chevron. We'll get the kid later."

"Yes sir."

"Don't forget the salt rub," Mr. Weis said.

"Okay," Wendell said, walking off.

"Oh, and we have that muslin bag to roll," Mr. Weis said, flipping his wrist to his watch. "In an hour. I'll show our new visitor how to milk a doe."

"Yes sir."

"I will see you later," Mr. Weis said.

Well, Wendell walked right out of the kitchen, and outside to the basement. Boy, then I really felt creeped-out.

That was when he looked into my eyes with a look like he was peering right through my head to the universe through the daylight. He asked Mara without looking to please get him a cup of hot milk—I guessed goat—so she went to the fridge and poured the milk into a baby-blue mug, and stuck it into the microwave. Wiping his forehead, Mr. Weis turned to me with that microwave still whirring.

"You are thinking, what is so important about goats? Nothing really," he said looking right into my eyes. "They are just animals. But it is an art in a way." I said it seemed that way. Mara sat down and looked at us, smiling sideways like she'd heard this ten thousand times before. "You must get a healthy, masculine sire and a good doe together. Otherwise, goat breeding is a terminal investment. It is vital that you find a doe with a thin neck, sharp withers, thin thighs and a springy rib, and most important—large teats, but not too large." The milk dinged from the microwave, and Mara gave it to him. He touched the edge of my shirt and led me out the door, back to the sheds. He walked slowly and deliberately, with his hands in front, and out of the side I could see Mara wave to me with her fingers, and looking curious with her forehead pointed down and only the tops of her eyes visible.

"Not only must you find a doe and a sire with healthy features, but you must find the best way to breed them," he said. "Inbreeding, for instance, can bring about excellent does, but it is a high-risk venture. The recessive genes can give you a nasty surprise," he said. He walked me into the yellow doe shed, and right to the stall with Saanen Twenty-six, whiter than white and almost glowing in the cool dark inside the shed. He put his hand out and Twenty-six licked the fingers and nuzzled his palm with her face.

"Linebreeding is another method. You breed your sire to your doe, but you must know your lineage well. The idea is to match related parents," he said. Turning his body to me so I could see his whole figure in my view he said: "But my favorite is really crossbreeding because you get the best of both worlds. The Toggenburg, the Saanen—these are nice breeds. On this farm our goats have a veritable orgy on their hands. It's paradise, controlled of course; family members are excluded." Then there was a silence, and we kept walking, listening to our feet move the grass. I didn't know what the hell to say next.

"By the way, my name's Phil," I finally said. He did his little nod, and pressed his glasses tighter on his nose with the back of his palm.

"So, I'm curious, Phil. What is your first impression of our operation?"

"Good," I said. "I think I like it here."

"Good. I don't want you to think I am strange, or that this place is odd. I own other buildings, and other land. I'm a landowner."

"Right, right," I said.

"I don't want you to feel strange."

"I know," I said. "I don't."

"Are you sure, because you look like you might?"

"I'm sure," I said, looking at the doe. I wanted to ask him more about himself and his buildings, but I was worried to go too fast with everything—I ain't that smart.

That's when everything changed for the better. First Mr. Weis opened the gate and we led Saanen Twenty-six out of the yellow shed into the sun, then into the milking shed. We walked the doe up the ramp and stuck her into this wooden contraption that held her still so she could feed on clover and alfalfa during the process. Mr. Weis called the thing a stanchion, or something.

Then I wiped the doe's udder with a damp cloth, like he said, to remove the impurities I guess, and Mr. Wcis got two more cloths and stuck them in a tub of hot water off in the corner. Then he stepped back up onto the platform and put the cloths on the railing and handed me a metal container, telling me to put it under her, and to get behind her.

"It's the old-world style. We're not going to be picky about a few dung particles."

"Okay," I said and sat on the stool.

"Now this doe has mastitis. We saw flakes in her milk a few days ago, which is why you're here. The milk builds up, especially this time of the year. Okay, grab the teat," he said. I did. It was hard, and not like I imagined. He told me to push up, then use just my bottom three fingers to push down.

"She's tender, be gentle. Give her love. Okay, squeeze it from the top down, strip it down."

I did like he said without saying a word, slowly, listening to the squirting. I've never felt anything like it, that breast growing soft in my hand, that bright white juice splattering into the can, filling up. I was taking something out of her and she was giving it with pleasure, with only a little bleating and shifting around. It felt natural to me.

So I did it, filling two containers, and Mr. Weis placed the containers in another tank, which he said was filled with cold water to keep the milk until it was done. Then I pressed the hot compress onto her udder for five minutes, and he said we'd come back in an hour and milk her more. He said the only reason he was saving it was to see if the flakes have disappeared.

"I'm glad you came," Mr. Weis told me, and his voice was gentle, boy. "I can tell you've been through something."

"Really?" I was surprised he said this.

"You see, it's not just goats. Mara," he said. "I have to look after her."

Mr. Weis said he would be glad if me and her spent time together because he knew she was lonely, working up at the all-you-can-eat place up on Route 40.

"College is a tough time, I suppose and she couldn't manage some aspects," he said looking straight ahead. "She'll be back, though."

I had so many ideas rolling in my head. I said I'd love to spend time with her, and I decided not to tell him nothing about my wife then. That's something I came to regret later, but it's another story.

We walked from the shed into the sunshine.

"I can tell you've been through something. Most of my tenants have been."

"Yes sir," I said. "I have."

"I'm sorry," he said.

"I am too. I'm very sorry."

"You'll fit in fine. There are two other women here in addition to Mara," Mr. Weis said, then he reached into his pocket and pulled out a ten and a five and handed them to me. I thought it was for the work I did, but it wasn't.

"I try to look after people," he said. "If you will take her to a movie, I would be very grateful." I was still thinking about Greta and all them things I did, and I was trying to not choke up on it. But then I decided the best idea was not to think at all. Listen and try to learn something, I thought, but I don't know if that's what happened either.

"Yes sir," I said.

Then Mr. Weis asked me if I would like a glass of milk. I said yes, only I asked him if I could have mine cold. He stood straight and he shook my hand firm before we walked inside.

THE KING OF TACO MAKERS

I show up late for work because my Dad was off somewhere looking for a job, and I can drive or walk three miles but I don't want to. I try to explain to the boss but she walks away, telling me to mop the men's room. Once I saw a giant wooden ostrich for sale in a store downtown, painted oak, with a red saddle. $5,000. My boss is like that ostrich.

"We shouldn't do that again," she says. "Should we?"

I shake my head no. I feel sorry for her because she's missing part of her middle finger. She says she lost it when she was trying to fix her mother's lawnmower. I wonder if her mother is still alive, and what she's like if she is. What if her mother never read her nothing? I tell her I don't like to be late. I like making tacos, I say. But I lie; I like making burritos. When I go get the mop this new girl giggles. "It's not like we're busy." I tell her I like mopping 'cause you can see the wet swishes where you mop, and the dry areas where you don't. The floor is yellow-tiled, maybe to look like corn. She says her name's Brandi.

My teacher comes over every morning at 7:30. Mom wants to get things going for me early. We do biology, English, or math. We prepare for the writing test required for Maryland.

Around 9:00 he leaves, sometimes earlier. Some mornings he's tired, and I think he's been up late. When he's feeling lazy or generous he shows me a video on killer bees or the great coral reef. It's not like real school, it's better. I learn better when people aren't around and things *have* to sink in because there isn't much else to think about.

This time it's writing. He says I can write better than I think I can. I'm not real interested in what he means, but I do it anyway. I'm good at doing what I need to do. I write on this grayish recycled paper.

Last year I also had Mr. Wilson but was too upset to work good. I broke down sometimes. We met at the Laurel library in a tutoring cubicle. They haven't painted over the gray cinder blocks there. I read *Black Boy*, and liked it. But I hated studying geology. I was angry then at my mother for leaving Dad. One day I made her write out a contract when Mr. Wilson could witness. Things are better now.

Mr. Wilson talks to me about flatworms and roundworms and microscopic parasites. He talks about scientists who discovered things, and we make small improvements. I like the guy with the meat who discovered flies don't come from nowhere like they thought. I think Mr. Wilson wants to do that, be a great somebody. He likes fooling with his change, and sometimes I think he puts it there just for that. He stands up, sits down, stands up. Restless. I like studying the monerans and the protists. We go back through the book the best we can and every other week there's a quiz. I like biology now, and I got a B last quarter.

I live in Jessup, near where all the warehouses for Baltimore and Washington are. I'm applying for better jobs, but for most of them you got to be eighteen. My dad's house has got pink furniture and framed pictures with gold borders of white women wearing green and yellow that he bought at Kmart. He used to have a nice leather bar in the living room corner, and sometimes I'd sneak a swig of something. Now the bar's a fake leather TV stand pressed against the wall. When

Mom left him last year the house went with it. Stuff everywhere. He smokes more now, and drinks more coffee. He says he needs something extra.

When I go to sleep I can hear the rigs rumbling up Route 1, and turning into the different warehouse drives. Some days I make tacos for the drivers who come in, and feel like I been to all the places they have. Like I can smell Florida on their breath, or wherever they get the stuff. I hand them their change. Sometimes my fingers touch their palms.

Someday I'll get a good job.

At work I talk with Brandi. She's younger, and she also makes tacos. She's the quickest there because she don't have no nails to drag her down. Her hair is cut short to her head, but she's cute anyway. She calls me Paige Thirteen, then laughs at her own joke. She says she likes to read novels and history, and on her breaks she sits at the pink tables and does her homework.

A couple years ago I saw my IQ test scores when my mom and the counselor went out to talk. It was around one hundred and five. I don't know how good that is. I've failed two grades. I think I'm dumber for getting into trouble than doing bad. My dad says I need to get wise.

I don't know why, but I've never been into sports. My teacher says I should be, but I can't imagine it. It seems too much to do without no payback.

I talk to Brandi about school when we make burritos and soft shell tacos. Her parents pay for her to go to private school in Baltimore County. She says she likes the teachers, even the uniforms. She says the kids are too snotty for her though, and they think they're better. She says she likes making tacos to even it out.

"What do you like to do?" I ask.

"I don't watch much television," she says.

At the end of the night she gives me her phone number. She has her own line, she says.

I'm in trouble because I sold pot on school grounds. I wasn't trying to be no dealer. I just did it a few times. Don't know why. I get into fights at school because the older kids think I'm a weakness. I'm not big, but I'm serious with a serious face. People think I got attitude. My mom is serious too. She borrowed money to keep the apartment for a year, so if Dad's swilling we can leave. Sometimes I sleep there anyway, when Mom and Dad are together. My mom says everything is up in the air.

My father's a car salesman. Last year he was fired at the Acura place because sales were slow after the magazine articles against them. He's trying to get a job so he drives off every morning at nine to look. Sometimes I bet he goes to the library and sits, or goes out for breakfast. My father don't want my teacher to think he's a bum. My mother teaches kindergarten in Prince George's.

When I first went to Hammond High I was beat up real bad. This group of boys called me a faggot, and pushed me around in the locker room until the teacher broke us up. After school they followed my bus in their truck and held me down while they hit me in the back and head with beer bottles and kicked me. They videotaped the whole thing until I lost consciousness. I called 911 myself when I came to. I told my parents I don't know who did it. I thought about joining a gang, but if I did I knew it'd be my parents who'd get me.

I got to go to court in my own defense. But I like the judge. He's a short little white man with a beard, and he seems to understand. I like people who listen to what I got to say. He says I have 500 hours of community service, and he doesn't want to ever see me again. My mother smiles at me during the walk back to the car. I want to tell her I think she has a pretty smile. She almost looks Asian to me sometimes because her eyes look a little like my grandmother's. Mom says she's proud that my grades are getting better.

"I like him," I say.

"Who?"

"Mr. Wilson."

"Is it helping? Don't you think you can go back to school? I want you to finish what you've started."

"I don't know," I say.

"Do you feel angry as much?"

"Mom. I said—"

"It feels good to have control doesn't it?" I think about the girl. I think about what my mother is asking me. It seems to be an important question.

"Yeah," I say. She settles herself in the seat. Mom's always trying to sit comfortably. It reminds me of when you're inside and it's windy outside and you feel protected.

"I think we're already past this," she says, nodding her head back to the court.

Saturday night my Dad and me go to the video store and get Coke and popcorn, and we watch a funny movie together and play cards during it. I like sitting on the rug. My mother says she feels sick and says she don't want to play.

"What are you thinking these days?" he says.

"Man, I'm too busy to think," I say.

He looks scared when I say that, then he smirks and says his son is growing up. I ask him if he's found a job yet.

"Ain't happened yet," he says.

"What are you going to do?" He shakes his head. Then he shakes it again.

"You could come make tacos," I say. We both get a kick out of that. I tell him he'd be a great taco-maker. He says he's sure he'll find something soon. He can feel it.

"I could be the *king* of taco makers," he says.

After the movies I give Brandi a call. She's still up.

"What are you up to?"

"Reading," she says. "I was going to go out, but my father doesn't feel like driving me to Towson. That's where most of the students live."

"You met some friends?"

"I met some, but until I can drive, you know."

"Yeah. I see my friends but they like, forget about me 'cause they don't see me everyday," I say.

"I know, don't you hate how people make school into a social thing?"

"It *can't* be a social thing for me, since I only see one person."

"What's your teacher like?" Brandi asks me.

"He does his thing. He doesn't get involved. He's no preacher, know what I'm saying?"

"I think that's what teachers should do," she says. "I'd rather just learn things."

"I don't know. It's easier because there's less kids around. It's not hard."

When my teacher comes and asks me if I had a good weekend I tell him nothing happened. We go over decimals and fractions, which are the toughest for me. Then he gives me a vocab quiz. He says he likes the way it smells in my house. My mother just cooked bacon. Once, he told me he's a vegetarian but that he eats fish. When we finish up and I go back to school, my mother will get him a going-away gift. She asks me what he'd like. I say leather gloves.

Then one day Mr. Wilson made a point. He talked about survival. Started out with evolution, then said he met a man who was in jail and learnt card tricks to pass the time. Said the man was the best card-tricker around, could fool anybody. It doesn't always have to be a useful thing was his point. I tell him I like my job.

"Do you feel useful?"

"No. I don't feel it," I say. "I met this girl I like though. That keeps me coming back."

"Is she pretty to you?"

"Kinda. Not really."

"What does she look like, Paige?"

"I don't know. She's a girl," I say.

He sighs and picks at his fingers. He stares at the window like he is looking for cracks.

"You don't seem too rebellious," he says. "When I was sixteen, I was harder to handle." I shrug. I want to ask him if he knows about any jobs for my dad. But I don't want to be a bum or nothing. I start thinking about Brandi as a kind of tool for me, but I decide to stop thinking about her that way.

I have one thinking place at the little park off Gerwig Lane. There's a little pond with a circular roofed-in thing next to it. You can see the carp circle around. I look for the dorsal fin. Usually I can only stay there by myself for a couple minutes before somebody come on down with their girlfriend or something. Then I walk back into the path, and sit on a log or something and listen to things. Even the sound of cars and people around is good. Things combine together. I like that about parks.

My family ain't been on a vacation since I was in elementary school. Back then we went to Virginia Beach for a couple days, stayed in a motel off the boardwalk. Could hear the drunk people shout in the night, and further off the waves, and even further off the ships headed to Norfolk where my cousin lives. I could see the lights of them boats from the motel, and the ones down the coast. Inside I told myself I'd like to be out in the open someday. I wanted to be able to see the horizon.

These days I make my own vacations. Sometimes it's a trip to the store. I don't have to go anywhere special to have an okay time.

The next Saturday after work I ask Brandi if she wants to come over to my house, and maybe her parents could come pick her up from Towson later on.

"Only my mom lives in Towson," she says. "My dad lives right here. That's why I work just on the weekends here."

"So could your dad pick you up later?"

"I could just walk home. He only lives off Holly Court," she says. Two streets down from mine.

"Why didn't you say something then?" I say. Girls always being so *careful* about everything.

"I had to see if you were worth it." She's teasing, I think. Then she asks me if I want to go to her Dad's place, then I can walk home. She says she don't like to walk home at night alone. I say no problem. I call my mom and ask her, and she says fine. She wants me to find a girl too. She left me a box of condoms tacked to my wall once. A smiley-face in red Magic Marker was on the box. I made sure to put the tack back on her desk. It was the pushpin kind with a pink top.

My mom picks us up in her jeep. Some loud jazz music is playing, and the drummer's into his solo. Drums are gay.

"How are you two?" We get in back. "Are you Paige's colleague?"

"I guess," Brandi says. "My name is Brandi."

"We're both colleagues," I say.

"You sure are." Mom frowns at us in the back mirror, the kind that means a smile. "Nice to meet you then, Ms. Brandi. Do you live around here somewhere?" Brandi tells her where. My mom sounds so formal the way her voice raises. She used to work as a secretary for the Howard County District Court, filing checks and answering the phone. "Well, I'll just drop the two of you off. Paige can come home whenever he wants," she says to Brandi. "You two should have fun." We pull out of the light, and onto Oakland Mills to home.

"My father will probably want to play Trivial Pursuit with us. He's obsessed with trivia games." Brandi circles her fingers on the leather seat. "He's a loon."

"He's a loon?" My mother asks.

"He was born in 1937. My father is almost sixty. He spends most of his time on his sailboat. It's forty-eight feet long."

"That's long. That's a big boat," my mother says.

"He's an idiot," Brandi says. "He brings his rocks along. He thinks he's a rock expert, just because he went to college and studied them. Like that matters." When we get to Brandi's, I watch my mom's brake lights turn red at the stop sign and blink out as she rolls down the road.

One of my brothers is older and lives with his girlfriend. Just moved in together last summer. He don't call me no more, and he don't even like her that much. When I do see him he's bitching she's too much a girl, wants her to be more like him. I try to tell him, man, you don't want her to be like you. You want to marry yourself?

I know they'll break up, and he'll come back. It's something about us boys. Soon as we find someone we can have, we don't want them no more. My dad begged my mother back. She told me he really got down on his knees in the driveway, and begged her to come back to his life. Now he's lazy again. I decide I'm going to see if Brandi's rich Dad knows anything.

My favorite meal is lasagna with spinach and lots of cheese. Tater-tots. Tall glass of milk with ice. Chocolate pie with whipped cream.

We go into the house and realize we smell like tacos and ground beef compared to the smell of paint and carpet everywhere. Flowers, everything smells like flowers. It's one of the big new houses I see passing by to our ranch house. Inside there's framed art and mirrors all over, and a huge wine holder in the hall. There's an office off to the side, and Brandi says he's asleep, because the light's off there.

"Let's go into the basement," she whispers. We do.

It's cool down there. She turns on the overhead. Goes over to the refrigerator by the outside door, and gets out two brown bottles, beer. She hands me one, and asks me to open hers. They're twist-offs. She's got to go change into sweat pants, she says. She asks if I want any chips or popcorn.

"No, I don't think so," I say.

"You can turn on the television. We have satellite TV." I do. It's on a business channel, and the stocks are streaming by on the bottom of the screen even this late at night. Her footsteps are light on the basement stairs, and once she is out the door I can't even hear her.

"I'll bring popcorn anyway," she says. I switch the channel.

"What's your Dad like?" I ask when she's back. I've finished the beer, and she has opened me another one. She flips the television to *ESPN*.

"He's a Dad."

"What kind of Dad? Is he good to you?"

"I don't know. What do I have him to compare to?"

"Yeah, that's true." I take a sip of my beer. It tastes horrible. But I smile and pretend. "My father's going to be famous one day."

"Really?" She hands me a glob of popcorn, and I eat the whole glob in one mouthful. I say I'm the Cookie Monster, and she laughs at that.

"He's a racer," I say.

"A runner?"

"No, a car racer. Stock car racing. That's where it's at. Not too many black racers out there, so he'll get some attention, you know." He's never raced a day in his life. I don't know why I say it.

"I hope he does do well. I'd like to meet him someday."

"I'll have to check it with his manager." I elbow her to show I'm kidding. "No, he's not famous yet."

"But he will be?"

"That's what I think. But you know..." I say. "You have any extra jobs if anyone's looking?"

"Me?"

"I mean your father."

"Oh, no. Not that I know of. He's not the boss anyway. Why?"

"No reason. My brother..."

Anyway I tell her I don't want to be famous, and that famous people are cop-outs. She says she'd like to be famous someday, but that maybe she'll end up as a teacher. I think of me and Dad.

"Everybody wants to be famous," I say. "What does your dad do anyway?"

"He's a computer analyst. That stuff is boring to me."

"Yeah," I say.

"No, I want to be successful or happy or something. That's different. Not just famous."

"What are you going to do?" I ask. She's quiet, and stops chewing on her popcorn. We can hear some muscley guy on television talking about the next season's shows. We haven't paid attention to the television at all. The man's wearing a bandanna around his head.

"I have no idea." She elbows me back on that, and we laugh. Later we get tired and turn off the lights. I hold her sleeve. She leans against where my shoulder meets the couch, and we drift off.

SAVING THE TREE

When we had dinner that night after we got in trouble, I told my parents about the man in brown, and they said that his name's Mr. Derwin Grove. Daddy said that he lives right next door and seems very, very nice. Addie and me hadn't met any friends yet except the tree, so we were kinda excited. My name is Dewey Nuttles, and I'm ten and one thirds, and I like wearing dresses and skirts no matter what Addie says. But Daddy said Mr. Grove's name quick like he didn't want to hold it in his mouth too long, and then said Mr. Grove showed him his big bunny collection, and that the man had lots of bunnies. Different kinds of bunnies. Different sizes and colors. The way Daddy made it sound was like the bunnies came in all different flavors like in Baskin Roberts, or whatever it's called. He seemed to want to talk about bunnies and not Mr. Grove.

But later that night when my parents were in bed and Addie and I were spying on them like we do—because it's fun and the only way to really find out what's happening even if you have to listen through the ruffles and laying-down sounds—Mommy said that Mr. Grove was the person who told Daddy that Carrie was too old and had to be cut down.

"The tree. I don't...We can't have it going through, Louise—"

"I know but I think...well."

"I just...We don't want problems right away," he said. "That doesn't mean that I like what he's doing." There was a long time when we could only hear more ruffling and talking.

"What makes a person do things like that?" Mommy said.

"Man's a power monger," he said. Whatever that means. Anyways, I think they agreed about some things. I just didn't know what. I didn't understand everything Mom said next, but it sounded like that the leaves with the little dot holes in them and the red ants and worms that crawl out of the bark and the big mole showed some friends of Mr. Grove that Carrie is too sick to live. And then Mommy said something about how Mr. Grove was trying to get them to change the way Bob looked for some kind of hysterical district. It sounded like they were afraid of the brown man, and that they were angry at him. I didn't know they knew each other so well. But suddenly I didn't really want to hear more. I don't know why. Plus my eyes were fiery-feeling.

That night Addie and I didn't laugh back into our room like usual and copy the funny slurpy sounds Mommy and Daddy always make after they are finished talking. We crawled back to our room really quiet and into our bed, and I explained to Addie what was happening to Carrie. After hearing me tell her things, Addie said that maybe Carrie is sick and should just die soon. I thought it was okay because it would be better than her being kinda dead for a long time.

"Carrie is sick," she said. "The branches fall down. Bam! Fall down. Dead," she said. She was right. The branches fell so hard when it rained that they crashed against the roof. The first time I heard it, I imagined angels were leaning over the clouds too much and falling over and landing on our roof. Sometimes I thought the angels had broken arms, and bleeding scratchy legs, laying on our roof, and asking each other if they have Band-Aids, wondering how they would get down from the roof without a ladder. Unless they just flew back up.

"If Carrie is sick that means Carrie will be cut down," I said.

"Will Carrie die?" she asked.

"Yup," I said. "Carrie's going to get it if we don't, you know…"

"Bugs die. Carrie is a tree. I don't want Carrie to die," she said. Then Addie started crying into her pillow with little choking sounds. I hugged her and we hugged asleep in our room that smelled like faded pictures and mildewy stuff. My parents hadn't peeled the walls in that room yet.

In the morning Addie and me came up with our plan. We practiced for two weeks. The first steps were the trickiest. We had to memorize a pattern so we could miss the squeaky parts of the stairs. It was left side, right, right, left, left, right, left, right, left, left, left, left, left. Thirteen steps to get to the front door. Addie and I made a song out of it following the pattern of Eenie, Meenie, Miney, Mo: a lily for each left, a rock for each right. I don't know why we chose those two things to stand for right and left, we just did. It went like this: "Lily rock rock lily lily rock lily rock lily lily lily lily lily." That way Addie and me could almost hop right down the stairs without waking Mommy and Daddy. We were caught a couple of times, but we just said we were going to get a drink of water, or that Addie had a nightmare and we were walking it off. We practiced every night.

The front door was tricky too. You had to turn the top lock to the right, then only open it a little so it didn't squeak. Then you had to squeeze between the tiny space and the screen door they just put up. Once you got outside everything was easy. You just walked over to his gate, and right in since he didn't get the lock fixed, then right up his stairs. Mr. Grove's steps weren't noisy I guess because they were rock, and maybe that's why we chose rock for the song, and for good luck.

Anyways, the extra-double tricky part was the rabbit cage. During practice we just went up there and figured out how to unhinge them without really doing it. We would do each one and then just give the bunnies grass. Addie and I thought that Mr. Grove might wake up the first time, but after that we figured out that he might be all the way on the other side of the house, so each time we went up there I spent more time practicing on the locks, then just giving the bunnies grass and petting them. Addie spent more time practicing the other thing.

We named each bunny. There was eight of them so we had Smushie, Crunchy, Boo-Boo, Oopsie-Daisy, Shoot, Darn, Booby, and Crap. Addie didn't know what the last two names were but I did. I like my name fine.

We got in trouble the first time because Addie and me were playing King of the Tree. The object was to climb to the first part of the tree before the non-climber person could count to ten or the non-climber person got to throw a tennis ball at you and even hit you anywhere they want. If the ball hit you then you were dead, and the thrower-person got one point. If it didn't, no points. Whoever got up to ten first won some prize that we made up. That one day when it happened, we set the prize as the one person had to catch a water-skimmer bug for the other person in a jar, so we were both excited.

Addie was climbing the tree, and I was counting to ten and squeezing the ball in my hand, and watching the blue vein in my wrist puff out, but she slipped with her tiny legs and scrubbled down the trunk then tried to get up again. I threw the ball at her when ten came, and it hit her in the back of the neck. Addie squealed a little, but my sister is tough, and plus she knew it was coming anyway. She hopped down and giggled and rubbed her neck and went to pick up the ball. That's when this man from the sidewalk started yelling at me. "That was a very nasty thing to do. Damn nasty thing to do. You apologize to her." I didn't even see him behind us on the sidewalk, so I was surprised. The man was wearing an all-brown wrinkly suit and a fat brown tie with wormy orange and red spirals on it and ruffled gray hair. And his face was crumpled and tan plus thin like a paper bag. He looked like he was an old tree himself.

The man looked mean and stared at me like Daddy does before he is going to spank us, so I said sorry, even though Daddy and Mommy say never to apologize if you don't mean it, and I didn't. Addie was giggling at the man. Then the man took a little bottle out of his pocket and took a sip of it holding it with his bottom two fingers. He put it back and walked away really fast like he did something wrong, or I guess, maybe he thought he did. And the funny thing was that his socks were different colors. One was kinda orange and the other one was black and white striped. And both of his shoes were untied. Plus he kinda had a beard, but not a real beard, just a kinda one. Addie and I laughed out loud about that.

Later Addie caught a water skimmer for me, only it died the next day, probably from not enough air.

Mommy made a big deal about our ages that summer. I was eight and my sister was four. This was back a couple summers ago. My mom said it was going to be the only time in my life I would be twice as old as Addie, which seemed weird. My sister was always asking if she could ever catch up to me in age, and I told her no but she didn't believe me until Mommy said it. I think that when I die she can catch up to me and pass me, or even double me. Or if she dies maybe I can double her. But then what if spirits can age too then nobody would really pass anyone ever? You'd be stuck. Anyways, now it's only five and a half years till I can drive.

That summer we had just moved into a one hundred and fifty-six year old house with a yellow flaking porch and shutters, and blue flaking everything else. We moved from Allentown, Pennsylvania and I called the house the dandruff house, but Mommy didn't like when I said that. She called it the fixer-upper. She said it wasn't nice to be mean to our new house, and that it might hurt its feelings.

"But houses aren't living," I said. When I hurt Mommy's feelings her shoulders would kinda hunch inwards a little like they would fall right down her chest to her belly. It made me feel bad, so I really tried to stop saying mean things around her. It didn't always work.

"You're right Dell. But it has a spirit," she said. It must too because why else would the old lady who sold it to us kiss the house before she left so that paint chips stuck to her silvery lipstick. I was still young and figuring those things out.

Anyways, my parents were busy fixing up the house that summer. They were always painting, or playing with the wooden floors that Addie and me liked to slide across if we were wearing two pairs of striped tube socks. My parents liked to scrape the tiles off the bathroom and kitchen floors with our shovel that we once buried Harvey our cat with. Mommy and Daddy flung the scuffed yellowy flowery squares into a pile so the squares spun in the air like Frisbees, and the dust and tile chips flung off them. They would do this a lot when they were around each other and smile at each other like they did when they were about to kiss or hug, but they were too busy even for that yuckiness so they would just stare the yuckiness like it could pass through the air invisibly whether they smushed together or not. They spent so much time on the tiles they had to tie old white and gray college T-shirts around their knees because they said it hurt after kneeling on their bones so long. And when they weren't working on the house they were reading some of the gazillions of books they had.

I liked when my parents got the wallpaper steamer, and they would press it onto the hallway wall, and the layers of wallpaper would peel off like apple skin. It would be so hot and steamy inside that it was warmer than outside, hotter than even the sun in July. And the whole house smelled like wet cardboard and stale glue. I liked looking at all the old wallpaper underneath. The peels would strip down, and you could look at the different designs and colors in the layers. You could see how old the house was, like counting the rings on the inside of a tree trunk.

Once they let me try the steamer. It felt like if I kept the steamer against the wall it would go right through to the next room. That summer my parents walked around in paint-speckled blue pants that whistle-talked when they walked by, and they wore red or gray checker shirts that looked like dogs ate at the cuffs. And when they were working in the attic or painting outside like they started to do later, they wore these mouth-coverers like doctors wear and their voices sounded like Darth Vader's.

When they were working on the house Addie and me would play in the back yard. We played lots of games. My daddy put a rope on the tree so we would swing on that lots until we'd get red scratchy rubs on the insides of our legs, and then we'd have to stop. We also liked to go play down by the creek. There was lots of neat stuff down there like old rusty tin cans and old brown or green or clear bottles with screw-on caps that must have been antiques 'cause Mommy and Daddy didn't have anything like them.

Addie liked to throw rocks at the water-skimming bugs. She'd throw the rocks and make a big splash and jump and say she killed them, but then I'd see the bug skimming over in the water near the creek grass. I wouldn't say anything though. I just liked looking at the bugs, and they didn't bother me, even if the creek did smell like when Mommy soaked Addie's stained clothes when Addie was a baby. There were also crayfish in the slow, side parts of the creek and we wanted to catch them and boil them and eat them like crabs, but Mommy said that crayfish eat the poopy stuff at the bottom of the creek so Addie and me didn't catch anything then.

But lots of times when it was too hot and sticky, Addie and me would just walk to the part of the back porch that faced the sidewalk by the house and sit in the shade and eat Popsicles. The porch had a screen but there were holes all in it, so from inside it looked like there were holes right in the tiny black checkers of the air. We watched the black and red striped bugs crawl in freckled little pie shapes on the rotting blue painted wood part of the porch sticking out. The bug clouds sometimes made scary faces with eyes and pointy noses and everything. They even crawled on the screen. The bugs liked to scare us. Whenever the bugs looked like this my sister would climb down and hit them with a branch and smash her foot into them hard over and over so they would either crawl away or die. Then she'd mash the ones that half-escaped. She'd mash them into the dust until they lost their black and red color and just turned dust brown, or she would pick them up and squeeze them, and laugh when their white guts spurted out like toothpaste from their heads or from the place between their wings. Mommy said she called the person that kills the bugs to kill all the mean bugs. He didn't hurry coming, but it was okay. Summers are fun 'cause they're slower and you have more time for fun, even if you have to read the King James Bible on Sundays from when Mommy says go until she says stop.

After she mashed bugs, Addie danced in a circle waving her arms in the air like a bug herself, or like those Indians out West we read about in school who liked to dance and sing a lot too. When Addie was doing this, I would always stand back. But she would tell me to help her mash, to stomp on the bugs and laugh. I wondered if there were any bug spirits, and if they lived in the dust or in the air. I wondered how the house could have a spirit even if it wasn't living, and how the bugs couldn't have one if they were. You couldn't tell by looking. My head would feel sweaty then like a big sponge, 'cause Mommy says it's so humid here. I would watch the dried mashed bodies, or the bodies that still squirmed in the dust so it looked like the dust was coming from them like the toothpaste did. I didn't want to kill anything. I'm not sure why.

But our favorite game was called King of the Tree. It was like King of the Hill, except you had to climb up the tree, and that was harder than any hill, especially with our tree. I told Mommy that the big people's house was the Fixer-Upper and that the kid's house was Carrie. The people who we bought the house from said the tree was older than the house, and maybe older than the whole town. It had a big fat mole on its side like Aunt Carrie had on her cheek, except no hair sticking out of it, so we called the tree Carrie. Carrie smelled sweet the way pancakes and syrup do, and when Addie and me climbed her we liked to just sit and breathe Carrie's bark and hug her. We'd try to flick all the meanie ants and worms off her. We had a brown plastic cave-man club that we hit the cicadas with. It even had fake wood lines that got all sticky from the bug guts.

Addie and me liked to name things with people names. When Mommy said we couldn't call it the dandruff house, we called it Bob because our Grandfather Bob was the oldest person we could think of. We imagined that Bob and Carrie were husband and wife and were married before any people lived in America at all.

It wasn't until a week later when Addie and me saw Mr. Grove again. We were swinging on the swing and jumping off to see who could get the farthest. Our backyard had a small hill and a rusty fence below it near the sidewalk where people walked. If you swung hard enough you could reach the hill in the air and roll down it. Just before you jumped you could see over the bushes and small trees near the sidewalk onto Main Street where the people walked by with shiny clothes to go shopping at all the nice stores that smelled sweet like Carrie.

Anyways, we saw Mr. Grove walking on the sidewalk again, and he didn't even smile at us, and we were just swinging. So I asked him "Mr. Grove, can we see your bunnies?" He stopped walking, stood there a moment and wiped at his eyes with his fingers, then made a mask from his fingers. I couldn't help but laugh a little. It was like he was playing peek-a-boo except he wasn't smiling. Then he took the little brown bottle out of his pocket with his bottom three fingers, and took a quick sip out of it then hid it in his pocket again. I noticed the bottle was actually flat like a square, and dull looking. Who ever heard of a flat bottle? And why would you need to hide something to drink in your pocket? But I thought it must be a secret and that it would be mean to ask. "We really like animals and stuff and we would like to see your bunnies," I said instead. Finally, he said yes.

So we walked over to his house. First he unlocked his gate. His gate was worse than ours. The lock fell off the soggy white wood into his hand when he opened it and he threw it on the stone path and said a bad word but we didn't tell on him. We followed him up his outdoor stairs to this platform also made of stones. His whole house was on a platform, so from his backyard we could see the top of Carrie and our roof. We could even hear my parents scraping away at the tiles. I wondered if he liked living there so he could see all the people around him, plus the ones in nice clothes.

Anyways, there in the middle of this outside platform was a big rectangular wooden house with a screen around it for the bunnies. Each bunny had a separate bunny room with little bullet bunny food thingies and water. Some of the bunnies were fat and looked more like oinkers than bunnies, but some of them were smaller and he said those were the newer bunnies. He said he just bought all of them. Mr. Grove was loosening his pink tie so it hung down over his stomach like a soggy branch. Then he took the little bottle out again. I thought it might be nice to say something so I did.

"Addie and me have seen some old bottles like that by the creek. We took some home even. Do you know how much money they are worth? We collected about a million of them." Then he seemed to get upset because his face kinda faded from us. It was very weird. I wondered if those bottles were once his and someone took them from him or something.

"You know, I come home and it's just not the same anymore," he said. "With nobody to share your life anymore it becomes meaningless. Pointless." His face became hard and knotty then. Then he said some more cuss words, but I won't say them because Mommy says if you say seven over your whole life you go to H-E-double-the-letter-before-M. "I can't believe she would do that to me," he kept saying. "The most selfish thing a person can do." I was afraid to ask him what happened, but then Addie asked: "She took your old bottles?" He laughed and even kinda smiled, but I didn't get it, and neither did Addie. His teeth looked like the fuzzy rocks in the creek. Mommy says the fuzz is good for the water but it looks like dirt to me. The man said that she gave him the bottle and that he doesn't even work anymore. Not really, he said. He doesn't really do anything. But he said he still enjoys dressing nice and just walking. Could have fooled me. Anyways he couldn't work he said, so he got those bunnies to look at when he was too lonesome, but he didn't look at them then. He just mumbled something about how bunnies are so dumb that they don't have any defenses from getting killed from any old animal that wants to kill them.

"Look at you two girls," he said. "Cute as cute." Then he asked us to go inside. So we looked at each other, then did. It smelled horrible, like if the smelly creek had to go to the bathroom real bad, but worse. I put my hands over my nose but Mr. Grove didn't notice. He had walked to the window and was looking out over the trees into the clouds. I looked at Addie, and she was holding her nose too.

"It stinks," Addie said. Then Mr. Grove noticed us again and looked around, then went over to open the window. There was food all over the sofas and piles of I-don't-know-what in the corner near the clock. There were lots of old things though to look at, and the wallpaper was old and greenish-gray. Dust swirled in the room when we breathed, and there was this little shiny metal man holding a flag and sitting on the table near where I was so I picked him up. But Mr. Grove got the window open and turned around. "Put that down!" he shouted. Addie started to cry.

"You meanie," she said. "Big meanie. You want to kill Carrie."

He tiptoed over to Addie and got on his knees in front of her. Then he put his bottle hand around the back of her neck and held her by the scruff like a cat or a bunny. I was scared for a second, and I almost ran to get Daddy. But then he pulled Addie to him and hugged her. But she pushed him away and squeezed under his arms and ran out of the room. I was about to run after her, but she was already down the stairs and I heard the gate slam, so I turned back to Mr. Grove.

"Why do you want to kill our friend?"

He stood up real tall and pressed his chest out. He told me to sit down. He brushed grapes and potato chips, carrot ends and brown banana peels off the sofa for me. I stood there. I thought maybe I should go check to see if Addie went back to the house, but then I decided she would already be inside. I sat down just a little.

"What is your name?" he asked.

"Dewey Nuttles."

"Dewey. I have two daughters too. Their names are Melissa and Christine," he said. "They don't live here anymore." I just nodded. "They are all grown up now. But when they were little they used to like to climb trees like you and your sister. That's your friend right? The tree? Right. But see, I'm a member of this little club. Actually I'm the president of it. The club decides what is and what isn't good for this town, and for the way the town looks." He was talking slowly and softly and gentle-like like the people on some of the radio stations my parents like with soft music. "Because Ellicott City is a historic town," he said. Then I understood what Mommy meant by hysterical: She says that's why no houses down here are pink or bright orange or anything like that, and everything is either white, or brown, or tan.

"When the people who lived in the house before your family sold the house, our job was to see if everything was safe for your family. We made many phone calls about the tree in particular and had special tree-people come and look at it. What they decided was that your tree is almost dead. Your father agreed. So, it will be done as soon as we can do it," he said. "I'm sorry. I'm really sorry." He said that was in three weeks.

"So," I said.

"So. What that means is that a dead tree is not very safe. And it is not very pretty, is it? Dead things aren't pretty, are they?"

"No," I shook my head.

"That's why," he said.

"But even if Carrie's dead, Carrie's still our friend." Then I stood up. "We don't want Carrie gone, even if she's dying," I said. "And plus, my daddy doesn't play on the tree. He just works on Bob."

"Who?"

"Our house," I said, then I walked outside too. I walked down the steps, onto the sidewalk, onto our porch, up our stairs, and into our room. And there was Addie in bed. She was asleep with creek lines down her face. I sat on the rug but I didn't cry. I just sat there and rocked back and forth without saying anything or making a noise, just figuring out what to do next. We had to change the plan because the first one didn't work. It only took me ninety-six rockings to decide what to do, then I woke Addie up.

We were ready when the night came after practicing. We decided. Addie had the stuff under our bed. Mommy didn't even notice because she and Daddy were so busy with painting, like always. We went to sleep first and then Addie woke us both up with her dream-alarm (she could just dream that she had to wake up, and then she would), and we went down the stairs and out the door. The song worked perfect.

When we got to the bunny cages I lit the sparklers and popped all of the locks, and put the bunnies on the ground, and Addie chased them down the stairs with the sparklers and an iron pan, which she swung. Some of the fatter bunnies like Shoot and Crap were slow to be scared, or to move at all. Addie hit Crap in the head right there near the cages. The bunny kinda rolled over and was shaking. The blood kinda leaked down its fur from its head onto its belly. Addie squealed with joy.

Addie tried to write each of the names of each of the bunnies in the air with the orange sparkler as they hopped down the stairs onto the sidewalk or street. I just watched her. My head still felt kinda soggy, but I knew Addie was doing good. Then she really chased the bunnies around with the pan, swinging at them. I think she hit Shoot and Oopsie-Daisy. After she hit both of them, Oopsie-Daisy just walked around in circles like it was trying to make itself dizzy, but Shoot started running. The rest of the bunnies just ran away too. But that was good too. Addie laughed and I hugged her and we both danced in the street and sung the rock-lily song. Then we ran to the sidewalk and threw the pan and the sparklers into the creek. The sparklers hissed in the water. Then we rolled down the backyard hill holding hands like a big log, so much our white nighties were green when we woke up the next morning. I don't think anyone heard us. We didn't think Mommy would notice anything in the morning.

Right after breakfast Daddy spanked us both, me eight times and Addie four times to match our ages. Daddy was so angry it seemed like his skin would peel off like the wallpaper when you steam it, but it was Mommy who did all the yelling. It was like Daddy was the boiling water and Mommy was the kettle. Then Mr. Grove came over and his face was so angry it seemed to be twice as big as usual. He didn't even ask if we did it. My parents didn't even try to protect us. It was so unfair. He looked at me and said, "I'm going to get it over with today." Daddy nodded right to him. Addie and I screamed. Somewhere in the screaming Mommy said that we would have to buy Mr. Grove his bunnies back plus two extras right from our allowance, or else he was going to take us to a court where they decide about bunny rabbits and how much we owe.

Anyways, Mommy made Addie stay in the playroom and sent me back upstairs to stay for the day. My parents were painting the ceilings then. I remember I had to smell the white all day.

By sunset time Carrie was all chopped up into little bits all over the backyard and the hornet sound from the chain saw finally stopped. And I couldn't even see anything from my room. I tried to get out and at least say good-bye to Carrie a couple of times, but Mommy said if she even saw me she would ground me for a month, so I didn't. I didn't even eat until dinner, and when that came, all that was left were Carrie's feet. We ate pizza but I kept staring at the sauce. I was glad we ate on the porch at least. I thought how sad Bob must be to have his wife die.

After dinner my parents let me and Addie outside, but they only gave us five minutes. Mommy ordered me to go down to the creek and get her pan back. By then none of the bunnies were still around, but we could still see the red smushes where they were. Mommy said a special group of people had to come by and gather all the dead bunnies in plastic garbage bags. She said that poor Mr. Grove had to pick some of them up himself. I could imagine Booby or Shoot lying there with flies all over them, bloody and goopy like Play-Doh. One bunny was right in the middle of the street with tire marks through it. Two other bunnies died on the sidewalk, and Addie said that Mommy said that another neighbor's dog was chewing on one of the dead bunnies until the owner dragged him off of it. I imagined the dog's face and nose all red and dripping.

Then I got my first look at what was left of Carrie. The sun was going down over the house. Mr. Grove was still in the backyard smiling at us. He was putting his saw in its yellow suitcase, and he tipped his invisible hat at us as we stared. He said my daddy was going to sell Carrie for firewood, and then laughed to himself mean, like his laugh was at us. Carrie was all cut up into little Carrie's. Her trunk lay like a huge sack of flour on the grass. Except it was all cut up like a giant sausage. Her branches and leaves were crushed into the dirt and greasy like used Q-tips. That's when I started to cry. I thought that at least my parents would let us have one last day with Carrie. But they didn't. It was not fair. At all. Carrie was just a stump and roots under the ground that we couldn't even see. I told Addie to stay put.

I ran and stumbled down to the creek. There was one more bunny down there, still alive, but bloody and wobbling around. It was sitting on a little grass island in the creek, chewing on the grass. I hated its guts and started throwing rocks at it. It hopped into the water and down the shallow water away from me. I followed it, still throwing rocks, missing, then hitting it once on the side and making it hop away faster. But then I saw the pan on a rock in the creek, and somehow I realized what I was doing, and it suddenly seemed silly and just dumb. The bunny wasn't hurt. It just stared at me. I think it was Smushie. I stopped and picked up the pan and dumped the water and creek mud out of it. Then I went over and picked up Smushie and put him in the pan and carried both up the hill to the sidewalk where Addie was, and then home. I put Smushie inside Mr. Grove's gate.

That night it rained really hard but I just listened to the sound of nothing falling from Carrie. Only the basement flooded.

The next day Addie and I woke up and my parents were down in the basement with yellow and brown buckets bailing the basement out. "This is why we can't keep anything down here," Daddy kept saying. Addie and me walked out into the backyard and just looked at dead Carrie all cut into bits. It looked like God peed all over the whole world and all the plants, and even houses were saggy and soggy. We just stood there for a bit and tried to figure out what next. The only thing we could hear besides the singing birds was the creek sound and the drip-drip-drip of water from everything onto the mud and soggy grass. Then all of a sudden Addie did something: She picked up the tennis ball and threw it at Carrie real hard.

"Bad tree," she said. "Dumb Carrie. We have to clean you. Died. Died. Stupid tree."

Somehow it was exactly the right thing to do so. I asked Mommy if we have scissors.

"Do we ever," she said. She came upstairs and pulled out one with rubbed worn red handles from cutting the new wallpaper. Then I ran out into the yard and started cutting all of Carrie's leaves off and any twigs that were small enough. If I could have I would have used the chain saw. We cleaned her up for her trip to the fireplace where the dead trees go. We sang the rock-lily song to Carrie. Then I buried some of her leaves and bark in the mud. We made a big mud mound for Carrie and stuck a branch with leaves in it so we could remember her. I guess Addie and me said good-bye to our friend that day, and hoped that whoever bought Carrie's body to burn would be warm all year round. It felt good once we were done. At lunch my parents said that they were very proud of the way we behaved.

Then after we ate two funny things happened. First, Addie and I tried to come up with a new game since Carrie was gone. We did play some tag games with Carrie's arms, and we pretended to count how many legs Carrie had underground, but the funniest thing was that we came up with a new game called King of the Stump. The rules were you had to stand on the stump while the other person threw tennis balls at you. You got ten tennis balls and however many balls hit the other person after throwing them all, that's how many times you would get to pretend-spank them with a pan. Daddy had to go out to the store to get some more balls for us. But I think he was happy to stop painting for a while anyway. The game helped us remember. And we named Carrie's stump Car, so I guess you could call the game King of the Car too.

The last thing was that later on that day Mr. Grove came by dressed up real nice, and his socks even matched, like he just came from church. He had a blue-buttoned shirt and clean white pants, and his hair was brushed back and slick so we could even see the places where his comb went. His hair looked like those roads with the grooves in them when my parents take us on a trip somewhere, but better. His shoes were so new they even reflected the living room lamps. He invited all our family over for dinner. He said that was his way of dealing with something like what happened. Mr. Grove said he didn't want to forget but forgive. I thought he was going to cry. Addie would have giggled about that before, but not then.

Dinner sounded like a good idea to everyone so Mommy asked him what would be served.

"Fresh crayfish gumbo," he said and winked at my mom. Then he smiled at Addie and me and winked again. "Plus fried rabbit." I looked at his feet and saw that both his socks were black.

And that's how we got to know Mr. Grove, the man next door. That night we first started calling him The Tree, for no reason really, just The Tree, even though he already had a person's name.

THE GAMBOL

Basically I don't belong here, and I don't care what you say. For one, I am a serious student, and I will attend the Naval Academy in the fall. That's in Annapolis, the state capital.

Okay, I will only repeat what occurred then if there is some understanding that I am not responsible for what took place. I mean, I understand America has an attraction, or whatever, towards blaming their problems on other people—which, I want you to know, I hate—but in this case I was a member of this club of victims, or whatever you want to call them. If you have to know, the source of the conflict arose when Mother decided to do what she did, and now she's being punished for it. But, since it seems like I have no choice, let me go back and tell you in the way it should be told.

See, my mother is a well-recognized dancer for the Washington Ballet Company, and she instructs classes at the university and also works as a volunteer at the community college. I think she does it because she still feels guilty about my sister, Nadia, who was the black sheep of the family. Nadia attended community college and never finished, and she's really skinny, even skinnier than my mom. Maybe Nadia has an eating disorder, not that anyone has ever said anything. Now she lives in Florida.

You have to picture my mother: She is tall and thin, with a small but wide nose and several freckles scattered on her face. One larger oval freckle is on the edge of her chin, and when I was young I would imagine that it was a boat sailing off the edge of the world. She is pale and wears dark colors and does her hair in a bun or pigtail. She wears hoop earrings a lot, and scarves. My mother loves draping things—paisley is her favorite pattern. I can circle her wrists with my thumb and index finger. A buddy of mine once said she is like someone from another century. I'm not sure if it was a compliment.

What's important to know isn't that my mother is a horrible snob, but that she seems to enjoy putting herself in a situation where she can be a snob. I know from experience because I used to play soccer at Oakland Mills, but despite the fact that she hated all the parents of my teammates, and wasn't afraid of being vocal to me about how much she hated them, my mother insisted on being an assistant coach for this team that I was on. My mother is polite to everyone. Just don't ask me to explain her.

Well, the main part of it all started because Howard County Community College was sponsoring a fall recital, or whatever you want to call it. This was only a small production, and every night after our olive oil dinners my mother would fiddle with her fake turtleshell napkin ring and dab the corner of her mouth with the corner of her napkin, and complain about the lack of artistic funding for dance. So one night she asked me to do her a big favor and videotape her dancers during a rehearsal so she could analyze and criticize their form, which she does to torture her students. So, reluctantly, I did what she asked me to do.

I was astounded at how bad some of the dancers were. Not only were most of the dancers simply not the right shape—overweight and short, mostly—but most of the ones that looked fine simply couldn't dance, and even I could tell that. They would kind of shuffle and hunch across the stage with their arms raised, as if they were trying to kick a soccer ball between their feet and smell their armpits at the same time. Then they'd leap across the stage, more like you'd do in gym than you were supposed to do dancing. In the car I asked my mother what that leaping move was called and she said it was a gambol.

As these students tried to dance, my mother's face didn't change at all, but I knew inside she was in hysterics. The students must have hated her because she was almost pulling her hair out, ordering everybody around. She'd grab her pigtail and tug on it like I've seen some basketball coaches do to their sweat towels. Whenever she was at HCC she wore her forest green leotard, and had this gray and green striped knit shawl draped around her neck and shoulders. I don't know why she tries so hard to be aristocratic. This is a community college I'm talking about, not Cambridge.

That night she continued to point to me and ask, "Did you get that? Did you get that?" I'd nod, and then she would turn back to the hostages, spaz out, or wince. "That's what I'm talking about. That's exactly what I'm talking about. You're not just dancing for your own release. Work against the grain. Don't force-feed the audience." Then they would mess up again and she'd respond: "Jesus Christ. Imply. Impart wisdom, not the God-forsaken truth. Dislocate your style! Jesus, don't you know your Novere? Again. Again. Do it again."

Obviously, I don't know anything about the world of dance except from what I pick up from my mother, but all I could think was, *What the hell?* I mean, the students that were involved in this project of hers bought their leggings at Kmart if that tells you anything. But noooo, my mother talks to everyone as if they were her manicurist.

So as I had my eye imbedded in the camera, I realized that Sharon Holbrook was standing in the corner of the room away from the others, with her Hair Cuttery shag flopping over her face. Sharon is my neighbor, or was, and we were friends in high school until my mother asserted her dominance and constantly reminded me of what other people would say. She called Sharon my "gal friend." I pretended not to notice Sharon, as she wiped her nose with her index finger, and picked lint from her sweater with her chipped, brown-polished fingernails. It was only afterwards that I discovered she was part of the ensemble too. I discovered the dandelions Sharon painted on her thumbnails while my mother was out visiting the land of dance theory. And that wasn't the only thing I discovered.

Farm View was a new development. The Holbrook's area was older, smaller houses with porches, and hardly any aluminum siding, mostly wood or painted brick with shiny aluminum roofs. Later I told my mother I hated Farm View because all the houses were trying to be different but the same, as if they were more interested in how the whole development looked than one house in it.

Sure, the Holbrooks were intelligent enough to know that my mother didn't like them. Sure. But what they never could have guessed is how far she would go to prove it, or why the woman would be so gung-ho in the first place. It was like Mother had a hypothesis that she thought she must prove. But who forgot to tell her that experiments are supposed to be at least somewhat enjoyable? Plus you're supposed to learn from them.

The problem for me was I always enjoyed the company of my neighbors. When we first moved to Farm View in 1994, we saw the Holbrooks yanking out their big red four-wheelers from their shed, whooping, and hollering, and playing screeching-loud head-banger music as they spun out on their lawn. I remember looking out the window the next day and seeing nothing but mud and thick tracks in the grass where their backyard once was. It was all gloppy and gray looking.

Randy gave me my first ever beer that next week, and discussed his theory: "Saves me the trouble of mowing the lawn," he proclaimed. I noticed Randy blinked a lot, like he always had something in his eye.

"Is this a regular thing?" I asked.

"Been doing it that way ever since I can remember really. We used to have a goat but he died. Name was Alvin."

"Like Alvin the Chipmunk?" I asked.

"No, it was a goat."

The Holbrook family consisted of Sharon, and her brothers Randy, Lyle, and Cody, and their pit bull Kiss, named after the rock band. Randy said they were before my time. Randy was nineteen, but in my grade. He failed as a senior twice. The first time I met him I thought he thought I was snobby because he kept looking away when I talked, but he was probably just high.

The Holbrooks were a wild bunch, that much was certain. Mr. and Mrs. Holbrook were both bus drivers, and also parked their vehicles on the lawn (it seemed like they had more vehicles than people). They had these poker nights, which were smoky, with lots of beer and drinks, and women for the brothers. Nothing fun got past them. The Holbrooks went deer hunting in Garret County, grouse hunting north of

Frederick, and fishing and crabbing on the Choptank three hours away. On a Friday night you could dangle off the old Choptank Bridge with the rest of the county, smoke cigarettes, and try your luck with the sea bass and eels. I should know. They took me with them once. Mother thought I was over at my old friend Pete's house that night. I told her Pete's parents gave me the bass from their fishing trip the month before.

And to top things off the Holbrooks weren't neat. They left cigarette butts on their deck, and beer cans on the curb. Their cards had pheasants on the back. My mother did not approve of any of this, but following her polite suburban graces, the night they moved to our neighborhood, my mother greeted them with freshly bought zucchini bread.

One day Mr. Holbrook cut down a tree that was struck by lightning on somebody else's property, and along with his sons they sawed it into logs, split it and dumped it near the fence adjacent to our yard. This seemed to be innocent enough, but apparently not to my mother. She was ordering chicken and cashew from the Chinese restaurant, attempting to pronounce the dish in pseudo-Mandarin Chinese with the phone propped against her shoulder when she peeked out the window and saw the woodpile. Well, she told the restaurant she had to go, and not to forget the chopsticks. Then she

popped her lips together in the bathroom mirror, and
stormed out the back deck down to the Holbrook residence.
Look out Holbrooks. Mr. Holbrook was raking the bark from
the pitiful patchwork of grass and mud they called their yard,
and I slipped through our sliding glass out onto the deck to
hear the conversation.

"Hi Earl," she crackled. "What is this? What are you
trying to say here?"

"What do you mean?"

"What are you saying? What is this? Is this a woodpile
against my fence? Because that is certainly what it looks like to
me."

"It's—"

"Release me from this situation, okay?"

Earl just cocked his head, like, *what the hell?* He said
something like we've been doing this for years before you
even heard of Eldersburg. With little pause, my mother
answered this with a tirade of if you don't move your termite
woodpile away from my nice fence I'll be forced to blah, blah,
blah. Like that. I was thinking, what could she really do? Give
them more zucchini bread? Earl did nothing except shrug his
shoulders, and go back to gathering bark.

"I mean it, Earl."

Earl did not move the pile, so one night my mother hired Henry—a thirteen-year-old neighborhood kid—and me to sneak over the fence and move the pile ourselves. The problem was Henry asked too many appropriate questions, like why were we moving the wood. I told him not to think, just work. "That's something you learn when you're old like me, and in high school," I said. He was one of these goody-goody kids whose parents nursed him on Disney movies and Bugs Bunny coloring books, and couldn't imagine what breaking the rules meant, just literally couldn't conceive of it.

That night I wondered if Henry was a dwarf because he was far too short for his age, even if he hadn't reached puberty. The problem with Henry was his arms were too long for his body, and he was always falling forwards, following the movements of his arms. He seemed self-conscious of his arms too because he crossed them a lot. O.K., so we moved the pile to the middle of the Holbrook yard, but I did most of the legwork. You'd think a kid with arms like his would be more help with carrying wood.

It didn't matter because I don't think the Holbrooks noticed the change.

The next thing that happened, which led up to the main event, was that Randy ended up, by some freak of imagination, doing yard work for my mother. I never did really get this. I thought maybe Mother was doing it so she could get back at the Holbrooks or whatever, but now I don't think that was the reason. Now, I mostly lean towards thinking that she hired him because she wanted to boss one of the Holbrooks around. Basically, Randy was the direct opposite of my mother. He told me once that hunting deer should be legal in the neighborhood since we got so many of them. Of course, my mother thinks hunting is for barbarians. Once, I saw Randy in an orange raincoat and I wondered if that was what he was doing, hunting. The only question mark was that he didn't appear to have a gun on him, but then he mentioned to me that bow hunting was the only real challenge as far as deer were concerned, so I thought maybe he was taking that a step further and attempting to wrestle a deer down with his bare hands. From what Cody told me, hunting was the one thing Randy was good at.

It definitely wasn't mowing lawns, that's for sure.

Mother hired Randy last October, and you know, it's still pretty hot in October sometimes. I've lived in this state all my life and I still think that month has odd weather. I always get lots of colds then. But what I wanted to say was that Randy cut the lawn like a just-grounded twelve-year-old who wasn't going to get his allowance until he finished. He would leave islands of uncut grass dotted all over the lawn, and that was when he did it on time at all. Most of the time my mother would have to call him to come over. And if she asked him to do anything else like prune the bushes or rake the leaves, he would forget and still mow the lawn, like he was protesting the change of itinerary. But I think he simply never understood the different instructions. I never said he was smart. Also, when he did mow, he would always find a way to mow over some flower or shrub my mother cared about.

The fireworks would explode every Friday evening when Randy would come for his paycheck (he was always on time for that, even though sometimes he thought he was there to mow again, then he would glance around the yard and remember that he just did it on Tuesday, or whatever). The pattern would be that my mother would ream Randy out— loudly—about something that Randy did or didn't do, and Randy would simply stand there and smile and nod, as if she was telling him about what she heard on *NPR* during her commute home.

"You don't deserve even half of this money," she'd say. Then when my mother was frizzy and displaced from anger Randy would say, "Well, see you next week then, okay?" and bounce away. "Jesus Christ," and a heavy Friday sigh would immediately follow from my mother's mouth. I think this was when I started to realize that my mother is basically a mean person. Then she'd ask where my brother William was. He'd usually be outside with his friends somewhere.

One time she said "Come on, let's snag some food, Alexander." It was a strange sentence for my mother to say, as if maybe the Holbrooks were rubbing off on her. "Snag," was not a Mother-like word. I asked her about the word once, and she didn't seem to know she even said it. In fact she told me she was sure she didn't use the word, but she did. Dinner would inevitably include more wine, for myself and her, but not William, and a cordless phone call to a colleague to discuss Doris Humphrey, Mary Wigman, Charles Weidman, Isadora Duncan, and their respective careers, or more often technique, and other related things I didn't care about. It was more interesting when she talked about other dancers. Then at least other people were involved.

"Right, it's really more a dance of the dead," she'd say. "That's what I think too. Rene disagrees though. Yes, yes, yes, you have to become invisible. Of course the choreographer must slip into the space, as it were. To achieve the Vestrisian goal, sure, sure. That's right. But this is just the theoretical basis. Now tell me about Pamela Lille..." Like that.

I remember hearing in a movie or a play—I forget which—that girls usually rebel by associating with people their parents don't approve of, and that boys rebel just by rebelling. I must have a feminine streak then because Randy and I became fast friends.

The funny thing about the Holbrooks was they didn't seem to care one way or another when a slap in the face was the issue. For instance, it could have been that they didn't notice the woodpile had moved, or it could have been that they simply didn't care one way or another where it was, or maybe it was that they just wanted it where it was. The thing I noticed though, was that when the boys rode out on their four-wheelers they simply rode around the pile as if it had been there all along. This cold-shouldered approach infuriated my mother above and beyond anything else. The fact that the woodpile (what the Holbrooks didn't burn) still sits in the middle of the Holbrook yard to this day says something about them, doesn't it? To my mother, the woodpile meant the Holbrooks didn't think they were overmatched.

So at this point, even though I found the Holbrooks interesting, I hardly knew them. This wouldn't last long. The Holbrooks left for Kentucky on vacation—which my mother said was the perfect place for those kind of people to go. "I don't mean anything by this but those neighbors of ours are T-R-A-S-H," she'd whisper to me. "They're just scummy people."

I got the house-sitting assignment because Randy and I were sitting in his room one day, yeah, smoking a bong if you have to know, when he told me about the vacation idea. I was surprised because from the way my mother talked about them I thought the Holbrooks couldn't afford to take vacations (but they must have *some* money, I thought—I mean they *do* live next to us). The important thing here was that, yeah, Randy convinced me to do it because he said I could come into his room and toke his bong whenever I wanted. He told me that his parents and him would arrange the bong hits as my payment instead of money, which was more than fine with me. Randy has these freckles that seemed to flare up on his face like little brown stars whenever we smoked.

Basically that's all that my friendship with Randy consisted of, smoking dope together and watching movies, or *MTV* with our eyes glazed over. We didn't talk much. But my mother was hesitant to even let me watch PG-13 movies, much less cable, so the whole thing felt good. But that's why I really liked Randy, because he didn't put a lot of demands on you. Plus, he was one of the nicest people I'd ever met. Plus, Mr. and Mrs. Holbrook didn't even care that Randy smoked dope, and Randy even said that his parents toked a few themselves at parties or when they had some beer, sometimes after a long day at work. And hell, they bought us all the beer we needed.

You can probably see where this is going. Yes, I watered the Holbrook's big saggy house plants, tended to Kiss, and collected their mail, which included assorted bulk mailers from antique dealers, used car dealerships, and a T-shirt somebody ordered from Winston Cigarettes—but also a piece of mail from the United Way, which surprised me. But then maybe I am easily surprised. A girl I went out with once told me that I'm repressed, but I don't think I am at all. I fed Kiss, just like the Holbrooks asked me, and gave him the appropriate amount of water. Then during the middle of that week, as I was sitting in my room doing my homework, my

mother approached me and asked me if she could help me
with the work at the Holbrook house, just to help. What could
I say? Was I supposed to say no to my own mother? Well, I
didn't.

I'll never forget the night she came to the house with
me. Now, I swear nobody snooped until my mother came
along. She was out of control, opening their kitchen drawers
and cabinets to look at their dishes, gazing into their
refrigerator, going into Mr. and Mrs. Holbrook's bedroom,
looking in the drawers for secret sexual items, bank
statements, jewelry. "Look at this hideous thing," she said
when she found a fake pearl necklace. I told my mother to
stop it but she was on a roll.

One of the things my mother liked to do besides
dancing and teaching dancing, was get away with little things
people didn't think of, or try things people usually wouldn't
do. To this day my mother loves to drive away from a gas
station without paying, or sneak out of restaurants, or make
free calls from public phones by dialing the operator and
saying the phone stole her quarter. She just gets a kick out of
it. I heard on the news a few weeks ago that scientists have
discovered some kind of gene that makes certain people more
likely to do wild or dangerous things. My mother is one of

those kind of people I think. But usually I blame her, not her genes.

One time in old Ellicott City she decided to follow these people around. We were getting Fisher's donuts (which she loves because they are made at a local bakery, not by some big grocery store), and she saw this couple that had a bag from one of the Maryland stores. They were eating cinnamon donuts. Mother took their presence as an insult—tourists. This was back when I was fifteen, and still interested in playing varsity baseball (which I didn't make).

Anyway, the couple was wearing crab hats, which I guess they also bought from the tourist store, and they were holding Orioles banners. Mother made me follow them with her, as the couple went from store to store. I was so embarrassed. Finally at one store—I think it was a crystal shop, or a palm reading shop, I can't remember—the couple said to us, in a smiley, kidding voice, "What, are you following us around?" The woman stuck out her hand to introduce herself to my mother, and probably tell Mother how nice it is to visit a quaint little historic town in Maryland, and how much it is like this other quaint little historic town near where they live. But Mother just smirked and said, "You know, Fisher's Bakery likes to mix ashes into their cinnamon powder."

"What?"

"Never mind."

"What kind of ashes are we talking about here," the man asked. "What are you talking about?"

"You know, mostly human ashes, but sometimes dog." Then she lowered her voice. "The ones that nobody takes."

Then she walked out and left me standing there watching their crab hats bob up and down in dismay. I didn't stick around for the aftermath though. When I finally caught up to Mother she made me drive, even though I didn't even have my learner's permit yet.

But what happened at the Holbrooks was like something out of the movies. My mother always carries the same purse—this huge, black and gold-trimmed purse—so I didn't think anything was strange, even when I went to feed Kiss and she was nervously carrying the purse in her hands in the living room, sifting through their videotapes, commenting on their taste in movies, which included *Bloodsucker 12: The Final Exit*.

When I came back she had a red spray paint can in her right hand, and a black one in her left hand, and I noticed she had dishwashing gloves on. First she started grinning, then she started spraying everything in sight: the television, the walls, the rug, the sofa, the plants, ceiling, lamps, closets, pillows. Her face was red and streaky from laughing so hard. I ran to her and grabbed her arms to take the paint away, but she sprayed my hair and chest and screamed, "It's my turn! My turn!"

I ran over to the telephone to try my grandmother, somebody, anybody, but Mother was now running and spraying like a banshee, and her hair was flailing behind her, and suddenly her shoulders looked wide like a football player's. She was shaking and rattling the spray cans, and spraying the kitchen, hallway, front door, and running up the stairs to the bedrooms, then out and down the balcony in back, and tossing the cans behind her. By the time I got anyone on the phone, Mother was probably at home, sipping ice tea from a wine glass. I tried to clean up, but I couldn't get any of the paint off and I didn't want to make it worse, so I locked up and went home.

Let me just tell you that when I was growing up I adored my mother. I thought she was the most beautiful woman in the world, and I remember thinking that I was glad

Dad divorced her because then I could have her all to myself.
Why would I ever need a girlfriend? I could just look at my
mother if I wanted to see someone beautiful—that's what I
always thought. But when I told Mother once that I thought
she was beautiful, she said, "Don't ever say that again!" I still
don't understand that.

And Dad, he wasn't even a real person to me, just
some kind of smoky figure, like the kind you see in a flashback
scene. To this day he only calls when he wants a favor, or
forgets to send the money, and lies about losing the address.
He lives in Missouri now. He's an animal rights activist, or he
was the last time I talked to him. I think he left because he was
whipped, and overpowered, and had no other choice.

But I swear, I didn't want to move to Eldersburg. It's
not even a real town. Just a strip with stores and fast food.
Mother moved us up here because, I don't know, maybe she
really liked to live near country folks (who she called
Scarletnecks—one of the many insults she sprayed on the
walls that one night) to feel superior, not that most of the
people living up where we lived didn't do the same thing as
her—commute to Baltimore or D.C. at six in the morning
and not return home until eight o'clock at night, if that.

I thought Mother had become a lesbian or something too, because she kept having her women dancer friends over late at night for wine or martinis, but then I have never seen another person here in the morning besides her. I tried to ask her once about her love life, but she shot my question down before I even asked it, by saying, "Yes Alexander, I have human desires like any other person. " That was the beginning and end of that.

I wish our house had a porch. If you have a porch you can sit out front and watch people go by, and talk to them if they are interesting. We have everything else but a porch. We have a deck in the back. I heard somebody tell me that Southerners would rather hang out in the front yard, and Northerners would rather hang out in the back yard where nobody can see them. If it's true, the Holbrooks and myself would be more Southern than Northern. I don't think Mother was running away from anything but the congestion when we moved from Gaithersburg to here. But then we get the congestion on Route 32 anyway. Mother got me a new ice blue Toyota Celica for my birthday.

Just to let you know, my mother always told me I should be a senator, because she thinks I have a stately manner

about me, or whatever. She said that. But I never understood
why she was so concerned about the appearance of what I do,
because she already has a prestigious job. Plus, I received
decent grades, and I was sure I would go to a reputable
college. What worried me though, was that she would try to
influence me if I ever did become a senator. I mean, my
mother reads books like *Women and Revolt: The Tenuous Marriage
of Marxism and Feminism*, and *Postmodernist Philosophy: Bridging
the Gap*, or *The Theory of the Body: Woman*. When I was in tenth
grade she called my teacher to argue that I shouldn't have to
read *Macbeth*, because it's sexist and glorifies violence. I was
so embarrassed. My teacher, Mr. Hollins, was a Pat Buchanan
supporter, and he teased me about my pinko mother for the
rest of the year. And I think because of my mother I got a B for
the fourth quarter, instead of what I deserved.

I didn't want to have to tell the Holbrooks it was my
mother who destroyed their house.

When the Holbrooks came back from Kentucky and
found their house trashed, guess what they did? Well, they did
call first, but they never insinuated they even suspected that I
was involved. The first question they asked was: "Hey there
Alex. You want to come to a party?" I said yeah, then we

talked for a long time about their trip and what they did—
camp, fish, hike. They didn't even ask about their house. It
was only later when they called back that they asked, "Hey,
Alex did you see somebody break into the house?" I was off
the hook. Of course I said, "Yeah, I did. It was Friday night."
They didn't ask for more details. They just called the police,
who obviously came and maybe dusted for fingerprints. Then
the Holbrooks called their insurance company, who
apparently couldn't cover, because they had the lowest kind
with a sky-high deductible.

The best part was that the Holbrooks had a clean-up-
the-graffiti-party the next weekend and they called to tell me I
was invited. I didn't tell Mother that was where I was going.
Instead I told her I was going out with Brad, my friend from
Columbia who she liked—even though I hadn't talked to him
in seven months.

That party was the weirdest thing I've ever been to,
and also one of the most fun. When I got there a lot of people
were gathered on the front porch talking about how great
Hammer Jacks was in its glory days. These were people like
I've never seen before up close. People with tattoos and long
hair, women wearing tank tops or little pink cut-off T-shirts
with tons of hair spray on, men with ripped T-shirts with

mummies, bleeding letters, and crosses emblazoned on them, and cut-offs. Tons of cut-offs. And they were yelling and downing beer like water.

I walked up to the porch and everybody yelled, "Hey dude, how's it going?" I walked past one fat guy with a beard and glasses who said, "Keg's back in the living room." I asked another guy if Randy was there, and his answer was that Randy was out with the band trying to make a pass at the lead singer. That's where I headed next.

As I walked back there, the balcony above me and people all around, there was a big smashing sound, and there was Mr. Holbrook holding a green broken bottle christening a motorcycle for Randy. The applause from all sides was almost overwhelming, like I was walking into some rock concert. I had no idea. People were handing each other gifts wrapped in newspaper—all gifts from the dollar store, apparently. They all joked about their junk jewelry, and chintzy coffee mugs.

I felt skittish, I have to admit, out of place, but also excited somehow. Randy saw me and waved over the crowd of people downing champagne in Dixie cups, and some guy handed me some, which I drank. Then Randy came over to me and said, "Hey, want a doobie? I was just going to spark one up." So that was that.

By the time I came out, my head was spinning, if you have to know, and I swear everybody was painting and wallpapering the walls, reupholstering the furniture, and scrubbing the appliances. Nobody was frowning, and all I saw were smiling people hard at work to help their friends, and all I heard were people saying stuff like, "It'll only make your place look better in the end, Bart. Ain't like you had no stellar place before." These were kind people. That was when I noticed the flypaper above the stove. I don't know if the marijuana took effect, but I swear they had about twenty flies on the paper, but why would they put it above the stove? I didn't even notice that before.

Then I heard the band. As I said, I was stoned, but nevertheless, the band was the oddest thing I think I have ever heard, all screechy heavy metal and flaring hair. The lead singer—who I first thought was a guy—was drunk out of her mind. She crashed on the lawn singing with a cordless mike, in the purple light from the bug zapper, and the band thrashed behind her. She was wearing a hot pink jumpsuit, I'll never forget. Then she walked into the bathroom in the house and started blabbing into the cordless "Singing in the drain. I am singing in the drain." That was when I saw Sharon.

Sharon was sitting on the motorcycle, drinking a beer by herself, her hair pulled back into a blue sparkly scrunchie. I think that was when, I started to, you know, like her. Because I was having fun, I think. She winked at me, and yelled something like, how come I'm not filming the party for my mother, and I walked over to her and we were talking, or whatever. She showed me her new fingernail job. They were roses. Then we started slow dancing, real close. I could smell her flowery shampoo. I think I spun her. I think she kissed me first. Then I kissed her, and held her, and we spun around and around, face to face. I remember she had flypaper tacked on the ceiling in her room.

"Those inbred idiots," my mother was saying after the first dance recital. William was there with Mother and myself at La Plata Grande in Columbia, this Mexican restaurant. According to my mother, the performance was a disaster. I was surprised, because even though the dancers were dogs, they still didn't do that badly, I didn't think. I mean, not that I like watching, but mother wouldn't listen to any point of view that included the least bit of praise. All she wanted to hear was that the whole thing sucked badly, and that she should just quit the arts and manage some T-shirt shop on the beach. I didn't feel like being the person to shed sunlight into her life.

"They were dancing to the music. *Still*," she said. "I can't believe it. After all the emotional space we explored, they still retained their dramatic form. There they were at their senior prom. Not everyone is a St. Denis, but for Christ's sake. It has to be an *experience* at least. Meet the minimum requirements." My brother William squirmed in his seat quietly. He just wanted to eat, but not Mexican food.

Anyway, she got up from the table to use the ladies' room, and the waiter came over to take our orders. He took mine and William's, then he saw my mother walk across the room, and back to her seat. When she sat down, the waiter said, "Oh good, the whole family is here." He turned to Mother and said, "What will the missus have?" I coughed, but the waiter continued his smiley banter: "Your husband ordered you a root beer, is that okay?" The waiter was still blinking dumbly at me, and at my mother. All I could do was grin, knowing what I was about to tell her.

WAC: THE ART OF

There's no story about me, only on Brent Trayo. He's the guy who shot my chances of being a millionaire down a notch, just for a sec, just until I catch my breath. Yeah, Brent's the motherfucker who thought he was too good for all of us, too good for Troy, too proud for money lifelined right into his pocket. A story's only on him, Troy says, because Brent couldn't gamble on a sale, and that's the way it is if Troy says it.

The first time I met Brent I liked him. I have to admit it. By the way he carried himself I thought he'd be good for the family. He had a nodding step, a flick of the hand to catch the time on his Mickey watch, a cool toss of his head to hear Troy point out the room where all the prints and lithographs were kept. From the first glance Brent seemed to be 100% salesman. Meeting people is like making a sale. First you have to take them for what they are or what they seem to be, then jerk them right out of it. What I jerked out of Brent right off was that Brent seemed to have the same kind of confidence that Troy had: the kind that can see the logic in a man, and sell right to it. For starters they both had the kind of eyes that lay deep in the sockets, closer to the brain, and the kind of eyebrows that didn't cover the facts over.

That day Troy led Brent into the room and told me to train him. From just looking at Brent I thought he'd come over, shake my hand, pat me on the back and say "Pleasant to meet you," and I'd tell him my name is Austin, then we'd get in the car and he'd ask "So this is WAC?" and I'd show him how it's done, and he'd be excited about it. Then he'd offer me a Tic-Tac, and I'd take two and say I like the kind he gives me even better than wintergreen, even though wintergreen is the best. But that's not the way it went down, no matter how hard I watched him.

The guy just stood there and didn't even smile or say hi, just shuffled his feet in the dust balls on the concrete floor, then bent over and picked up a dust ball—which must have been there in one corner or another since I came to WAC—and rolled it between his middle finger and forefinger into a sort of dust ball snake. Then he looked at me, looked down, rolled it tighter, gray and brown with flecks of glass or something (I couldn't tell), looked back at me, grimaced, and dropped it into his pocket. Odd. I said hi and everything, and had him grab some art prints, then I walked out to my Bronco with him following, dragging and scraping his feet on the asphalt.

Brent came a month before I was going to be promoted to manager. That was my best dream. On the day he interviewed me, Troy said: "You'll be a manager in six months, district manager in a year making a hundred grand. In two years you'll make a mil." He scratched his cheek with his long pinky nail that day and said that "WAC is making a lot of young people make a lot of money. WAC wants to cover the world in wholesale art." WAC stands for Wholesale Art Corporation, he told me: "No frills here," Troy said. "None." Troy told me that my turn in the grand money wheel was next. He said I would have a few goals to meet: fifty, seventy-five, one hundred sales a week for two weeks each. He called it "learning." Then he slapped me on the back and led me out of his white-walled office. It never bothered me that he didn't have any art or Disney up there. It didn't bother me that he slapped me on the back. Troy was Troy.

I'm sure Brent heard those same encouraging words of wisdom from the master, but something in his head didn't register the same as me. The first time I took Brent out to show him the strings, he kept asking me about serious things like the job, and health insurance or whatever, and what Troy is like, really like. I told him, "Man, chill out. We don't like to be so gloomy around here. It's like Troy says, we should grin every time we see the poster glass." As I straightened a few Monets and Disneys and elephant prints tight in their glass black frames and gray cardboard-edge protectors, I told Brent everything there is to know about WAC, which wasn't much because WAC is so simple, so down to earth. A lot of young people our age are making a lot of money, I told him. Then I told him that he will be a manager in six months, then that we want to drown the world in twenty and thirty dollar art.

But Brent kept pushing, kept rocking the canoe. By this time I was driving around the beltway towards Annapolis, and my hands were sweating and itchy, and the radio sounded fuzzy so I switched it. Every time I wanted to hear music there was no damn music on. I mean nothing—only opera, or damn space-age art rock. Brent asked me if WAC just worked by commission, which was the question Troy told us to keep secret, so I said, "Ask Troy." Then Mr. Persistent asked me what about the cut-off sales idea, which was the other secret-Troy-question so I gave him the same thing. That was when I exited onto 97 and told Brent "You know, we really have a family at WAC, a team." And I tried to smile, to soothe him by smiling. But he just stared out the window, at the construction on the highway, and didn't smile at all. I remember that. I thought he needed cheering up so I said, "Cool that they're expanding this road here, huh? Maybe I finally won't have to fight the traffic the whole time." He didn't say anything, just looked out the window as if he was looking at a Nazi death camp. What a black-ass, I thought. I guess that was the moment I started disliking him. There I was trying to be nice, and there he was trying to be a black-ass. How is he going to sell if he's so serious all the time? Customers see that and run like it really is Death come to tote Matisse. You have to be able to smile to sell anything in this world. "Yeah, ask Troy," I said. "Troy knows."

When we got to the strip I was working, Brent didn't hesitate in tagging behind me to train. Obviously driven. The strip was where all these haircut joints were, the kind cheap enough to buy our prints, but not so cheap that they couldn't afford anything on their walls. Haircut joints are the milk of the crop because the women and fags can't buy just one. Easy pickings. I took two sample prints out of the back, a Monet and a sailboat, and we hit the first joint. I told Brent to pay attention. "Good morning, madam," I said to the lady up front in bright yellow heels and a red miniskirt. "We just came from an art sale at William and Mary College, and we're selling this beautiful art today at discount." Then I flipped the prints from back to front. Very dramatic. "Today we want to make your day," I said. I never said 'lucky.' People usually seemed suspicious of us peddling luck *and* art.

"I don't think so," she said. Then I knew I was going to have to force a sale. I just had to hit her logic. High heels, I thought, red skirt. I walked over to her, put my arm around her and took her hand ever so nicely. It was small, so small it felt like I could crush it into dust.

"Honey," I said softer, "Maybe your husband isn't being nice to you, if you know what I mean? Don't you think Van Gogh would give him a go?" She half-laughed, half-squinted at me. I surprised her at least. But she shook her head. "But I bet Ansel Adams would," I said. Then she let out a stomach laugh. Bingo. She twisted in her heels, dropped her scissors on the counter, and stepped away from her customer.

"I'll take a look at what you have," she said. "But make it quick, honey, I'm trying to earn my chow, hear?"

I took her to my Bronco and Brent followed. Yeah, I showed her what I had. She ended up picking out four Ansel Adams, which was all I had of him that day, and then after she paid, another lady from the back of the joint came out and said, "*Mine* likes Mr. Gogh." Then she winked at me. Brent mumbled something about Mr. *Van* Gogh, but I cut him off by getting the lady to also buy a Goofy, for—nudge, nudge—afterwards.

After she ponied up, I said, "You see, it's just like potato chips at these joints. The sheep can't get enough of them." Then I told Brent about Troy's rule that we have to get three *no*'s from a person before we give up on a sale. That's the way to do it, I said.

"What other rules does Troy have?" I shoved the samples in back.

"I don't know, man." He moved closer to me, around the Bronco to the driver's side.

"What?"

"Well, one is that you should get them into the habit of saying 'yes.' See, you have to feed into the way the animals think."

"To me a salesperson should put the customer at ease."

"Look man," I said. "I don't know if you got all these ideas in college or what. All I know is if you don't screw the customer they'll sure as hell screw you."

"I just know I wouldn't want to be pushed," he said. I was going to start a battle right then and there, but I decided to shut up instead, to just let it go that time. I got in and started the engine. We went to the next joint after that. Right next door. I sold twenty that day, total, which was good, okay, it was.

Unfortunately for me though, Troy said Brent had to tag along for one more day of training. I told Troy in the morning meeting how skeptical and questioning Brent had been, and Troy told me it was my job to convince Brent that he *had* to work for WAC. "But it's hurting my sales," I said, even though it really wasn't. The truth was that the guy made me uncomfortable. Plus, even though I sold the day before, when two people come into a place it seems more of a scam than if it's just me. It's hard explaining someone just for carrying prints and watching. Troy dragged me off to his office and made me sit down. He closed the door and told me to stare at the white wall. I thought which one, but didn't say anything.

"What's going on, Troy?" I asked. Troy didn't answer. I stared at the white. I thought of when you lay in the park staring at a cloud and you and the babe next to you both get different things out of it. Except I didn't get anything out of the wall.

"Austin, I don't give a shit that you *think* you're not selling," Troy said suddenly. "You know our policy towards new recruits. What is it?"

"We keep them, man."

"Right. We keep them. They come, they stay. Brent's a smart guy. He's been to college. He's like a tomato plant, just needs a stake next to him to help him along the way. Tell him he could be as rich as me. Tell him he'll be a millionaire. I don't care. Just get him." Troy was only twenty-three and some said the best salesman ever to live on this earth and that was before he became manager where he was making close to a hundred grand a year.

Then Troy pushed his nose into my face. I could feel his breath jam my own breath back down my throat.

"Goddamnit Austin," he said. "You'd better keep this asshole. Tell him that I said he could be manager in three months if you want. Make him love his fucking job with every cell he has. I don't care how. Just do it. Do it."

I promised I would.

Then he led me out of his office right into the morning chant session.

Before each day Troy would make us stand against the wall and work ourselves up like each day was the Super Bowl. The family called itself "The Warlocks." That morning after our talk Troy started screaming, "Isn't it great that you'll all be millionaires?" over and over and over again. Then we'd scream "Yeah!" and pound our fists together. Then he asked, "What are we going to make today?"

"Money! Money!"

Sometimes it'd get pretty wild and I'd start slamming into everyone, and we'd work ourselves up into a froth. It helped sales. Troy even wrote some poems for us. One went: "There once was a man from Amoco who said 'no, no, no.' So we sold him a Van Gogh, Gogh, Go!" I loved those morning chant sessions. It was beautiful seeing the family there riled up, pumped. Larry and Todd and Greg and Hankie really got into it too. Then we'd yell, "I love my fucking job." Everyone did.

We were selling to everyone then: to heavy security industrial parks, to banks, to Denny's, to Kmart, to whorehouses for Christ's sake, to everyone with four walls. We would have sold to churches if they weren't so stuck on their snobby religious paraphernalia. The fact of the matter was that raking in five bucks out of every twenty and ten out of every thirty wasn't bad at all. We were our own bosses every day, and also part of The Warlocks. That's what I told Brent. Maybe the chance to be rich bothered some people. Maybe the tax-free income bothered some people. Or the fact that Troy got five for every five that each of us made, not doing anything except for ordering more prints when we got low, but mostly staring at the wall. It didn't bother me. When I was in middle school I sold magazines and candy bars and won two ten-inch TVs for the most sales of both. I never knew what to do with two TVs except try to watch two shows at once. My mother always said, "Selling is a job you can do anytime. It's just that some people are too proud to do it." Frankly, the ones that didn't like it at WAC, they kept their mouths shut, or we made them. As we should have.

As soon as Brent came along though, everything went to shit. I think it was because he had short preppy hair unlike the rest of us. And he wore prep too. And he didn't have earrings. And he didn't like comics like the rest of us.

Like on the second day of his training he was ten minutes late, and I told him that Troy doesn't play with lateness. He said his car ran out of gas or some bullshit excuse, and I said he better have a reliable car for this job. Then I took the butthole to First Annapolis, then Annapolis Savings and Loan, then to Citibank. I made sure to point out the "no soliciting" signs in red and black, and made sure to point out how I whistled one Goya from this woman clerk at the first we stopped at, and two Dali's from the second. And that was with only a glance from the cop coming up because of the manager calling. "This is nothing like the time the cop punched me out of the pottery store," I told him. Selling to the banks was what Troy called a *rip*—a difficult sale. "Cut some rips," he'd say, shaking his hair from his eyes.

Brent followed on my heels that morning and I finally made him carry the sample prints into the restaurant strip where it was a no-go all over. I showed Brent how to push them hard, to get three *no*'s before stopping, and to make sure to ask everyone if they needed a print for home, if not for the restaurant. "Banks and restaurants only early, never Fridays," I said.

"We should've been here earlier, I told him. I was all over his case for being late. I had to force Brent into WAC or Troy might not make me a manager. Troy might just grab me by the shirt and throw my ass out in the street.

Later when we went to McDonald's for a ten-minute lunch-sprint (Troy's name) Brent asked me about the manager bit.

"Oh yeah. You're guaranteed to be just like Troy in six months. Just taking in the money. Just living," I said. Brent looked down at his McChicken sandwich in disgust. I wondered if he ate McDonald's much.

"Really?"

"Eat your sandwich," I said.

Brent ate every bit of that sandwich, chewing it in the side of his mouth, even eating the wet-rag pickles. I do have to admit that. Then when I was finishing up my lunch, he touched my shoulder and looked at me, almost to my eyeballs, not around the edges, not looking away, and he asked, "How do you lie to these people?"

I hate when people touch me.

"I don't know what you mean," I said.

"You lie. You have to lie. It's not as if what you sell is necessary to anybody. It's all in museums or corporate offices or some rich person's house anyway."

"So?" I really hated the guy then. Why didn't he just do what everyone else did? Why didn't he just go to some place where they were like him? If there is such a place. He always thought he was right.

"I mean, the mask," he said.

"Man, what are you talking about?" I squared off to him.

"You lie to yourself to make a sale," he said. "You have to. Because it's not in our nature to sell things. How can you live with yourself?"

"Why don't you just come to work on time? This is a team here!"

He stood up, turned away, crumpled his sandwich paper, then back-kicked dirt towards me from the floor, walked over to the trash can and threw his garbage out. Then he walked to my Bronco, and before I could get to him he sat on the hood.

Brent started selling on his own the next day.

I can't say what he did off his own selling, but from what Missy told Frank who told Hankie who told me, Brent was basically afraid to sell. The wuss. Hankie said he saw Brent in Patapsco Park reading, and not even at lunch, but during the prime hour of 10:00 in the morning. And Brent only had a little piece of shit Chevy, hardly enough room to fit enough prints to sell to one hot haircutting joint. And Hankie said that he heard that Brent owed Troy some money, and that was why he was with us, but that Troy was still positive Brent would be a manager, no matter, and that Troy had faith in all of us. Personally I knew that Brent talked to himself because anybody who said the kind of things he said to me must.

But after two weeks Brent didn't meet the weekly fifty sales limit, so he had to lag back with the new recruits. Troy was on Brent's ass, yelling at him to sell more, yelling, "Have you got the right stuff?" with Brent mumbling back, then Troy getting more worked up but still not admitting a bad thing about Brent's selling abilities to me, just saying he had potential, smiling, grinning, running his hands through his hair, looking right past me through his white office door with no art prints, no Disney, like he was looking at some invisible person about to appear out of his own imagining. Troy got where he got because of his faith, I thought.

After another week Brent wasn't chanting in the morning, and was just moaning, "I like my job," in the afternoon sessions, and that's when I really started to want to hurt the prick because he was affecting the family then. I could see it in their eyes.

One morning Troy left to catch a nap (he deserved one), and Brent was my task before the whole of the Warlocks because, as Troy said, I'm the right hand enthusiasm-man. Brent was really loafing, not even looking at the other Warlocks, as if he was better than all of us, and for no reason since he had only netted some pitiful twenty-seven prints in three days. So I got in his face.

"Hey, wuss! Quit feathering it and cut some damn rips," I said.

"Yes sir," he said, saluting me.

"You're setting a poor fucking example for the recruits. Why's that?"

"Why don't you ask Troy?"

That was when it all broke inside for me. I pushed him against the wall and grabbed his faggy little prep green and red Polo.

"You have no excuse for not selling. You're such a little girl. You can't even take a single *no* without feeling bad, I bet. Go out there and sell to those animals," I said.

That was when, right in front of everyone, he did something completely unexpected: He punched me in the stomach. It hit me like a parasite tunneling into my gut. I dropped to the floor, right next to the O'Keefes. I could feel the dust balls that Brent hadn't picked up fluff against my clothes, the shamed stares from The Warlocks, Troy's invisible shaking head outside and above the vision of the room. Then I could hear Brent walk over and pick up prints from the stacks.

"You're wasting your time," he said. "When I sell, it's because I feel it out there lurking, waiting for me. But most of the time, I feel nothing. If they buy it's because it's already out there and has nothing to do with you being a good salesman. It's not an art. It's only because you had the luck to hit the right spot that day."

Then he walked to his car to start his day, and nobody stopped him. They stood there and stared at me like they had never seen anybody on the ground before.

"Luck," I said. "Fuck luck."

I only sold five prints that day. That shit, that little shit jinxed me.

It went like that for a few more weeks: I mean quiet antagonism, and little selling. My sales were up and down, but on the whole down, even with me smiling till my cheeks hurt. It was that prick Brent who started the slump. Brent was a nagging doubt-fly in the whole Warlock oatmeal. And he kept opening his trap too, saying that the market was over-saturated with cheap art, and that no matter what we say ours is about the cheapest, saying that there *is* a difference between a Disney and a Velasquez, saying that how could there be enough room in the world for each of us to be like Troy, and that all of us being young millionaires is out-of-this-world-impossible. But everybody knew that Brent was just negative, and selfish, and just making excuses for not being a good salesman, and that he just thought he was right about everything. Everyone in the Warlocks wanted to kick his ass, but only they didn't, to keep that team family harmony flowing like usual, to not let a bad pear like him spoil the core. That's what I think.

But a cancer like Brent is too much for any good
in this world. When more new recruits came in and Troy told
Brent he'd better keep his trainee because he had faith in him,
that was it. Brent had lost new recruits the week before,
probably because he told them his version of truth, which was
no truth at all. Then in came this other skinny faggot with
short hair, no earrings or nothing, strutting around with his
white tennis shoes and a fat mole on his chin like he was Mr.
Sales. Brent took him out to train him, and maybe they
humped each other. Who knows? What's important is that
Brent got this recruit so worked up that he whined to the
police on the phone, saying that WAC purposefully "Breaks *no*
solicitations, threatens its workers with a cult atmosphere," or
some chick shit like that, and that WAC blackmails its
salespeople—"salespeople," I'm sure he said.

That was a Wednesday. On Thursday when Brent came
in, Troy took him into his office. I'm not sure what Troy said,
but Brent walked out of there without blood on his face, no
black eyes on him. And Troy scuffled out pulling his hair back
tight with a blue rubber band. I pictured it as Troy giving
Brent the boot, finally losing that strong faith in Brent, and
Troy so angry that he comes to the end of his argument, and

just gives up. Brent probably philosophized at the mouth then, tore into poor Troy with his luck-theory shit. I pictured Brent talking about lying, and honesty—not of the religious kind, but of some higher quality, and then Brent not even picking at his teeth with his pen like Troy did, but just straight-up telling Troy that he couldn't stand to see Van Gogh peddled off to Essex Travel Associates, even by himself who knows little about Van Gogh but wouldn't mind learning. Then I bet Troy made a fist in his left hand, and Brent said that anyway when it comes down to it, money doesn't really matter, and how can us bunch of neo-hippies get into such a scam? And then I bet Brent said that he cuts deals anyway, not rips, by selling the thirty-dollar lithographs for twenty, and the twenty for fifteen because they're worth even less than that. Then I bet he lied about that in the records anyway by misnotching the number sold. And I'm sure Troy just sat at his desk looking bored but silently angry, thinking when he could get back to his new townhouse and girlfriend waiting there for him, and Brent just stared at him and asked if Troy had listened to a single thing he had just said, then Troy yawned and said, "When will I get my money back?" And Brent had it all right in his pocket next to the dust ball snake he'd kept as a lucky charm. But all that's

just in my head, and not worth the print it's papered on.
Brent, Mr. Selfish-Money-Hater, Brent, Mr. I-Cannot-Tell-A-
Lie went off to chop down a cherry bush. I hope he eats fried
beans the rest of his life, without any refrying even. I hope
he's so poor he has to eat McDonald's forever.

There's no story on me, there's no story about any of
the Warlocks. There's only a story on Brent Trayo. It's a
shame: He could have sold somehow. That's what I failed at
showing him. Troy's right.

It was a year later into WAC though that I started not
thinking about Brent exactly, but just working out a few
strategies he seemed to know about selling despite himself. I
told the idiots right off that I was selling right out of the back
of some truck and one room warehouse joint, and that I was
getting five bucks for every twenty, and ten out of every
thirty, "So just fucking buy." That actually worked for a while.
And Troy told me every morning that he was setting up the
new store for me to be manager. Except then he came up
with this new cut-off that the Warlocks had to sell a thousand
in one week as a team. We never did. For some reason the
sales started dipping way down below forty a week for me,

below five hundred a week for the Warlocks, and after a month of poor sales Troy had to finally let me go. I don't blame him. I owe Troy everything. Troy just said that I lost it, and that happens sometimes. Troy is a good comfort. If he was only a girl.

I wonder though what "it" is that I lost. I wonder if it was another me who messed everything up. I wonder if there is another me out there. You know, you hear there's supposed to be a carbon copy of each person somewhere in the universe. I hope there's not one of me. If there is I hope my other me is with Brent, burning in the canyons of hell or something. Right there where I can know where he is.

Whatever it was I lost, everyone stopped selling. The Warlocks stopped selling. Even Troy couldn't—I heard he had to go out there again. I'm sure WAC survived though.

But it's good. Everything's good. Now I'm into a whole new challenge. The dealing kind of selling. You know, Chevy's.

YESTERDAY WAS RIVET

Phyllis is on the screen in the dark. I'm chasing Orange around the Coke machine, and by Dee, the fish tank, in-between "Ghost Town," and back around the couch in the glow of the screen. "Little Cricket" is on again. Videos. Videos. I'm sick of...except when the man talks fast, fast, fast. TV. "Deal valid until—void where prohibited—special offer only until." The colors and sounds are right for you. They tell you exactly what to do. "First time buyers programs available—treat yourself—on sale now!" And when that happens I don't want to chase Orange. I don't care how much he nuzzles, or licks.

"Stop that Ryan," Phyllis says. "What did I..." Her voice fades into the sounds of the screen. Bleeps, blips, bonks. Bloink. Bleeop. Whooosh. Shooch. Her screen flashes a different color from my screen, and a beeping sound, and a whooshing sound flash. She types so hard it sounds like when Freedy rivets. Freedy likes loud sounds. I don't care what Dee says, I'm calling them what I want. The floor is sticky.

"But they aren't friends," Dee told me. "You're supposed to respect the people who bring you in." Dee has a nail through her tongue. I want a nail through "Little Cricket."

In the morning, Phyllis tells me we're flying to Boston. In a day. I think maybe we're moving, and "I don't want to move," I say. "I like it here with Freedy."

"We're *all* going," she says. "It's just a trip." She tells me it's my first trip. She says her first trip was when she was seven. Her parents didn't take her anywhere, she says. "You're lucky." I can hear the screen buzzing and zipping downstairs. Phyllis smells like Freedy. Sweat. I want to chase Orange around and around and around and...

"I don't want to play with toys," I say.

"You have nice toys," she says.

"I want the screen."

"The screen is not a toy."

Dee tells me that we're going to visit someone Phyllis met on the screen. She tells me Mom found friends without even leaving the house.

"What kind of ball would you like to be, Dee?"

"I don't know," she says. "That's—"

"I'd be a beach ball. I'd want to float."

"Beach balls don't float in the air."

"They do if the air is in the water," I say. I have to wee-wee. The floor is sticky.

I saw Dee find the turtle. It was swimming in a creek behind from where we live. She didn't see me. She was looking for her secret plants back there. I've seen her. She told me never tell, but I might if she hits me again. She is careful not to hit me. Dee lied and said she bought the turtle for Mother's Day. She put it in a shoe box and told her. Phyllis stopped looking at the fish tank when we got the screen. "I can do things faster," she says. She sighs when I try to tell her the turtle is eating the fish eggs. She presses down harder on the mousie. She says fish eggs are good for turtles. But we have fish too. Before she watched the fish. Before that she listened to the wind chimes. Freedy rivets too much to hear them now. He makes folding chairs and sends them out in the mail to a company who wants folding chairs. They are silvery, like the fish. He says the company is bad because they make him stay at home. I want him to stay and rivet. Don't find any more turtles anybody.

"We need to clean," Phyllis says.

"The floor is sticky," I say.

"Right, we don't want to come home to the mess, do we?"

"Maybe the screen can clean it," I say.

"They can't do that yet," she says. "Someday." She looks at the light. One of the light parts hangs. "Someday all the screens will be one screen."

"Then I can use your screen?"

"By then we'll have two screens," she says.

"Phyllis, I hate 'Little Cricket.'"

"I don't care. I told you not to call me Phyllis. Call me Mother," she says. "Please." She points to the mess. Clothes and food and papers are stacked. Freedy is out getting supplies. I can hear the wind chimes. I can see the sticky in the right light. Her shoes go shcheeee, schuump, shcheeee, schuump.

When we get there, fifteen people all sit around and say who they are. I'm wondering if these chairs are from Freedy.

He isn't looking at the chairs. Nobody knows each other. Everybody is looking off away from everybody else. They all say their screen names. It's like Miss Hoffman tells us to do with our names if we're out visiting in the zoo, walking around outside and around.

Nobody asks who I am. Dee has her headset on, but not too loud. I can barely hear it. She's drawing in the corner. I ask her if I can draw. She tells me she wants to get the hell out of here. I want to go back and eat some of that creamy stuff with the spinach in it. With chocolate bars over there on the table. Freedy doesn't make tables.

"It's difficult to meet people in this closed-off society," the small woman says. "Even at work. Everyone has their own set of friends."

"We need to do this every month," the big woman says. The women clap. The two men look at each other and smile. Freedy watches the other man uncross his legs. He's the only one in shorts. The other man smiles bigger, and he looks away from Freedy. The other man stares at Phyllis. Back at Freedy. He bites his lip, and then looks back at Phyllis. Phyllis looks at him and smiles.

"Who's gonna pay for that?" Freedy says.

"We all will," the big woman says.

"So you're gonna get a job?" he says to Phyllis.

"I have a job. It's called housewife."

"That's the kind of job that don't pay," Freedy says.

"Maybe it's gotta start then." Two women clap, and nod.

"Maybe when you work for somebody who can afford you," he says. Freedy stands up and asks Dee if she wants to go get ice cream. I say I want to go too and he waves me on.

The store is freezing. I wrap my shirt around my legs. I'm eating a cone of Moose Tracks. It's brown. It's dripping on the table. I lick it from the table.

"I try my best to be a good father. I'm just not going to waste your college money to come up here twelve times a year. No way."

"I don't want to go anyway," Dee says. "I don't like school *now*."

"You're going," he says.

"I want to be a welder," she says.

"Welders are stupid," he says. "You're not stupid."

I lick the Moose Tracks off the table and Dee smacks my head. Freedy stares at the light above us.

"I'm putting a ban on that damn computer," he says.

In the plane back he tells her. She screams at him. "Not unless you want me at Ginny's." She says she'll file suit. "That's a right," she says. "I know my rights."

"Let's just slow it down," he says.

"The opposite, Freedy. I'm doing just the opposite of that."

Freedy has dried ice cream by his lip. He slumps his shoulders and cracks his knuckles.

"I don't know," he says. "What'll I do then?"

"You just mind your own business," she says.

The turtle still doesn't have a name. Nobody calls it one thing, at least. Freedy calls it Wastrel. And I call it Little Cricket, but Dee calls it Nil. For Phyllis yesterday was Rivet. She calls it something new each day.

I DIDN'T SAY ANYTHING

The man asked, "Ever play the lottery?" That's what he
asked, because the most important thing on the trip didn't
happen in Florida, it was on the airplane sitting there with that
man talking, waiting to take off.

My father and Brady and Shelly sat together on the left
side, and my mother and me sat across the aisle from them. I
could hear Brady's headphones from where I sat, and it was
playing some dancy-rappy thing. He was nodding. We were
some of the first passengers on the plane, and the five of us sat
together not talking. People walked in and we didn't look up.
We looked at the magazines in the seats in front of us, fooled
with the safety brochures and with the blue mini-pillows, or
looked out the window of the plane like we were off the
ground already. My mother stared at the seat in front of her.
Her face was tight-looking around her eyes, and she picked at
her arms, then flipped through a pet magazine. I wondered if

she had a fight with my father before we left, but I didn't ask. This was seven in the morning on a Saturday.

Then a man sat next to my mother on the empty aisle seat. First he put his black leather bag in the compartment above us, then he sat down next to her, blinking and smiling. He was a thin little man, maybe 130 pounds, with silver-rimmed glasses and reddish hair that was cut short enough so I could see nicks on his head, and his face was covered with a thin layer of peachy hair like a girl's. He wore this dark green suit with a yellow T-shirt underneath that I laughed at inside because it made him look like Robin Hood, or the Green Lantern, or something like that. The man smiled a lot at a weird angle, and after a few minutes the man smiled right at my mother, and blinked a lot, and my mother kinda half-smiled back. The whole thing seemed so direct or embarrassing or something.

Then I looked at my dad, but his eyes were closed and his arms were crossed over his stomach like he ate something bad. Then a stewardess walked by and told us all about the seat belts and taking off. I heard the man say something to my mother about the way the woman moved. That little man had a squeaky little voice, and a quick laugh like a little boy. I was fifteen at the time, and I sounded older than that man. My name's Jim Wesley.

"Where are you headed?" the man asked. He didn't say "you all," or "your family." Just "you" right to my mother.

"We're going to Florida," my mother said. She flipped into her work voice, real flat and even sounding. "The Keys."

"Great. Great. Let me tell you, you will love it. Really. I'm from that area and I just adore it. You will have a great time there." The man talked on and on about how well he knows the Keys, and how we should visit this restaurant, and that beach, and he blabbed about fishing, and certain coves, and other sections of the islands, and talked on and on about how she has to spend at least one night at this certain hotel. I wasn't paying attention exactly, but I was listening, and when I looked across the aisle again I saw my father had leaned back in his chair, squinting with his eyebrows curled down, his arms still crossed, and his head cocked in the direction of my mother. His whole attention was directed across the aisle.

Then the airplane took off, but that wasn't important because the man was still going on when it seemed like he should have stopped.

What happened next is the man and my mother started talking about work, which made my mom switch back to her normal voice, and slump her shoulders, even if she wasn't trying to. I thought the man was some kind of travel agent really, and that he could relate to my mother because maybe she wanted to escape too. The man leaned closer to her in his seat, like he had a secret for her. It wasn't one of those slippery plastic seats though, and they might have been sitting on the couch or kicking back on easy chairs. The man had his head resting against the plane seat and they were talking about everything concerning their jobs, and I wasn't really paying attention to either of them then, just looking out the window at the other planes and the greasy runway. It was a gray cloudy day, and the sky was spitting gray-looking rain.

Then I turned for a second and suddenly the man talking to my mother looked familiar. It was really strange, but I swear I knew him from somewhere. Maybe he was one of my teachers once. But then I would have remembered what class he taught. Maybe he was a coach I had once, because I played basketball for a couple of years, but I would have remembered him right away. I couldn't figure it out at all, but I didn't bring it up.

"Ever play the lottery?" the man asked my mother suddenly. I thought it was a strange question because I thought only poor people bet money on that sort of thing. I didn't think we were poor, or desperate for money, but maybe I was wrong.

"No," my mother said. "I don't like to gamble."

"I do," the man said. "I even won. The lottery I mean. The jackpot."

"You did?"

"Yeah."

"You're kidding."

"No. I won it. See this suit," he said, shaking the sleeve of his jacket. "One thousand dollars."

"No." My mom was circling her hair in her fingers.

"Yeah. I'm telling you."

That's when my dad jumped in from where he was sitting.

"I won some things," my father said. "Some stuff." The man and my mother turned toward my father slowly, and nobody said anything for a moment, until the man put his hand under his chin.

"Is that so?"

For a second it was like my father was the stranger, not the other way around.

"Yeah. I won film. Lots of film," my dad said. "Free film, and lots of other stuff." At first his face was concentrated on the man, but his body was still loose and relaxed-looking. But when he said "stuff," it was like he ran out of ideas. It was true about my father's luck though. At that point my father was the luckiest man I ever met. He won everything—NCAA tournament ladders, bets on boxing and football, horse racing, Little League—everything except those bets with Mom on the Cowboys, because they knew they shouldn't bet on the Cowboys if they both rooted for them. Another time my father won a year's worth of free gas from the station off Route 108. My sister and him would drive ten miles back from 175 just to go there, and they'd bring gas back in milk jugs and stack them in the basement for safekeeping. I never heard of Mom using that gas.

"Is that right?" The man turned back to my mother and touched her on the hand with his. "That's nice," he said behind him. I don't think he knew it was my mother's husband.

"I get fifty thousand for forty years," the man said to my mother. "Taxable, of course. But do I have to work?" The man shook his head in quick little movements. I watched my dad. His thumb and pinkie rubbed together, and his feet were flat on the floor of the plane. I thought he was going to get up and punch the guy, but he sat there like a rock. Like he was paralyzed or something.

Finally the man and my mother kind of ran out of things to say, and the man napped, or pretended to while my mother leaned back in her chair and stared up into the little reading light they give you. She was staring into it, and for a second it made me think of being at the dentist's or something. But she had thoughts in her head, I could tell that. She asked me if I was excited to be in a plane, then picked at her fingernails, not listening to my answer, which was yes, and her eyeballs were shifting back and forth, and I could tell she was thinking to herself, and that it was something important. When our flight landed, my mother held out her hand to that man like those fancy old-time women do when they want a man to kiss it. The man took it firmly, held it with both hands, and kissed it. He didn't turn around when he got his bag. The man didn't look at me once when he got off the plane, and he didn't look at my father either.

"Hey, who wants to go to the Keys?" my father said one night. It was dinnertime. This was one of those times when everybody was together, which was unusual, and we were eating Mom's spit roast, and potatoes, and we were sitting at the table like most people do, I guess. Brady was flipping the television from *MTV* to *Entertainment Tonight* then to *ESPN*, to *Comedy Central*, then back to *MTV* when the commercials were over. I guess I think TV is okay, like the way that one woman on *MTV* talks—that chitter-chatter is pretty funny sometimes, even if it's stupid. For once Mom and Dad weren't arguing about money or anything.

I helped with dinner that afternoon. Mom bought one of those electric spits so you can cook meat while you're at work, and we had beef. I watched the roast after school, that orangish-brown meat looping around like a clock. The thing had this electric hum to it, and the meat sizzled so much it seemed to talk. Anyway, I was setting the table and Brady wasn't out playing soccer, or football, or wherever he goes, and Shelly wasn't out with her boyfriend Ted Youngston, doing whatever they did. They were both lying on the couch watching the thirty-inch St. Paul's bought me for my sarcoma. My sister and brother had the bass on the sub-woofers thumping so hard I could feel it in my stomach, but nobody said anything. I wasn't complaining 'cause Mom actually cooked something that you didn't have to take out of a wrapper, and then my dad came home and leaned back in his chair with his hands curled around the back of the knobs, and he took his watch off and dropped it in his white shirt pocket. This was in our townhouse in Columbia.

"Smells good," my father said.

My mom curled her toes on the tile, and tried not to smile, and sat down and put the food on the table, then dished it out onto everybody's plates without asking how much we wanted. We all had Cokes with ice. That night my father even said thank you, and didn't scratch at his face once. My brother and sister sat down and leaned into the table like they were trying to eat as fast as they could, and nobody talked for a while. My dad's face looked red and warm when he was chewing, and he looked around like he was relaxed in his own home. He's kind of a big man with red hair and a large cushy face. His smile didn't even look planned or like plastic or anything, like it did sometimes when he had that layer of selling on, or whatever it was that made him look farther away.

My father worked in public relations for this company called Ginkgo Star—some chemical agricultural company. He hated his job, and he told me so all the time. He told me just about every day how much he hated answering questions like a telemarketer, and how someday he'd find something better. Then I wouldn't ask anything more. I knew he didn't want any more questions about work. He didn't want to think about it. At dinner usually he'd make us turn the lights down so low we could hardly see our food or each other—the ones that were there.

"We get the phone bill yet?" My dad licked the meat juice from his fork.

"No," my mom said. "Not yet."

"They better have taken that Chicago call off," Dad said. "I told them nobody from this house makes calls to Chicago."

"Yeah, okay," my mom said.

"One thing I'm going to do this month is cut access to those 900 numbers. You can do that now. How's that sound, Brady?" Brady didn't say anything because it wasn't really a question, and Brady didn't like to answer things like that.

"And one thing I want to know—and nobody tell me right now 'cause I'm in a good mood tonight—is who keeps dialing that star sixty-nine crap? Just think about it. Okay, Brady?"

Brady didn't even nod. Nothing.

"Maybe you can write it down if you can't remember," my dad said. "Okay?" He paused.

"Okay, so anybody interested in a vacation? I was thinking Florida."

Everybody looked up from their food at this. That wasn't like my father to ask us something like that, or think it. Usually it was something about the Cowboys if it was fall or winter, making wagers on Sunday's game. Both my parents loved the Cowboys because they were everything nobody was in our house, and Mom and Dad would be real competitive about it, even though they liked the same team. They were always yelling for this player or that one to do good, and once they bet one hundred and fifty bucks on whether this one player would score in the game. Mom won that time, and she spent it on a trip to Bennigan's for all of us, and Dad only ordered a root beer float in a mug, and made fun of the decorations on the wall. My parents had something in common. Me, I hate sports.

My dad was always saying how we were just scraping by, and asking us how we were going to make it once the college bills start rolling in. Maybe that's why Brady dropped out and went into tattoos. I would too with all that buzzing around. Anyway, we had only been to one family vacation before, and that was just to that beach in Delaware—Rehoboth. It wasn't run down, but I remember the lookout towers still there from World War Two. I wanted to go in one, but you couldn't. I didn't feel our family was close then, and maybe we never have been, so a vacation was an odd thing for my father to ask about.

"What do you mean, Daniel? " My mother closed her eyes and breathed deeply.

"I mean, let's go snorkeling, jet skiing. Florida. The whole kit-and-caboodle. Florida," he said. "Won't that be nice?" He said *Florida* like nobody had ever heard of the state before. For once, his voice sounded excited, and *real*, and not like a salesman or something.

"I don't know. What about school?" my mom said. But nobody was listening to her. For a second, I felt a sparkle of excitement in the air, and that was unusual. I could hear it in the way nobody was chewing fast anymore. Even Brady seemed to be excited for a few minutes. For a moment there were images of clean warm beaches, and clear blue water with fish swirling in it, and pretty girls in lime-green bikinis. God, I wish. But I was honestly excited, and I think my father could tell.

"I want to go," I said.

"Good, good. I'm calling the airline tomorrow morning," he said. "And I'm calling travel agents for advice. Damned if I'm going to pay them to do what I can do though." My mother grinned at him like she was saying how can we do this trip money-wise? She looked worried, but he didn't want to notice, and he shifted back to me instead.

"It sounds like fun. I want to go," I said.

"You will go," he said. "We're all going. It will be a family thing, and we will all go." My sister and brother looked at each other, but didn't change their expressions when they scraped their plates—the ones with purple and white flowers twirling on the sides. But they were just pretending. Brady shoveled his food into his mouth, and said "Sure Dad, whatever." Brady was wearing his dumb green and yellow plaid baseball cap with his gold chains drooping everywhere, trying to act cool. Shelly shrugged, and Mom didn't do anything except ask who wants more mashed potatoes. There was no gravy, but I was okay.

"I know it will be great," my father said. He gave a little bounce in his seat. I watched him watch everybody else out of the sides of his eyes, but I could tell he didn't want to think about them. Instead, he smiled at me. I was his favorite. I don't know why. Maybe it was because I didn't say much, and I did what I was supposed to do. Brady and Shelly left, and the table was empty except for me and Dad and Mom. It was a huge round pine table, lots of wood in-between. Except the wood looked shiny in the light that night, and the sun was down. This was in December, two weeks before Christmas.

"I think it sounds fun," I said. My mother stood up to clear the table.

Then my father stood up, and took his plate over to Mom, holding it gently on the edges like it disgusted him to even touch it. He walked over and flipped through the junk on the counter, and he found the phone bill tucked under one of my mom's romance novels for protection, and there was a bill from the car insurance company too, which started it all up again.

See, one thing I don't tell many people is the first rule in my life now: I hate my family. I mean, I really hate them. I just keep it quiet, hidden. I didn't feel this way before the trip though. Things changed down in Florida.

Now my mother is a fat slob who sits around the house all day watching the television and painting her fat toe nails red, painting her little white porcelain pigs she keeps scattered all over the house along with her birds and little fish bowls. That's when she's not answering the phones, and filling appointments for Dr. Olen, and wearing too much makeup so she looks like some kind of carnival clown. My mom is one hundred and eighty pounds and Milt's mom is one hundred. No woman should weigh more than one ten, maybe one fifteen.

Milt and I got it set up so that I gotta pay Milt a monthly fat tax for my mom—ten cents for each pound over his mother. Last year I lost fifteen some dollars, but my New Year's resolution is to get my mom on one of those weight loss programs, even if I have to help her pay for it. It's either that or send weekly cheesecakes over to Mrs. Shriver. It's a good long-term deal as long as Milt and I are friends, since he has to pay me a dollar per pound if his mother gains weight.

These days my father is a pretend-nut who lives in Seattle with some live-in nurse, but I know he's lying. He says it's his duty in Vietnam that got to him, but I don't buy that crap. My sister rides her racehorses all day, and brushes her hair in the mirror, then shoots it with lots of hair spray that smells like cantaloupe or watermelon. She's twenty-four and still lives at home, which I think is pathetic. But I can't blame her much because her boyfriend used to beat her, I swear. He wouldn't marry her, and then somehow he got custody of their kid, Andrew, who is six. Shelly is starting to look like a horse herself—it's her bushy red hair and big teeth that does it. My brother smokes pot in his room, listening to music with his girlfriend. If Mom is really tired, she'll go down there and smoke some too. Maybe Brady's her favorite.

I'm the youngest kid and I go to school. I hate it, except for algebra class. Algebra makes sense. The polynomials, simplifying, all that stuff. Factoring. Bring the GCF down, factor it through, the FOIL technique. I love it. It's simple and easy to do if you follow the directions. I like it that way. A year from when we all went to Florida, eleven months from when my father picked up and left, and I'm still doing algebra like it was going out of style.

I get so lonely sometimes; it feels like I'm a rock, and there's this coal-digger machine tunneling through me with its diamond tip. It starts when I don't want it to, and it comes through me in a way that scares me and makes me want to just lay in bed and never get up. Sometimes I can just forget about it, watching the television, listening to techno, but that empty feeling always comes back when I'm not expecting it. Sarcoma's a kind of cancer that starts in the soft areas, like muscles. That's what Dr. Olen tells me, when he's not too busy talking his medical talk so I can't understand a word he's saying. Sometimes I think he tries to confuse me so I won't ask questions. He says my cancer is near my sartorius muscle. Sometimes when I'm tired I call the cancer the sartorius and the muscle the sarcoma. I get them mixed up sometimes.

I don't talk to anybody in depth except Bear. He's just my dog, but he's really my best friend—even though it sounds lame to say that. One thing though: He leaves his yellowy hairballs all over the house, and my mom is too lazy to pick them up. I have a couple of other friends, except I always have to call them first to do anything, and that gets on my nerves. Plus they act kinda embarrassed to go out with me when my hair is half-gone. It's like I have to sell them something every time I call them up. Except Milt, my second best friend. He's stuck it out with me the whole time, even when I was bald from the chemo and could hardly sit up. Milt never made me talk about it. Last winter his sister's husband died in a car accident.

I remember when we drove to BWI that morning, my father asked me if I wanted to sit in the front seat, and I got to put my Orb CD in, which calmed things down for him. He had been fighting with Mom for days before, and his voice was cracked. I was really surprised I got to sit up front because I always had to sit in the back—usually in the middle too where it's all humpy and I'm stuck between my brother and sister. I really feel like the youngest when I have to sit in the middle, and sometimes I got car-sick when it smelled all stuffy and stale, and I had to ask them to roll down the windows. Mom was in back.

But this time my father asked me to sit in the front, and I think it was because he didn't want to get down about the trip and wanted everything to work out. Nobody else except me really wanted to go. They were just going because he said it was a family trip, and if they didn't go it might mean they weren't part of the family, and they wanted to be part of something. This idea changed too when Dad left. I thought the trip might be a time to improve things, and I was looking inside my head and trying to think it would work out. My father usually ignored problems that came up and figured they would work their way out on their own somehow, but this time he seemed to sense things were wrong in a way that bothered him, and that made him want to fix it.

We flew into Miami so we could drive Route 1 down to Key West, and so I could see why Dad wanted to come here in the first place. We were skimming along the water, and if I didn't look across or down it was like we were driving right through the water, or were in a floater-boat and the water was all around, blue as anything. But then I'd look across and I'd see all those blue and yellow billboards for hotels, and restaurants, and places to go fishing and stuff. Then I'd see other people in other cars also looking out at the billboards and tropical trees and boats in the sea, then I'd look back up to the tops of the power lines buzzing.

We were all sitting around a table near the hotel pool eating fries and the ham and cheese club sandwiches we ordered, drinking soda and trying not to think about the rain. We had been swimming, but when the rain hit we huddled under the table umbrella. All of a sudden Dad scooted away from the table with his sandwich still sitting on the plate. He snapped his shirt off and dove into the pool, rain or no rain. It was his olive-green shirt with a pinhole rip in the back, and it was soft-looking sitting on the concrete. Dad didn't even eat the chocolate chip cookies they brought us, but maybe it was 'cause the waiters looked as us funny for being out in the rain. I ate mine first like everyone does at school, before the sandwich.

"I thought it was supposed to be sunny here," Brady said. We could hear Dad splashing around as if he was having the time of his life, but I could see he was just trying to inspire something besides boredom. Out of the corner of my eye I could see him try underwater handstands. It looked like somebody was shooting the pool water with a machine gun.

"It can't always be sunny," I said. "Otherwise it would be a desert."

"Shut up."

"You," I said.

"Both of you shut up," my sister said.

"Shut the hell up yourself," Brady said.

"I'm going to shut you up," she said.

"Let's all shut up," I said.

"Shut up," they both said.

When Dad was done he came back over to the table drying himself, and his swimming trunks clung to his legs, and his legs were dark with hair. He looked at me and nobody else. It threw me, but nobody looked at him strangely.

"You want to go someplace?" That's what he said.

"I guess. Where?" I felt like I was a woman he was asking out or something.

"Someplace out there. I don't know, maybe we can play pool. Let's get a breath of fresh air."

Nobody thought about it much, or really looked up even, but it seemed weird to me to go inside another building to get a breath of fresh air. I was getting sick of sitting around that pool though, so I went with him to Café Bayamo.

So, like I said, it was that man who brought all the other bad things that happened to us during the rest of the trip because all we got was rain and cold while we were down in Florida. I mean, it was sunny for maybe an hour total, and that was the first morning at sunrise before all the rest came. Those travel agents are a bunch of liars.

You want to know what we did once we got to Key West? We sat around the hotel pool watching those scruffy people and gay guys walking around. The few who would come out in the rain. It was depressing because we had all these plans to go jet skiing and snorkeling, but the water made us shiver, and at Matt's Sea Haven they said the waves were too rocky for good jet skiing. So we pretty much just hung out around the pool in the hotel, which was okay with some of us because it was a nice heated pool and wasn't too chloriney or warm like somebody just peed in it. They even had a spa inside. No pool table though.

The only one that seemed okay was my mother. Now that I think about it, my mother seemed happier down there. I guess she liked not having to cook, and I was glad for her. Brady and Shelly whined about the whole thing, even though they were older than me. They said, how are we supposed to meet anybody if we can't even go outside? Shelly didn't even swim in the pool, like it was her own protest against things.

My dad said go ahead, go outside. But nobody did. It was raining so hard the water was coming down sideways. Even the surfers weren't out, and the Keys didn't look like much from the window, and nobody wanted to go fishing. Plus the Everglades were closed from the government shutdown.

It was my father who took all this especially bad. I guess because it was his idea and he felt responsible for the weather. Day One he frowned and said at least we can catch our breath from the jet lag. Day Two he was surprised it was so rainy in Florida. Day Three and he was talking about heading back. It was Day Four when he looked desperate and took me to Café Bayamo in the rain.

When we got inside Café Bayamo my father bought two beers in brown bottles and we sat down in a booth off to the side. He put both beers in front of him, then turned and made sure nobody was watching so he could slide one to me. I had beer before with Brady, but I told my dad I hadn't and acted surprised and happy because it seemed like he needed to feel better about things.

The bar was dark and sleepy inside, and it had dark wooden walls with wooden booths, and fake stuffed fish on pine frames on the walls. Mostly dark though. I remember that, not being able to see much. I thought this was weird for a beach bar. I remember there were two tan ladies wearing tank tops sitting near us talking softly and looking through the paper. There was a guy by himself at the bar in a nice blue shirt eating lunch. Then off near the bar were a bunch of waiters with name tags sitting around talking and smoking. I wondered what it must be like to be older and live down there. Anyway, at this point it was raining so hard we could hardly even hear the music inside.

My father drank his beer and I drank part of mine then, and gave the rest back to him to drink.

"I have to take care of something," he said.

"Okay."

"I'll be right back, okay?"

"Yeah, okay," I said. He seemed like he knew he was doing something he shouldn't do. But he went ahead anyway.

I watched my father walk to the bathroom, and I sat there listening to the different sounds in the bar. I heard music, the laughing and sounds of silverware scraping on plates, and more talking that I couldn't make out. It was a while before my father came back, but I figured he was just in the bathroom, and I drank some more beer.

When my father came back, it looked like he had four or five tickets in his hands, and two more beers. I thought at first they must be tickets to some kind of event or water show. I kept hearing about the porpoise jumps. But when he laid them out on the table, I could see they were all lottery tickets with different numbers on them. I was surprised.

"Where did you get those?"

"Up at the bar. Think your old man got lucky?" I thought it was weird that he would say "got," even though we didn't know yet. But to him it was obvious.

My father was lucky, but he never won anything of real value. That's where he went wrong on the lottery idea. I remember he didn't look up from those lottery tickets for maybe fifteen minutes. He just sipped his beer. He flipped through them like each one held some kind of magic in it.

"How many did you get?" I asked. He didn't answer, and his eyes were glued to the tickets.

"How many, Dad?"

"What's that?"

"How many tickets did you get?"

"Five," he said. Then he looked back down at them. "I got five."

"Why did you get those?" I asked.

"Why do you think?"

"I don't know."

"A little adventure," he said. "Nothing wrong with that, is there?"

"Did Mom put you up to this. I mean that man in—"

"Got to take some chances sometimes," he said. "Take some chances in this life, or you'll wither up."

Only a month later it would be his idea to buy two thousand dollars worth of tickets, then go up to Atlantic City and lose ten grand in a weekend. When none of his tickets hit, he left. "Just a public relations thing," he told me. Sure. Right. But that's old news.

You can imagine the rest. I got sicker two months after he left, and chemo was a month after that. Before the first time I had to get chemo I threw up. After that I fazed in and out of my mind for weeks. I threw up all the time. I still don't remember some of the things that happened during that time. I do know I hate doctors though.

I don't exercise much these days. I do sit-ups sometimes because I don't want to get fat like my mother, but

I'm never going to war—I don't care what they do to me. I'm going to be different than my parents. Except my guidance counselor at school tells me I'm showing signs of depression. She doesn't know about my father, but if she did I bet she'd wonder if my father's problems were really from Viet Nam. If Mrs. Gregory asked me that, I'd tell her I have no idea, and that the only thing I know is that he's freaked out because he left his family, and nobody's supposed to do that, ever. I'd also mention that my father told me on the phone that he has a new girlfriend, Kristen, who is some nurse at the place where he is staying. I wouldn't smile if Mrs. Gregory asked for more, and I wouldn't get angry or upset. I would just state the facts, because that's the way it is. Then I wouldn't want to talk about it any more. Anyway, I only went to the guidance office for information on good math colleges, even if Milt's right and it's too early to be thinking about that sort of thing.

My mother is fine. That part's the worst, because I wish she was angry. She's too tired to hate anybody, she says. Last week she tossed me a tan plastic bag after she came back from work. It was from the mall. Inside was this Cowboy's mug that plays their song if you hold it to the light. Mom says it's not a mug—it's a stein. Whatever. She gave me some white tube socks too. You know your socks are raggy if you can't tell if they are inside out or not.

Now we're really scraping by, so Brady got a job at the taco place in the mall to help pay the bills. My father calls maybe once a month. Maybe. And he doesn't ask me many questions, even when they discovered the tumor. He just doesn't want to talk about it. But he is having me visit next month to meet his new friend, and go swimming.

AMANITA AND BOLETE

Laurel Newton is miserable and she knows exactly why: her stuffy podiatrist husband, her mid-level paper-pushing job, the dowdy Falls Church colonial, the dog dying of bone cancer and old age, her insane Anglican family, the loneliness, the lack of passion and verve, sporadic stomach ulcers, mild anorexia nervosa, the spark of her own childhood decomposed into close to nothing.

She's in the grocery store, glancing at the community bulletin board as she withdraws money from the bank machine. Ads for baby-sitting, tutoring, lawn service, wedding planning, mushroom hunting, catering. Mushroom hunting? She snaps up her money, crumples the receipt instinctually, not wanting to know how much she does or doesn't have. She owes thirteen thousand on four credit cards. Laurel reads the ad. New members welcome at the Falls Church Mycological Society. Meeting at eight on Friday night at the St. Paul's Methodist. No dues, just come.

Laurel walks away, spends a hundred and fifty on groceries, and in two trips, lugs the bags like a pack animal across the burnished black parking lot, drives home listening to a review of the show at the National Gallery, then doesn't feel like cooking. Without emptying the plastic grocery bags she piles them into the refrigerator, orders a pizza for dinner. Her husband works late. Laurel assumes Gil's too cautious to have an affair although just last year she seduced a twenty-one-year-old intern in the janitor's storage room. She eats one piece of pizza, watches the news, turns off the phone, tosses pizza crust to her parakeets, crunches the rest of the pizza into the garbage, leaves the empty pizza box on the table for her husband, and walks the dog.

Wolf limps along, peeing, then barfing blood on the sidewalk. Laurel can hear the dog's bones creak and crack with each step. The veterinarian told her she should put Wolf to sleep. But Laurel would miss her; she's owned Wolf for fifteen years. She doesn't believe in euthanasia for dogs. Live and let live, she thinks. Wolf won a ribbon at the Fairfax County Dog Show ten years ago. The best-groomed Lab, first place. Laurel's life was different then. She remembers feeling more essential, less guarded, younger *and* wiser.

A sickening moaning sound curdles up from the dog's insides. Wolf quavers to a stop, slumps on the concrete. Laurel kicks the dog's rump and yanks the chain, tells her to get a move on. "I have things to do, Wolf," she says. "Come on." Wolf's eyes roll back into her head. Laurel can hear the crickets, the wind through the trees, the sounds of tires on the road, engines shifting into high gear. She can feel the winter in the air. Wolf sighs, collapses into the grass in between the road and sidewalk. Laurel stands over the body, unsure how to react, at odds with her natural emotional reach. "Goddamnit!" She leaves the dog's body on the grass strip until Gil gets home.

Laurel leaves a note for Gil to put the dog in a trash bag and to leave it in the garage for now. She doesn't know why, but her nipples are sore. Waves of exhaustion roll over her. Maybe she should eat something. She orders a movie on Pay-Per-View, then falls asleep fifteen minutes after the credits fade. When she wakes up, the yellow striped afghan is crumpled over her head and the television is off. The afghan smells like tomato sauce.

Laurel takes a week off from work. She tells the FDA, officially, that her sister is sick and in the hospital even though she got more out of Wolf than all three of her divorced sisters combined. Two days later she buries Wolf in a pet cemetery. It costs $6,500, but money is not an issue when it comes to death. Wolf's coffin is lined with red satin. They hire an ecclesiastic from the National Cathedral, who offers a eulogy worthy of the dog of an employee of the federal government. Laurel and Gil stand together as the rites are read, the crisp edges of their fingernails white in the sun. Halfway through the burial Laurel realizes she's standing on her own foot. She brushes the dirt from her pumps as Wolf's body is lowered into the ground. Under a pine bower, a man leaning against his shovel watches her.

"I think these rituals are important," she tells her husband at lunch. He hasn't been to church with her in years. Her eyelids are still smudged with mascara as they eat at the kitchen table. Gil nods, and asks her to pass another low-fat frozen croissant that she had heated in the toaster oven. He smothers it with honey, and pats the top of her hand. Laurel recoils, says it is only a dog. They argue about their only son, who is nearly failing college. Laurel has considered disowning

C.J.; Gil wants to give him more leverage, let C.J. make more of his own decisions. "It's sink or swim time," he says. Eighty percent of Laurel never wanted children. Professionalism is more important, she thinks; what you do in this world is your mark. What else matters? She has brothers and sisters if she wants trouble. Gil hasn't made love to her in a month, and she hasn't missed it. He doesn't even undress in front of her. He brought up the idea of sleeping in separate beds, in separate rooms, and she was more than happy to oblige.

"I saw something interesting a couple of days ago," she says.

"What's that?" Her husband doesn't look up from the business section. The part in his hair is exact. His slacks are ironed perfectly. His tie looks as if it is painted on his puce ironed button-down.

"A flyer for a mushrooming hunt, or some such thing. Why would someone want to hunt for a fungus?"

"I have no idea," he says, eyes still glued to his cautious utilities quotes. He lost fifty thousand dollars of his retirement in oil stocks when he panicked in '87, and Laurel knows he worries constantly about what will happen in five years. His pension will be relatively small, all things considering. Is this why she married a doctor? He should have never joined that damn HMO. She thought her own measure of spunk would balance his circumspection, but maybe in the end she was ultimately wrong.

"Birds certainly, but mushrooms? They just sit there and grow and die."

As soon as she says this, Laurel knows she is actually intrigued by the idea. This may be her husband's primary function now: He is a sounding board. If his interest is not piqued, then maybe hers *should* be. Laurel decides she will go to the meeting. To spite him maybe, to insert a measure of impurity. Their marriage is one big fucking impurity, she thinks.

"I've never heard of a more idiotic idea for a club," she says. Her husband nods, and asks her if she has any fruit besides bananas. Laurel usually stocks a large bowl filled with fruit. She buys so many bananas that half go bad and have to be thrown out at the end of the week. Then she buys more anyway.

"Is there a problem with bananas?"

"No," he says. "I just feel like grapes or an orange or something different."

"You earn money. You're welcome to go shopping yourself," she says.

Her husband stares at her, holding his glance, swishing food in his mouth. He crosses his legs under the table. He is a stoic to her, cold and rational as a neutron star. A stoic who doesn't appreciate sex anymore, or intimacy, or love beyond the bounds of comrade-in-arms. Her defense is two-thirds distance, one-third resentment.

"What? Don't stare at me," she says.

"I wouldn't know where to start," he says.

He looks back down into his paper, mumbles that he won't have any fruit then. Laurel pushes away from the table, changes into sweatpants and spends the rest of the day in the basement piecing together and labeling a "Wolf Photo Album," sniffling, wiping her nose on her sleeve.

Friday. A wiry Polynesian-looking man stands at the front of the church meeting room in the basement. His name tag reads "Renton Fillis," which doesn't sound Polynesian to her; he must be adopted. Laurel's mother used to threaten to give her up for adoption; Laurel could only wish. A crowd of thirty or so sits in plastic chairs connected together with metal clasps. The sign behind Renton reads "Mycologists Have More Fun" in smeared red marker. Laurel sits near the back, wearing a mauve sun hat, hoping nobody she knew would be there, pretending to look at her watch. The man is talking about the hunt on Sunday.

"For those of you who are new to us, of course, we have to watch out for our friends the Amanitas. I have only seen them here and there, but that's been enough for me. The problem, as some of you know, is it looks so much like our common white mushroom that people eat it, and white death doesn't take any prisoners." This reminds Laurel immediately of work, where she upholds the appearance of covert health dangers while knowing herself that her greatest risk is a paper cut. Her work entails mostly analyzing fuzzy medical photographs of kidneys and endless data on the subject of kidney disease. She falls asleep at her desk at least once a day. But Laurel knows that appearance and reputation are, in this world, everything; and *still* death can rise to the top of the ordinary if you aren't careful.

Renton talks about the tools they need to bring, the cautious frame of mind they need to maintain in the field. "Of course, don't eat what you don't know," the man says. Laurel likes this man, his calm insistence, his lack of dim pensiveness. No need for explicit histories of each and every mushroom. The man self-mockingly seems to know that it is only mushroom hunting, which makes it more than that somehow.

He hands a stack of papers to the person sitting at the front. He says he is passing out a leaflet for the novice collectors that details the possible effects of mushroom poisoning. Laurel scrolls her eyes down, skipping the introduction:

"MMH: Bloating, nausea and vomiting, bloody diarrhea. Orellanin: Renal failure, kidney damage, kidney transplant can be required. Muscarine: Heavy tears, perspiration, salivation, fall in blood pressure, blurred vision. Ibotenic Acid and Muscimol: Delusions, staggering, hyperactivity, deep sleep. Amatoxins: Diarrhea, abdominal pain, kidney and liver failure, death."

The man mentions what they might see on the trip. September is the best time of year for mushrooms, he says, because you get the Boletes and the Giant Puffballs. "You'll see both of them, if you're smart and know where to look. Let me put it this way, the King Boletes are selling this year for a hundred a gallon pickled. Easley Prolen is still buying for twenty a pound. So you can have a little fun and make some money. Or you can eat your butts off," he says. The man mentions a mushroom cookout and drying session when the bus returns. "6:30 sharp, tomorrow. Don't be late."

The woman sitting next to Laurel smiles as they rise to leave. She asks Laurel if she had ever been to a meeting before, and Laurel says she hasn't. The woman sticks out her arm and Laurel quickly shakes the tips of her fingers.

"I'm Nellie," the woman says. She is a short woman with a curly crest of hair tucked under her green visor. She wears a tan crosshatched vest over a black athletic T-shirt-and-shorts-ensemble. Laurel can smell apricot or peach on her breath. The woman is friendly; Laurel wonders if she has been drinking.

"I'm Laurel."

"Great. You know, one thing I wanted to tell you that Renton didn't mention was that you should bring a pole, or fishing net or something like that."

"Okay, what? To…"

"Well, I think it's a good thing to do," Nellie says. "In case you, I mean I, see a polypore up a tree that I'd like to sample, so it's not a bad idea. Some people go for the biggies. I like to collect the different ones myself. Some of the tooth fungi are interesting."

"Right, right."

"I have a big old branch trimmer I bring, the kind you know, you pull the lever, then you cut whatever you're going to cut. I've gotten some real doozies that way."

"Right," Laurel says. "Very interesting." She lifts her voice to fend this woman off with a dose of over-politeness.

"My branch trimmer is named Zachary, which I think— don't you—that, that's a good name for a trimmer?"

"I have no idea," Laurel says. "I suppose—"

"Oh, okay, listen, I want to give you something to look over before you come tomorrow," Nellie says. The woman reaches under her seat and yanks her backpack onto her hip. The bag is stuffed full and the straps are frayed. Laurel thinks the whole mess is unseemly and sloppy looking. The woman is some kind of hippie-eccentric. Nellie unzips the bag, digs around and pulls out a folded swatch of newspaper.

"Just read it, and tell me what you think. Tomorrow. See you, okay. I've got to get to the library before they close."

"Right," Laurel says.

"Return the videos. It's two dollars a day, and I've got four of them."

Laurel nods, saying she is glad to meet her. The woman is most likely a dyke, she concludes. She opens her purse, and folds the article into it, stuffing it next to her checkbook.

During the drive home Laurel slows down in front of the tract mansions under construction in the court across the street from her development. They will sell for five hundred thousand minimum, and the backyards will be maybe one eighth of an acre. Twenty years from now Laurel hopes the county informs the buyers that their properties are built on an imminent sinkhole, and they have to cut their losses and sell out to a masonry company for half the purchasing price, pitching long and acrimonious lawsuits that amount to little or nothing. Pain and suffering for all.

Everything Laurel knew to the bone feels so far away. The Newton family name that goes back to 1680's Virginia seems tacked on to her existence, irrelevant now. Her ancestors grew up with the Washingtons, for God's sake. But her Virginian heritage is now parceled out to housing companies that will put the soul of her state on the auction block. She longs for the old elite. It is okay to treat other people as a means to an end with this reasoning. Laurel wants to be seen in a good light. She didn't battle her sisters all these years for nothing. She didn't tolerate her mother's obvious liaisons just for a sliver of the middle class. There is something more to this existence.

Two years ago Laurel's son stopped speaking to her when he found out she used fifteen thousand dollars of his inheritance money. She didn't understand why he was upset; he barely knew Aunt Brida, and had only spent a few weekends helping her clean her house before she moved out to the nursing home. Laurel was the one who had sat there tape recording her life history, organizing her correspondence, reading to Brida when her eyes glassed over with glaucoma after her stroke. Yet Brida only left her a fraction of what C.J. received. She told Laurel she was giving to the younger generation; so, Laurel was just equalizing. Who was the one paying for his tuition?

When summer brought C.J. home from college, however, Laurel cooked him steak, green beans, and potatoes, his favorite meal, and he seemed to appreciate the gesture. She helped him carry his things upstairs. They played cards that night. He drank three glasses of wine; she had two. Laurel both loathed and reveled in the fact that Gil barely noticed his son; he spent that night in his study reading, and listening to Ornette Coleman, or some abstract, sprawling jazz that she loathed. What a selfish man. He should learn how to cook, she thought. He needs to address the basic issues of independence. What would he do without her?

Laurel spoiled C.J. that summer, buying him shirts, CDs, beer, concert tickets, anything he wanted. She never showed him the closet full of power suits she bought with the money, never told him of the "business trip" she took. C.J. appreciated it, seemed to forget about the inheritance money, or at least devalue it in his own mind. The blind date she arranged for C.J. was a success. The woman liked him and spent nights with C.J. drinking and, Laurel knew, carousing after she fell asleep. At night she could hear them bumping around in the living room, laughing and humming in pleasure. She barely saw her husband at all that summer. If he was eating, she would stay in her room. If she was cooking, he seemed to stay in his study. They didn't watch television together. She began to live vicariously through C.J. She wanted to *bond* with him.

When her son left for college at the end of the summer, Laurel was crushed. She tried to call him at his dorm room, but he wasn't there most of the time, and when he was, his friends were there too. When she did get him on the phone, their conversations were short; he didn't want to share. His emotional state seemed increasingly brittle. She wrote him; he never responded. She thought about buying him a pager, but didn't. Laurel started wondering if he was sinking back into what he came from. The family matters more, Laurel told him. "I thought you said that school is my lion's share of duty," he said. Laurel lied and said she never said that. "Right Mom, okay," C.J. said. Last summer he stayed for summer school. C.J. hasn't called home in three months.

Gil is in his bed. Laurel is in hers, in what used to be the guest room. Propped against the headboard, she flips through her bird book, remembering how she used to go on bird hunts ten or eleven years ago. Sometimes Gil would join her. He enjoyed the woods themselves and became interested in the subtleties of each ecosystem, later bringing a notepad and pen, sketching a fern or a magnolia tree while Laurel scoured the woods for hawkweeds. The sun left a space around her eyes whiter than her skin. Laurel can hear him ruffling through papers in the master bedroom, worrying about bills. The bed is an Art Deco she inherited from her grandmother. It has a certain solidity that she likes. The tops of each post are rounded with a quarter moon. Shooting stars are carved into the base of the bed. Are they meteors or meteorites? On the headboard a girl wanders among the stars, her head arched skyward.

Laurel thinks about knocking on the door, entering the room. But what would she do *then*? Say she wishes they weren't like this? Admonish him for being such a frail, uninteresting man? Let her nightgown slip to her feet as he watches her squeeze her breasts in her hands, feel the soft plush carpet under her toes, hear the air conditioner clicking on, and the faint twitter of her birds in the kitchen? Feel his skin on hers, his chest hair into her back, his exhalation in her ear as he sighs in?

She feels sorry for Gil, for herself. She remembers the article, and opens her purse. Her motions seem to be more vibrant somehow. She is aware of her hands unfolding the creases in the newspaper. She is aware of her position in bed, the covers, the bed frame.

The article is just a short AP report, surrounded by jewelry ads the lazy woman didn't cut off:

Homeless Man Dies After Consuming Toxic Mushroom

MIAMI—A man authorities claim was homeless, ate a mushroom commonly known as a Witch's Hat and died last night in a marshy field in the suburbs of Miami.

The Miami police department believes that a group of college students at the University of Miami paid the unidentified man to search for hallucinogenic mushrooms. Frank Halter, a spokesperson for the University of Miami, said that he knew of the homeless man, who apparently had been housed by certain fraternity houses prior to the recent incident. The Miami police would not comment further on the relationship between the man and the fraternity house.

"He had a picture of a brown mushroom in his pocket," Detective Grimble stated. "It was Friday afternoon. Somebody wanted to have some fun, illegally."

Grimble said that the homeless man had been arrested before for buying alcohol for minors in a certain fraternity house, in exchange for a place to sleep. The small brown mushrooms, Hygrophorus conicus, reportedly caused four deaths in China over the last two years.

--Associated Press

Laurel folds the article back into her purse, and snaps the reading lamp off, eyes open in the dark. She imagines a huge, hulking, disgusting man with hair down to his waist, speckled with warts and lesions, his scraggly beard hopping with mites and mosquitoes. The man walks across the field, drunk, picking mushrooms and putting them in his pockets. He has a sense of duty and gratitude, but little else. He is so hungry he decides to sit down and eat a few. He only has a vague notion of why the kids want the mushrooms exactly. He walks away, picking more mushrooms, then as he's walking back towards campus, strange visions whirl into his head.

Giant mouths snap at his head, needles jab into his nostrils, cows scuff his face with their hooves, and spores rise into the wind, millions of spores. They needle into his legs and arms. The man collapses into the field, and passes out with his face in the slime. Mushroom heads catapult their load of spores over his decaying corpse, giant Amanita and Bolete seed spores sink into his stomach lining, in the fetid bog of his intestines.

The house sounds quiet without Wolf clanking around, snarfling his water. Why did Nellie show her this garbage? Why should she even waste her time with any of this? Maybe, Laurel thinks, she *is* paying some kind of penance, but for what? For what?

Laurel sits on the stairs, tying her tennis shoes when Gil scuffles out into the hall.

"Going out on a walk?" Laurel hasn't told him about the meeting, about the whole idea. Luckily though, she already prepared her fungi basket.

"Yes. I'm actually going down to the park, and I'll be back later."

"Fine," he says. "I'm getting some breakfast."

"Coffee's made," she says. "Help yourself."

"You have something on your face," Gil says, passing by into the kitchen.

Laurel goes to the bathroom, clicks on the light, looks in the mirror. A pink welt sits smack in the middle of her cheek, possibly a large mosquito bite. She considers a Band-Aid, but decides to layer the bite with makeup and a touch of rouge. She considers a hat or scarf to provide some distraction. At least she is thin. She tucks her beige blouse tighter into her pants. She decides to let everything speak for itself.

Laurel walks back into the kitchen, takes the basket from the table, thinks about kissing her husband's hair, but brushes his shoulder instead. His breath smells like bell peppers.

"Picnic by yourself?" He glances at her shins. "That sounds fine."

"Glad I have your approval," Laurel says.

"You don't," he says. Gil's ears are red. His eyes are still gunked with sleep. "You do whatever you want." Laurel doesn't know if that is a statement of fact, or a complaint. The lines have blurred.

"Yes, I do," she says cheerily, turns, and is out the door.

Saturday's bus ride is long and hot. Nellie is nowhere in sight. A group of men (Renton included) in the back of the bus joke, chortle, play cards. Two women across from her talk about work. Several families sit together with earphones on, or faces down into a book or magazine. The bus driver talks to a man in a baseball cap.

The gravel drive the bus takes is winding, scraggly, and hilly. Laurel watches the pricker bushes and honeysuckle go by. Eyes in the brush, movement. A raccoon, or maybe a fox. Gil would love this, Laurel thinks.

The last time Laurel was on a bus was in Turkey for vacation. She called her secretary once from Istanbul, and had her leave a message for Gil that she was alive, but didn't bother calling otherwise during her week and a half away. When she got home the refrigerator was nearly empty, and she yelled at Gil for not taking care of himself properly, for not stocking the refrigerator. They didn't speak to each other for three days after the incident. Once Laurel made a list of all the things she hated about her husband, which she keeps in a folder in her closet, just in case. One night she thought she smelled a strange perfume on his shirt, but didn't say anything. He's too craven to do anything, she thinks.

The drive simply ends facing into the woods; a path leads away through the trees. It's too early for the leaves to turn, although the poison ivy runs up the trees in red veins. The air is warming, and will reach eighty-five, the newspaper said. Renton pops up from his seat, and asks everyone to follow him. Laurel follows right behind him. An aqua hatchback pulls up right next to the bus, and Nellie pops out. Laurel feels better at the simple familiarity. She looks in her basket to make sure she brought everything she should have: lidded basket, knife, wax paper for spore prints, magnifying glass, notebook, paper bag. She didn't bring a pole, although one of the other women did.

"Feel free to roam at will," Renton is saying. "We will meet back at the bus at noon." As soon as he says this, three of the men scatter off the trail, chanting "Puffballs! Puffballs! Puffballs!" Two women and a boy wander off to the right, quietly eyeing the ground. "I'm going for the fairy rings, whoever wants to come along. I know they're up there," Renton says. "They always are." The rest of the group follow him. The trail becomes increasingly narrow and soggy. Feet squish on the decomposing bark and pine needles. Laurel will follow the leader.

"So hi there, Laurel," Nellie says, swaying up to her, the limb cutter bobbing on her shoulder, and brushing the low branches.

"Good morning." Laurel winces at the woman's insistent friendliness. She wants the trip to be about *her*, not this other woman. Nellie looks like she's wearing the same clothes she wore yesterday. She smells like burnt oregano.

"I'm telling you, is this a great morning to look for fungi or what?"

"Yes it is," Laurel keeps her politeness in check. Nellie introduces Laurel to her branch cutter, and Laurel grunts.

"Look at that," Nellie says, suddenly crouching off to the right. "What a cutie!" The woman in front of them turns around and asks, what is it? Nellie reaches into her fanny pack, withdraws her mushroom identification book, rifles through the pages.

"It's either a well-developed Water Club, or..." Nellie flips through the book, brushes the pine needles and decaying leaves away. "It could be a Swamp Beacon." She finds the match in the book. "Right, I do think it's a Swamp Beacon." Renton and the others are farther up the path looking up into the trees at something else. Birds chirp, the wind whistles softly through the trees; Laurel can smell the piney marsh. The skunk cabbage and rotting birch cloak the smell of Laurel's companion. She remembers that the joy of this type of activity—hunting for birds, trees, mushrooms—shuts everything else out. You put fungi in a special place in your mind, and the rest becomes background. The natural surrounding accentuates what you're looking for.

"It's not edible," Nellie says. "I'm not cutting it either. Look at that thing." The other woman stands, smiles at Nellie and lopes ahead towards Renton and the others. Nellie bounces up from the ground, slips her identification book back into her fanny pack, but doesn't zip it.

"Isn't this great?"

"It's different," Laurel says. "Yes."

"Who would have thought mushrooms would be so exciting?"

Laurel knows people don't change. And not only that, they don't try to change. People are static, stubborn as anything in the natural world. The only thing dynamic about humanity is the broad sweep of history. The ins and outs of daily life are more or less the same as ever. Who would have thought she'd be working for the federal government? She wanted to be an artist, and she spent much of her time in college painting large watercolor portraits. She simply didn't want to live the *life* of the artist. She wanted money, comfort. Stability. The regular things that regular people have; art could be a hobby, she thought. Then what?

How much of her life had she bolstered with a sense of meaning that she didn't really believe, didn't even *want* to believe? Perhaps this was a self-justifying measure, to conduct her own life outside the bounds that she initially set for herself. But then could you put a price tag on that? Everything seems flat and ultimately unimportant if you look at it through the lens of finance. Although it is seductive. Greed is a strong motivator. Is she really a disappointment to her own conception of herself? Perhaps she is more loaded down with her own false dignity than she realized. How many friends did Laurel even have anymore? She could count them on one hand, and she spent little time with any of them at all. It makes her swallow hard to think that Gil is the person whom she could depend on most.

Nellie and Laurel slosh through the path together, to where Renton talks about zoned phlebia, which dots a beech to the left of the path. Nellie whistles, and bobs her pole up and down like a piked sentry on duty.

"I mean, how I would identify this is, it's reddish, it's a crust," Renton says. "If you can put things in categories, you can narrow it down. It's not a Puffball, as you can see. And it grows on a tree, which cuts most, I said *most*, mushrooms out, right? So I'm sticking with Zoned Phlebia."

At noon Laurel returns to the bus with her basket filled with fungi, some for the collection she decides she would build, some to eat. Nellie is still suspect, but the farther she walks into the swamp, the more Laurel allows herself to revel in the lack of perfection, to be at home with herself and not worry about ultimates for a day. She is always surprised by the lack of symmetry in nature; the mushrooms are themselves— they don't have to match a pattern. Why shouldn't she have a life too?

Laurel examines Blue Staining Cups, Carbon Balls, Wolf's Milk Slime, Stinkhorn. She enjoys the different shapes and colors of each organism. In a marshy field, the group first found Granular Puffballs, which Renton said were edible, but only if you liked eating sand. As the group fanned across the field, Laurel tripped over the first Giant Puffball. She yelled out to the others. Nellie and a tall man raced over to where she stood, and immediately said it was a Giant Puffball. "Wait, there's another one," Nellie said, pointing off to her right. "There's one," Renton said going a bit farther. Laurel felt a shiver of actual pleasure, part of something, a unit. How much of this was against her own will?

They found a fairy ring of Giant Puffballs, one the size of an infant's head. Each person cut one from its rhizomes, wrapped it in wax paper and nestled it into their baskets. On the way back Renton's group met up with the group of men, and the women with the boy. The men said they found so many King Boletes they couldn't carry them all, and that the rest of the group should go collect some for themselves. Laurel ran at the head of the pack, knife in pocket, ready to cut as many as she could.

The group then builds three small fires in the gravel road, and they drag logs from the woods to sit on. Renton obviously promised the bus driver some mushrooms because he brings out his frying pan and oil to sauté the Giant Puffball slices. Laurel watches the women sliver green onions, chives, basil, and parsley into the pans. Renton says the Giant Puffballs had probably two or three trillion spores each. "They'll be back," he says. "They're here every year."

The man in the cap brought a case of beer, and Laurel drinks one. She eats half of her own Puffball, closing her eyes to taste the herbs and onion and the soft meat. Like some of the others, Laurel would dry the Boletes at the drying session, which Renton says really brings out the taste in that particular mushroom. She wouldn't sell any of them. As the day winds down, she decides to give Nellie her phone number. Maybe they could have a drink together someday, she thinks. Standing in the parking lot, her basket filled with mushrooms, Nellie thanks her for the company and scribbles her phone number on Laurel's unused scrap of paper bag.

"You don't look so sad right now," Nellie says.

"I looked that way?"

"Yeah, well things can be transitional."

"I guess I can't see myself," Laurel says.

"It's okay with me," Nellie says. "You can frown if you want. You do have a mean-looking scowl."

"Yeah, maybe. I don't—"

"It's just good to see you having a good time."

"I did have a good time," Laurel says.

"You're allowed that—it's okay." Laurel looks at her feet and nods.

Laurel pulls into her driveway, actually disappointed that Gil isn't there. The note on the table says he went out to the hardware store, that he didn't know when he'd be back. He could be screwing the perfume woman for all she knows. Either way it's immaterial; Laurel will surprise him with the fresh Puffballs. Even better as a surprise, she thinks. For dinner she'll make sautéed Puffballs to accompany the broiled trout, and the chard. She'll set the table with the nice linen and candles. She'll confess where she went. They will actually talk, address concerns, maybe touch each other. Laurel is ready to see through these things.

But she needs onions. She drives to the grocery store, wonders what C.J. is eating for dinner. Laurel buys a bag of sweet onions and is ready to speed through the express line. She stands in line, her load is light, and she's ready to shift forward. She sees the navel oranges on sale, four for a dollar. She decides that seven could be enough for now.

MY APRIL

The world has imploded since you left. They roared in from Washington, D.C., and stole the McGregor's Bronco, and broke into the Duffey's house to steal their stereo and Sony VCR, and tore up the Carlyle's deck for fun. In one year. Everything I read in the *Post* tells me Washington is a ravenous goat, and it's not stopping to look before it eats what it eats, and it's stampeding for us in the suburbs. Last month they carjacked a BMW from Linda Tilly in Elkridge, a friend of Tim's, and dragged her for a mile hanging from the front door, pinning a blood tail on Route 175. In front of a McDonald's they flicked her infant from the car like a candy wrapper.

April, I'm trying so hard to stabilize, as I am now, walking out of the house, from the quiet into the loud dank of the spring night. I know how hard it is to keep my baby Ashley snug and nursed, and Rebecca and Bill in school and snug in bed at night, and Pete at home where he never is, and myself anywhere where I can just *be*. I get so tired. Yes, here I am walking the neighborhood watch, which I must do despite not having a baby-sitter. I'm sliding the deck door locked, walking down Holden Drive, with my Radio Shack walkie-talkie smacking my hip, and my baseball cap askew with "Columbia Heights Fights Crime" in orange. Tim McGregor just called saying, "Here comes one," and I stride my walk confident to keep them away, and I bounce to show them I'm tough, and I pin my arms to my hips because to swing them is to be overconfident, so overconfident it's the opposite.

Here comes a car, and oh, lucky for them, it's the Dopson's jellyfish-white Jeep. I wave. They smile at me in their red and green striped polo shirts and roll down their window. They ask me if Bill wants to go swimming at the Jackson Community Center with their little Davy tomorrow. I say yes, automatic, intent, and I can't control these things, and I don't even like little Davy because he says *shit* instead of *shoot* like I taught Bill. Then Sally Dopson asks me how I am doing, gesticulating even with her sprained wrist she got from pruning her bushes, or so she said, because her husband won't help. She's a liar. She says it all because she has to, and I have to string the words back out of my mouth in short threads. I wish I never had those neighborhood parties, and I wish I'd never been so friendly or enjoyed myself so much, April, and now I'm paying for it. They ask me, "How is April doing?" Of course I lie to them that you've moved down the street to Oakland Mills, and that you're just really busy with your new job at NSA. "We really liked April," he says. But not enough to check and see where you live, and their skin looks so thin I think I can see the blue-green veins in their faces, and they pull out before I can ask Sally about her wrist, and I tighten and contract, and I tidy my teeth against my gums, smell the azaleas and dogwoods and try to smell the pansies and geraniums layered in their smooth green lawns, and listen to the wrens rustle in the dogwoods and locust trees, blue-gray in the after-after glow.

It is 10 PM on Saturday, May 2nd. April is done. Soon the water sprinklers will sprout and jet. Soon the trees will cluster and cloud so thick I won't be able to see the sky. Soon the residents of Columbia Heights will be tan as Mexico. The summer always makes me think of you, April, and wonder how you are in the Rockies somewhere, where you really are with your pretty carnation dresses and your dark leather thick-bound sandals. I know that you *are*, April, you are one, you are *closedness*. I know that Frank does hate you, and that you could do nothing else but come to me when you left him, and could do nothing else but despise my hospitality when you stayed that summer to argue with me every night on the deck over vodka and lemonade in yellow and brown plastic cups. You would tell me I'm drinking too much, and that I had no right to tell you how to be with Frank, and that you *had* to say what you said about Pete, and *to* Pete, and April I blame myself, and I know you're angry, and that it's not Frank— Frank's not important—but we were, and no matter what, we both know the most crushing news is to learn that self-awareness can't change a thing, even when you are like me and can't tell the difference between the clouds on the inside or outside.

Tim McGregor started this. It's his fault. Last July after the carjacking, he called a neighborhood meeting, and we all met at the Barton's blue aluminum shingled house that you know looks just like mine (it even has the same mailbox). We all drank Hi-C and ate Chips Ahoy on the little red paper plates left over from Jinny Barton's birthday party that said "You're Great!" and Tim steamed and boiled: "We must protect *our* nests at whatever cost," he said. "It's natural, they are hunting for our cubs," he said. "It's time to fight for what's ours!" Our children, our Volvos, our invisible fences, our lawn sprayers. That's what he meant. The Duffeys and Carlyles agreed of course, then everyone else did, and we decided that the community watch would be mandatory for each household, rain, or snow, or sleet, or hail, and that each of us would be responsible for two hours, one night a week, and that all we have to do is walk up and down the neighborhood, up to the *Columbia Heights* sign on Clover Drive (where you know the only entrance is) and back, and watch for unidentified cars entering the neighborhood. If we see one we are supposed to radio Tim who lives on Dandelion Court with a view of all entering cars, which despite his telescope he can't see because of the oak between the window and the street, or so he says. He still has that "astronomy" telescope in his bedroom window prodding sometimes at Mrs. Harry's bedroom, and he has the listing of the community license plates, which he flips through, smudging plate numbers on the tips of his fingers. I know you think Tim is a waste of flesh. "The duty of the community watch is to get those license plates," he says, and to buzz him on the Radio Shack walkie-talkie, because it's the best brand. And if he thinks the car is suspect he radios in to the police who come and snoop, and poke, and peep in their whistle-white cars, and don't find anything, or anyone, anywherc, and even if they did there's that new statute that says no high speed chases in residential areas, so what's the point? Tim always blows his top, his face rashing and his skin tight, and the cops tell him he's off base, and if he doesn't calm down they're going to ignore him forever, and that's what frightens him.

I think you're right, April, we haven't caught anybody but ourselves. I think Tim is what you wanted from me. "Just relax," you said. "Don't let Tim get *into* you," you used to say. And despite his flare-face Tim is not a bad guy. But April, he's not a replacement, he's a stick figure, a Taurus-driving mannequin, a pot-smoking pot-luck dinner host, and maybe that is what we really wanted from Pete and Frank—not those Hallmark marriage proverbs: "emotional partner," "love for life," "soul mate." We just wanted space fillers, soul potato chips. When we talked about our men in those day-long country car rides west into the Appalachians, we both agreed that they were not as important to us as we were to them, and that men have to strive for some ultimate, and if they don't they wither, and part of marrying them, we said, was in realizing how we had to pin ourselves under that; even though we cared less, we still had so much more at stake. Just because. We both agreed that the worst thing is having a man kiss your hand, because that meant *everything* we don't want is on the horizon.

Remember when we both decided to marry non-hand-kissing men, and better two men like that to get in our way than just one hand-kisser. That one time we drove all the way to West Virginia and lost ourselves in the strip mining overviews, and gray mountains, and exposed granite, and it felt great. Remember early on Pete and Frank would rent a sailboat, and take us out on the Chesapeake, bring beer, and subs, and rippled crab potato chips, and devour them first, without napkins, without offering us anything, assuming we'd just grab our own. And they'd flick the trash under their armpits to the water. I would turn to you April when I would watch their beer bottles bob and dunk in the water as we sailed away, and I would know the dusky water would ripple into the glass mouths, and sink the trash to the bottom, to rest.

So here I am, strutting down Holden and turning onto Gray Grass Drive, walkie-talkie smacking my thigh. I'm wearing black except for the hat, and I'm zipping my eyes, sniffing the air, and really looking, because I don't want to sack my neck onto their chopping block, and God, April, I don't want to end up a thin little red trail on the cement and ground glass. I'm trying to be tough, April, but this uproots me, and Tim McGregor tells us that on average one hundred cars rush into Columbia Heights each day, which means, on his Radio Shack calculator, 8.3 per watch period. So I have 7.3 to go. What is that .3, April? Is it the one that escapes? Is it the dust ball behind the Eazy-chair? The carrot end in the garbage disposal? That word that never completes the journey from the brain to the tongue? The present? I have to make it until midnight, and then I can return home and lie in my whistle-clean empty bed, and think of Pete at work where he never is not. But at least I have my Radio Shack radio, and a Velcro grip so I don't have to hold anything. At least when I'm walking I can see, and rest, and try to stabilize, and at least I know Tim McGregor tilts on the very corner of his father's mahogany rocker that he inherited last spring, and that he is sipping decaf—he is always conscious of his chemical flaws— and reading *Consumer Reports*, threading his telescope in and out of the *O* of his left hand, waiting for each and every one of my calls, tennis-eyeing the street for those two circles of light.

I walk past the Gordon's house and the Jackobsons, who are grilling ribs on their deck this late, and eating potato chips and spear pickles. They wave to me with charcoal fingers, in the blue light of their bug zapper, and I call Tim and tell him where I am, and he says, "Just look for the license plates, license plates, license plates, Tamara. Over and out." I kick the grass blades and clover that have breached their lawns. When I find weeds I rip their souls out, and step on them because at least Pete does mow the lawn every Saturday, and I can rely on his basic aesthetics at least, even though he thinks he has a market in beauty, and that I just plant stuff, or so he says. I pass the park with the swings that Bill fell from last week. He scraped his knee so bad I had to wrap it in a Spider Man pillowcase to stop the bleeding. It's the park where we play softball on Tuesdays at 7:00. Then Tim calls back and says "Here comes one," and I think then of how you smoked those home runs into the honeysuckle when you stayed with me that summer, and how you could hit the ball harder than any woman I've ever seen, April. I suppose all that softball practice in high school did us some good. Softball is there so that every week, I know I can chirp with the ladies, which I am trying to do less and less of, April, and it's there so that I can get annoyed and put on the catcher's mask and squat there digging balls from the dust, getting dirt stuck under my fingernails, tossing the ball back to the pitcher in slow fat arcs. I have become involved in the neighborhood whether I like it or not.

The next car coughs through the night. The headlights are murky through the mist, and I can't see inside, even though the windows are rolled all the way down. A hand flicks a cigarette into the Jackobson's lawn, and the hand doesn't wave, and it is a sedan, a gray Olds. He saw me. Oh, yes, it's just the Benningtons and Gary is probably asleep in the back, and that's good because Gary is a little brat, and he hit Rebecca with a yellow wiffle ball bat last summer. Henry Bennington is a louse and a drunk, and has a brother who plays minor league baseball in Frederick, and I wonder where they are coming from if it's not some sleazy bar in Baltimore. He pulls up to me and asks me how you are doing, April, and I shake my head, and say you're fine in Oakland Mills, and Harry says that "April is such a good kid," then he pats my hand and I can smell the tobacco on his fingers, the kind of husky cigarettes your father used to roll on the deck. I tell him I'm in a hurry, and he says he'll drop by when I get back, but I tell him it's too late tonight, no drinks for me, and that "I'm getting a headache from thinking about headaches, you know, has that ever happened to you?" Then he weaves and waffles home. He wants me but his wife doesn't seem to care. They must have some sort of arrangement. I'll think about it.

I turn onto Broken Branch Drive. I walk on. Tim calls and tells me there's another coming, and I tell him that last one was just the Benningtons, and he already knows, as he does sometimes. With Pete owning TSA now, and trying to get it off the ground level, you know he's never home. He was never home even when you were here. And sometimes, April, I feel like I'm married to what I think of you instead, and that can be a comfort, but still I feel crowded, and jumbled. I go in to see Pete in the afternoons and help him with finances, paperwork, letters, coffee, lunch, dinner if he wants. I lost my job at the community college since Ashley, and April, what am I going to do this summer when Bill and Rebecca will be home from school all day? And of course there's Ashley, and I won't even have time to work as Pete's runner. Pete stares at his computer screen for twelve hours straight some days, the way you did when you put everything you had into every paper when we were roommates at

Towson. Pete comes home and his eyes are remote, and his mind vanished long over the Rockies to our honeymoon in Estes Park, and near where you are maybe, and he sweats and shivers wet sheets next to me at night, gone by 6:07 AM. April, when I'm home I can't find closedness anywhere. Ashley is teething, and I never remember teeth being so aching. But at least Ashley has her spots, even if they're beneath her gums.

So here comes a car with its brights on. It's weird Kathy Donovan's yellow Bug, and she beeps at me. It's O.K. She's twenty-two, and in that rebellion-against-her-mother stage, though still living at home with her parents. I nod at her, but she almost runs over my foot as she squeals around the corner. In one hand she vacuums her Big Gulp through her red and blue striped Slurpee straw, and flips her maroon dyed hair over her face. She's not really weird; she just pretends. Kids these days. At least she didn't ask me about you. Then Tim McGregor calls. "What's the news?" I tell him nothing. He says I'm the only one he calls on the route, and I guess I should feel special. I don't answer. He sounds like he's trying to act bored, but he's the one boring me. He says that it is 10:27 and that I should keep my eyes peeled for Amanda Hayes. Then his voice rises again, "Because she's the next watch," he says. "If she comes early and she always does, then you can pop on over." I should tell you, I've been going over to Tim's to drink, and at first he was eyeing me, and then I eyed him, and then other things happened, April, and I'm so *embarrassed*. What makes it worse is that he's divorced (his fault), which makes him pathetic, and me even worse, and now he's pushing me, and I'm too tired. Got to do something to fill the time. 4.333 to go, April. "Over and out," I say.

Then right away before I can walk two steps, it comes. It rabbits past me to the stop sign behind me, and I turn. I run into the Walters' lawn, and duck behind a boxwood, and it jolts to a stop. It's a Cadillac, black. I can't see inside. It has tinted windows, and two antennas, and one is a car phone pigtail, and the rap throbs, and he has a *Public Enemy* bumper sticker, and April I'm scared. The car backs up into the Walters' lawn and idles. Just sits. I rip my walkie-talkie from my waist. I whisper to Tim. It turns right. "Maryland PWT 575," I say. He has a list of neighborhood cars, and the cars of friends and relatives. He tells me they're O.K. "It just looks like a city car," he says. "Yeah" I say. "Why didn't you tell me he was coming, Tim?"

"It's just the brother of Kevin Carlyle," he says, "Don't freak out."

"Figures," I say. "I'm not coming over, Tim. Over and out."

April, I am sorry about Frank. He still calls me once a week to ask if I have heard from you, and if I know where you are, and if I have then I'd better tell him, because he says, "I'm her husband and I still have some rights." I tell him that you are out in Mexico, and that you are not coming back, and I imply it's all his fault for being so negligent of your feelings in the first place, and that he should discover his cowardice and break out of it, and so on. I'm sorry he hated NSA, and didn't want any *brats*, and reminded you of your father when he drank and flushed red, and burped his vodka into scentless clouds. I do talk to him for you April just like I did when you stayed with me, just like you stood up to Pete for me. Remember when I told him he should stop grubbing for money and spend time with you? And even though I hated you at times for interfering when you stayed with me after Frank, even though I argued with you every night on the deck with our vodka and lemonade—you telling me to back out of your business, me wanting to know what was wrong, you telling me you just wanted to leave and that you felt netted in, me pushing more—and even though I slammed the door on your fingers once, and said it was an accident even though it wasn't, and even though, God, I wanted to smack your face that last time when you wheeled out in your old Honda hatchback, telling me, "Why don't you stop stopping me, Tamara? Why don't you stop sapping my energy," I did appreciate you. I did. And I know you hated the parties I threw with tiny pink paper umbrellas and streamers. You left seeing me lying as only I can do at parties (you remember the time I went on and on about Tim, and Tim's brother who I hadn't even met, and Tim's brother-in-law who I also hadn't met, because I wanted so hard to *seem*. You blinked and blinked and clicked your teeth with your tongue). What dumbfounded and impressed everyone here was that you didn't play that game. The proof is here: Now nobody wants to talk to me about me, only about you. April, you must know you have always been oxygen to me.

I breathe deep and put both my hands in my shorts pockets. Bill lent me his sling shot this afternoon in case of emergency. He wired it on the school bus with a coat hanger and rubber bands. "If you shoot for the eyes you can kill somebody," he said. Can you believe Bill is ten now? His slingshot gives me comfort for some reason. I take it out of my pocket, and bend down and pick up pebbles from the street, and they feel warm, and smooth, and I protect their exposure in my palm. April, do you remember how I used to grind and flint my hands together when I was a girl? And crack my knuckles because I could? And gross you out? I did it when I asked if your birthday was in April, like your name. You said May 7th. Next week. Now my knuckles ache when I write letters to you, and my legs are tired of walking this winding neighborhood with a thousand streets.

I'm walking down Hayworth Drive, and I'm smelling the pines, and the spring-cut-grass air, listening to the baseball announcer shouting the game from the Galloway's deck, and listening to Tim calling again saying, "Tam, another one," and smelling the air hot with water, and thinking about the time when we went fishing at Centennial Lake, which, like all lakes in Maryland is a man-made ditch with man-bred fish. You would cast first, rocking the boat, spreading yourself all over so that your legs dragged in the water, and you would toss the extra worms into the lake at the end of the day, and watch the bubbles balloon and blimp to the surface. You liked to prance around naked in my room, goose-stepping and rumba-dancing to the Temptations when I wouldn't take off a thing, and you stuck up for me when your Dad lost it in his vodka when we were girls, hiding us in the cellar when your dad called us little tramps, chasing us with his Louisville Slugger that one time. I never understood why your mother let him get away with what he did, and luckily we were quick runners and stuck together then. Now I understand your mother. April, you could do this community watch with a shotgun hot against your shoulder, and make these cars *yours*. But I can only walk down Hayworth Drive with shuffle steps, smelling the azaleas, the iris, the onion grass, listening for car rumbles against the air and the wet night. Distracted.

I have to pee. Who cares about Tim? I knock on the Ryan's house. They let me in, and talk to me about the storm that is supposed to be coming our way, and about Bill and their kid Greg's Cub Scouts. They offer me lemonade, with sugar, and they want me to look at their Jamaica photos. I tell them I have to pee and they let me pee, and I want lemonade, and they don't ask me about you but they smile like they want to and Ed Ryan scratches his beard with his thumb and smiles. Goddamnit, this time I want to tell somebody, even if it's Ed

Ryan. But it will take too much time, and I think of Tim and his walkie talkie, so I down my lemonade and leave. I think they are offended and she crosses her arms. Oh well, I walk out the door. I do think it would be nice to have a beard to hide behind. Then the car steams by, and I miss it. Shit. I mean shoot.

Tim calls and asks, what is it? "I had to go the bathroom," I say, and then he blows up and says I better run after the car, and that that one could be the one, and that he can't believe I was so irresponsible, and I say "What can I say, Tim?" I turn him off and keep walking, and I turn onto Rice Weed, and the Lafts and then the Parks drive by and wave to me, and Stephen Laft rolls down his window and offers me a ride, and then a beer, and I tell them I'm on duty, but they insist, so fine, I take a Corona, and guzzle it there, and Stephen nods because he never goes to the neighborhood meetings. He's not bad looking either. And who knows what Tim is going to say to him, or do to him—Tim can be so impulsive. They drive off. 1.333 left. Tim calls back and cusses at me again for the car I missed, and cusses himself right out of the conversation. Then he calls back, tells me he called the police, and cuts out. I walk onto Clover Drive, and look across to

Dandelion Court and can't see into Tim's house so I keep going and stop at the sign and feel the rough brick against my thighs and buzz Tim again and say, "I had to go to the bathroom." Tim crackles, saying that it is twelve of ten, and that I should wait at the sign for a while and to "Hang tough until the cops come." I tell him again that it's natural, and that I had to go, then that I'm scared, and he spits back, "Toughen up, Tam. There's no order to Saturday nights, pumpkin." I can't help giggling at how his voice sounds like the pit-faced fiend you see in half the world's macho movies. For a second I think I hear his real voice from his house, but I don't. "Over and out," I say, and cramp behind the sign in the spring grass.

I mole my fingers into the loam, loom my fingers through the mulch to roots torn from their souls. I smell the soup of sour boxwood and tulips, and I am safe here. I am. I grip Bill's slingshot. I am crouched and curled. When they come, April, I am going to shoot for the whites of their eyes right through to the bones of their brains, and I will stand here being everything you have always expected me to be. My God, April, they are swarming from the city to eat us alive, and I have to keep Pete's dead weights in front of the door so they won't come in. I bought dead bolts for the children's rooms. I sleep with a butter knife. Sometimes I sleep in the basement near the warm whirling dryer to keep me company, and the basement is dark and brown like this sign April, pretty and tasteful with brown and tan letters.

April, it helps me to think about when you moved to Maryland from Ohio when I was eight, and your parents moved next door and your dad would come over and talk to my dad, and they would drink and play chess on the deck, not worrying about anything, and you and I dug a garden, and would squat and plant cherry tomato seeds, and watch them grow, and pick them early sometimes and bring them to our mothers in our shirts like we were kangaroos, and when it was July we'd bite into the small red heads in the afternoon, and the hot juice would jet into our mouths, and we'd laugh at the sting on our chancre sores, and you'd tell me all you really wanted was to be Audrey Hepburn. Why did you give it up for Frank? When you were a girl you said if you didn't have that dream, some dream even when you were married, you wouldn't know what to do with your life. "Acting must be the bestest anybody could do," you'd sing, and twirl your pretty pink carnation dress in arcs, the dress you hated, the one that your parents would make you wear even if you held on to the banister so tight they couldn't rip you to church. Afterwards we'd sneak into your cool basement, and it would be darker there and still, and your shadow was always bigger than mine, and prettier, and when I dropped my guard you'd creep behind me and scratch my back with the sheaths of your long fingernails, and screech *boo*, and later you'd hold my hand, and it was bigger than mine, like a new softball glove, or the swollen inside of a pumpkin. Only you could do it. I knew I wouldn't let anybody else in. And you knew this, and I curled inside that *closedness*, and let the door swing wide open. You left for the mountains, April, or so you said, and I want to take this horticulture class with you now at the Jackson Community Center, and if I wasn't such a liar, and if I wasn't so afraid of those moments when you lift the cover then maybe you would be here, and maybe I could know what nobody else knows, how it feels to be you, and April, my April, forgive me.

I used to dream that you died in a car wreck, and that I was a happy martyr's friend, forever rooting you inside, all mine. And April, I root in the soil, and find jagged rocks there. I look for the skulls of animals, and when I'm walking I look for road kill, and if I find it I take pictures, and then I paste the pictures in the book, and your name is in the book, and that makes me smile every time I see it. The car's fog lights cloud Clover Drive. The trunks of the pines, and sycamores, and red maples are yellow then black, then yellow, and I stand up, April, and fling a rock into the foggy lights. He must be upset about you too, April. It misses. So I put the beer bottle in the sling, and fling that, and it hits, and splinters the windshield glass or itself or something. Home run! The car slams on its brakes. The driver steps out. I duck behind the sign, and pick at my head with my fingernails, and crackle to Tim "I hit it! I hit it!" I'm exhausted.

I hear the driver walking towards me. Do I know him? Is it Frank? Pete? Tim? It's cloudy. There is not one reason why you left. I don't know. I don't know. I can't see through these lights, and Tim snaps back to find out what's happening. I tell him "0.3333333 left." I tell him that. Footsteps. I think I have a headache. I think I have dandruff. I have a gray scalp flake under my fingernail.

Yours—

Tamara

AND THEN WE CAN DECIDE

After twenty years Franklin Multher gets an anniversary party at Crispy's Seafood—his years of washing dishes and scrubbing pots in the steam finally amount to something. He could be manager by now, but he wouldn't cut his hair, and that seemed like a battle worth waging back in '78.

He walks into Dining Room One and the place explodes: "Surprise!"

The gathering is a mixed lot. The real surprises are Carl and Ellen from back in '80, big supporters of his band, the Whirligigs. Now Carl and Ellen own their own interior decorating business. They get by. Calvin McKay, fellow dishwasher and confidant '81-'83 embraces him, tugs on his hair. He's a regal pediatrician in Kansas City these days. The Finney twins shake his hand, and introduce Franklin to their husbands whom they simultaneously wed back in Pittsburgh. Marriage has kept them away from Crispy's. Who can afford eating out these days? But all the regulars are there. All of his friends from Harrisburg are there.

And the ones like Healy Brown—who parted on uncertain terms—are won over, even though they approach him with reserve. But Franklin can't hold a grudge he can barely remember. They shake hands and the band strikes up. Everyone lifts their glasses, and downs the bubbly with strawberries from the crystal centerpieces. They smile at the rose petals sprinkled on the tables, and sing and dance, and stumble against the tables, and clutch the tablecloths before they happily stammer home.

Patti has worked as a telemarketer for ten years. Sometimes she tells Franklin she's surprised *telemarketing* is ten years old, much less her stake in the job. At their house on Rowe Street they watch *The Jerk* for the fifty-seventh time, and make love as the credits roll. She will take him to the lake tomorrow and they will camp under the spruce knobs. Swim in the lake.

"No, that wasn't on my mind at the time," he says.

"Not that I mind. I don't mind. I'm no victim here." They tread water in the center of the lake, nobody around.

The September leaves fall into the lake around the edges of the water. A circular curtain of falling leaves. Where they swim it is leafless.

"Why exactly did you do it?"

"You remember. It was important. I'm not going to be—"

"A part of something you couldn't agree with."

"Right. We've talked about this," he said, circling his arms in the water. They are both relaxed.

"And I'm not disappointed. I just want to make sure I understand."

"If you want to think of it this way you can: I never wanted to be important," he says.

"What do you mean, *important*?"

"Part of something. Lording over people. I never wanted to be in charge. This isn't new."

"No it's not," she says. "I guess I didn't either."

The shadow of the moon is a pinhole in the lake. The lake is smooth and silent. Around the lake the leaves fall in the dark and the frogs croak. The summer winds down. They are camped at the lip near a cove that melds into a swamp by the entrance road. They light a pipe and Franklin takes a hit.

"No," she says. "I'm wrong." He hands the pipe and lighter to her. "I did want to be important. I didn't want to be a telemarketer. I know that."

"Are you talking about when you're a kid and the teacher asks you—"

"Yeah, that's what I'm talking about," she says.

"What did you say?"

"I said an actress." She holds the pipe in the open face of her hand, and flicks the lighter twice, getting a flame. They smell pine and spruce, and the dank wetness of the ground.

"But did you want to be an actress or did you think you wanted to be an actress?"

"That's just it," she says. "It's hard to know, isn't it? It's hard to figure out what I really wanted in my core. It's hard to know where that Hollywood shit starts and ends." She hands the pipe right back to him.

"I don't know," he says. "I can't see you at a bunch of fancy filming parties or anything."

"True," she says. "But I didn't see myself as a telemarketer either. I could adjust to something else."

"I couldn't," he says. "I'd disappoint myself too much. No. No way."

"I don't think I'd disappoint myself if I was trying something. It doesn't have to be set in stone. I could go back and do something else."

"Hey, you're still young," he says. "You can do what you want. We've always said that."

"I know," she says. "I'm just saying that something new isn't anything certain really. Patterns are..." Her voice trails off. She picks at her finger. "I don't want to be serious. This is supposed to be a celebration. Forget it, Frankie."

He hands the pipe back to her. She shakes her head. He lights the bowl up again and takes a long hit. She stares out over the water. She strains to hear the leaves.

They wake up. The treetops waver in the cool morning wind. The sky is the color of Windex. Patti suggests they take a hike around the lake. Franklin agrees, and they take the tent down and gather their belongings. They stick everything in the pickup.

They hold hands as they trudge through the brambles and trees. The county never built a trail around the lake. Franklin had always suspected they wanted to limit loitering and date rape. He always thought they should have a trail anyway. He touches the small of Patti's back, and she shoots forward with a start.

"That surprised me," she says.

"Sorry," he says.

"Say something," she says. "You're so quiet."

"I'm just thinking," he says. "I am. I guess I'm thinking about what you said last night."

"Yeah." She squints into the trees, listening to the birds and the wind.

"I don't know what the truth is. I don't regret my decisions though."

"I'm not asking you to either," she says. "I think it's important to lend a little perspective. That's all."

"Yeah," he says.

They walk on either side of a tree, separating, and returning back to each other. The leaves crinkle under their feet. He clears his throat.

"Do you think we should do something different? We can. We don't have to stay here."

"No," she says. "That's not it. Whatever we do we're going to do right here. Everybody we know is right here."

"Okay," he says. "Let's do something different right here then."

"I do have a suggestion. It's symbolic, that's all. But it's a start. And then we can decide."

"What's that?"

"Let's cut your hair."

"My hair?"

"Yeah, what's the point any more? You made your stand. You won."

Franklin smoothes his hand over the top of his head, and runs his fingers through the long strands. He has thought about this before, but he didn't have a reason to take action. She's right; why not? He has to admit, he likes the idea. Who would want to become status quo to himself?

"Let's do it," he says.

Franklin kept it hush-hush. He mostly didn't want to call attention to himself. Patti agreed with this approach, since she wanted it to be about *them*, about them as a couple. But she didn't want to cut it herself. Patti didn't want that responsibility. She called up Andy Limbaugh and he said he'd do it, and he'd keep it low among Franklin's friends.

But somehow people found out the whens and wheres, and the next thing they knew twenty people were over at Franklin's smiling through the living room windows to see how Andy would do it. Somebody brought cigars. Willie knocked his way in and handed one to Franklin. Franklin bobbed his head.

And when Andy picks up the shears and starts in on the locks around Franklin's ears, somebody yells out to Franklin, "What are you going to do now?" Franklin knew that was coming. More than anything else he was proud of his legend. This is worth something, he thinks. Standing, Patti touches him on the shoulder, and Franklin shivers. He was something beyond a mere dishwasher; he knew that all along. Something beyond mere.

"I have absolutely no idea," he said. He grins and lights the cigar. Patti sits next to him and crosses her legs. Andy smiles from ear to ear. She runs her fingers through her hair and says, "Andy, when you're done with him, can you get a little of mine too?"

THE BROWN DATSUN

Pulling onto the shoulder of Route 70, she stops behind the Datsun. The knotted white T-shirt on the driver's side door handle snaps in the wind. Macy flips a page of her pad where she tallies the make and plate numbers written neatly in black ink. She writes "Brown Datsun: CMN 189" on the top line and looks inside the car for signs of the owner's name, a credit card receipt, a letter, bank statement.

Despite the age of the car, it looks relatively clean. Scraps of shredded paper and a pen cap rest on the back seat, and paper clips and pennies cluster the space under the parking brake. The dashboard has a thin veneer of dust. She can make out a red umbrella handle under the passenger seat. But otherwise the car is clean. Macy isn't surprised by this; exterior appearances are hardly foolproof clues to anything, much less any sort of soul guide. She notes these things anyway, like some dutiful reporter hoping to join an editorial staff.

She needs to buy more tinfoil, and more videotape. The recent excursions have eaten into her stock, and she will need more.

This is mid-April, and Macy has been hounded by her usual spring allergies. She hurries back to the safety of her leather interior. She sits there, a woman of fifty-three in her Ford Taurus—engine running, ragtime swing soft on the back speakers, staring at the abandoned car. Eventually it usually does come to the worst, she thinks, it usually does.

But is this her usual martyrdom complex rearing its head? Effort does pay off if that's what you want, she thinks. This is not just an optimistic position. This is the result of extended experience. We have more time than we can fill. The challenge is to occupy yourself, Macy thinks. But how do you do that with meaning? You can work yourself silly. You can dive headlong into some hobby or pastime. But what if you don't find pleasure? You can easily get stuck in some kind of middle ground, where the enjoyment itself becomes work.

For ten years Macy was a statistician for the county planning commission. Among other duties, she collected the numbers on growth and development in the southern region. It was laborious, and menial, and time-consuming. She took one week of vacation over that time. And then she took a six-month mental health leave. Her husband didn't ask her to work. She just did.

Although she never lived on a commune, years ago Macy did live in Boyd, a small town in South Carolina where she worked at a health food store. She enjoyed the physical pleasures of working in a store: the smells, and textures of the food. That year she did meet several friends who unfortunately dropped out of her life after she left. Now Boyd seems like some kind of concentrated purity, a burning dot in her head. Macy rarely felt pressured to do anything, or to be anything those days. A "professional" life was the furthest idea from her mind, as was a husband.

Somehow, a greater American reality intruded. Macy conceded to this, although in some way she knew that it was a welcome guest. She was born in Charlotte into a family of hard-working entrepreneurs who bought up half the town's restaurants and bars before the growth explosion. Her father owned a statewide restaurant chain. Her mother was somewhat of a socialite, and in those days that meant cocktail parties. Fancy clothes. Macy accepted the comfort and sense of entitlement. Even as a young girl she knew she wouldn't have to work nearly as hard as her own parents; she felt that was their gift to her and her sister Prella.

Unlike her sister, however, Macy had difficulty with the practicalities of her upbringing. She usually found some way to mess up her hair or crumple her dress. Macy was barely allowed into the common area during a party. She would ask the guests frank and embarrassing questions. Her parents tried to take her to church, but she would feign coughing and sneezing so much that her parents were worried they would become the scourge of the congregation.

The problem came down to the fact that Macy was too pragmatic for faith, or thought she was. But at the same time, Macy knew she needed the benefits of a life of extended effort. Love had something to do with this. Her friends in school told her how great it was to be in love, to be loved by someone, a man. She didn't understand this. In the abstract she knew that this was important, but the feeling itself didn't poke through. A romance wasn't interesting in itself. The radiation of love was what she was interested in—how it could affect her daily life, what she could get out of it. But that's not what they meant by "being in love."

Macy turns the ignition and listens to the low rumble of the Taurus engine. Women were not supposed to give a thought to automobiles when she was growing up, and her father didn't encourage her. But this had nothing to do with the cars themselves. Now she will accomplish something out of her attempt to preserve, in her own way. One can only do so much, but maybe something internal will be captured out of the quiet fervor. The workman-like saints—the ones Macy admired—were very much like this. Emily de Rodat was one Macy read about as a girl: a woman who simply opened a free school in the 19th century. It was not a broad action. Stigmatas and visions did not enter into her head; she was a worldly person who kept one eye on something beyond.

The shopping center is only five minutes away. The sun glints through the windshield. May is quickly approaching, and Macy is stunned by how quickly the trees have blossomed and shifted into a bright green. Pollen encases the car in a fine powder, which dusts away as she accelerates to fifty-five. Groundhogs nuzzle into the grass along the side of the highway, a crow lands on a high branch of a dead tree, and then she passes them. Life in a blur—patches of pink, and purple, and green. The gray highways go straight to where you want to go, even if they were designed so the army could respond to the Russkies.

Whatever is built for one reason is used for another reason. Tennis courts are used for street hockey. Gymnasiums are used for church services. Cars are used for makeshift beds. And God is in things, not just people: All atoms are equal. Macy agrees with the Spinoza she read in college, and identifies with pantheism in general, in any form. But she realized this first and foremost when she sold her first car when it died, a 1969 Nova, to the junkyard. This was the end, she thought. And then two years later she saw it on the side of 695. She knew it was the same car. She could feel it. The owners must have put a new engine in the car—but the body was fine. But when she called the junkyard, they professed to have no idea what she was talking about.

When she pulls into the parking lot, Macy opens the door and sits sideways in the seat, staring at the asphalt and feeling the warmth of the sun on her face. Another winter is officially over, and the slow rise to a new season is ahead. How does she survive? At one point she used to volunteer for a cemetery preservationist she knew from work. But she knew too many people. The work was too close to memorialization. She agreed—the developers had no right to knock down a headstone, and much was unfortunately lost to neglect, not just conscious destruction. But...the effort felt not exactly too conventional, but too close to everyday death, and disease, and decay. She could feel her body too acutely tugging at the thistles clouding a headstone.

As Macy locks her car and strides across the parking lot to the retail store, she feels functional and earthly. Yet her curly hair feels somehow too excessive for her body. How could her neck be so short in comparison to the tendrils that cascaded to her shoulders, how could her legs be all tendon and bone? She couldn't even make a mark on her waist from the teeth of tight panties. Her eyelashes are too small. Her mother expected her to fill out as she got older, but the process seems to have reversed itself. Not that other women don't have their own hang-ups about their bodies, their weight. For Macy, it's length. Even her teeth seem too elongated, as if she were stuck in a fun-house mirror.

The man at the counter does not seem preoccupied with this, however. Like the best service employees, he seems to be a person who can maintain a conversation about anything. This is why the argument about the disintegration of contemporary conversation does not seem to hold its own water to Macy. Managerial pressure is certainly applied to push the customer through, but the greater pressure is philosophical—to appear friendly, to be talkative and extroverted. All of this improves conversation, not to mention customer service.

Leon asks her how she will pay for the aluminum foil and the three packs of blank videotapes. Macy says she will pay with a check, if that's okay. Leon says it is more than okay, and he asks for her driver's license. He sees the Westminster address, and says he too lives in Westminster.

"Is that so?"

"Lived there two years," Leon says.

"And you come all the way down here to work?" Macy says.

"I like the drive. Want to get *out* of town sometimes."

"Understandable. I've lived there all my life."

"You've never lived anyplace else?"

"Except as a child and young adult. I've lived there since I've been an adult, I guess."

"Wow," Leon says. "That's unheard of these days."

He hands her the bag, and her driver's license, and tells her to have a good day. She says she hopes he does too, and means it. She wonders if she will ever see him again. She doubts it.

When she gets home she checks the mail—bills and magazines and junk—and changes into a pair of shorts and one of her husband's flannels. She wonders how he's making out. One more year and his assignment will be over. He will be back. But she is also enjoying the solitude, of course. She can't deny that. Or maybe enjoying is the wrong word...surviving. This is not what she expected out of a marriage. She gets the video camera, and pops one of the new tapes into the slot. She hasn't told him about the project. He'd think she was entering into some post-career crisis.

In the garage Macy squats over the mountain of tinfoil, placing the camera off to the side for now. Her idea is to surround the mountain with copies of the abandoned cars, not actual copies, but impressions, miniature models. Something close to what the traditional Mexicans create—a shrine. The mountain is loosely based on Mt. Rainier, which Macy fell in love with when she visited the Seattle area.

She rips a sheet of foil from the roll, and bunches it into a ball. The entire operation takes half an hour, depending on how much detail she wants to put into the model. She pinches the wheels, and tries to get a general configuration of the Datsun with her fingers. The brown spray paint is in the cupboard, and she places the Datsun on the workbench, slides a sheet of newspaper underneath, and closes one eye as the nozzle releases a stream of brown.

When the car has dried, Macy will return and add the red umbrella with a brush, maybe a silver powder for dust—details so she can remember the lost car. She will type a thumbnail description into the computer, and number it 112. When she has finished, she will turn the camera on and hit *record*. A slow pan across the tinfoil mountain will end with a close-up of the Datsun, but the speed has to be the same. The time has to be at least ten minutes, exactly ten for each addition or alteration. The mountain of cars will grow from where it is, to where it should be.

BEIGE IS NICE AND REGULAR

Sedwick's favorite things are right there. The helmet bank filled with pennies. The baseball game humming in the living room one hundred and sixty-two days a year. The newspaper and coffee in the morning.

And nobody can say he lacks dedication: He gets his oil changed every three thousand. Dentist checkups every six months. He invests money in mutual funds, no load. But not too much. Let the company take care of the rest. Jogs three times a week. Once a week he'll catch up with an old friend. Maintain all aspects of his life, starting with that morning paper.

His last payment to the newspaper was on time, but a computer glitch erased his file. Or so the computer said on the computerized answering service. The computerized voice wouldn't tell him how to register a computerized complaint. "Delivery of your newspaper is terminated until further notification," it said.

Sedwick looks under the boxwood, and in the neighbor's yard, but his paper is nowhere to be seen. The sky is dark. The air smells like a garden hose. His neighbor steps out of his front door. Sedwick doesn't know the name of his neighbor. Sedwick watches him unlock his car trunk. The neighbor watches Mary Hopkins across the street unlock her car trunk. They drop their briefcases into their trunks simultaneously. What happened to the booming fad of telecommuting? Is this why traffic is so bad?

Sedwick likes watching other people watch other people. He can see Mary's paper is still in her yard. He goes inside to get his keys to drive to the store, to purchase his own paper. He is not a freeloader.

The store is five blocks down Wisconsin Avenue. Sedwick will drive: It will feel quicker. He wishes he could read while he drove. He could accomplish more. He could listen to morning radio, traffic reports, and read the paper. Who doesn't look forward to creative advertisements? French Roast when he returns.

But the sky opens up when he turns onto Wisconsin. The traffic lights blink yellow, but the next set is red, red, red. Nobody goes. The cars beep at each other in confusion.

Nobody knows what to do. Sedwick sits in the line, listening to the advertisements, thinking it will change, but the light isn't cooperating. He drives through the intersection after the others, and buys his paper. In the store, a man is wearing a tank top. Everyone can see his muscles underneath. What is the point of that fuss? Sedwick wants to get back to where he keeps his favorite things. He tucks the paper in the plastic bag under his arm so the deluge of water won't intrude. On the way back the radio station is out. The light blinks green, green, green. Everybody stops.

Sedwick has the day off. And on his day off he wants to take care of the business. Joseph, his cousin, asked him for a favor. Joseph is impotent. The meds think he has prostrate cancer, though they aren't sure yet. Sedwick has heard his cousin tell them he'd like to just gouge his genitals out.

They sat in Joseph's living room two weeks ago. *One* of Joseph's living rooms. He has one on each floor. The house has five floors. They were on the second floor, in the living room with the faux sixteenth century Chinese porcelain, and faux lapis lazuli statuettes from the height of the faux Ottoman Empire. When Sedwick asks to use the bathroom Joseph mentions that he has nine of them, by the way. Eight televisions, unless you count the wall-sized as two.

When Sedwick returned, Joseph said: "You know her. And Amira's very attractive."

"Yes. Yes, I think she's, well, she's...pretty." His fingers smell like cinnamon toast, which is mystifying.

"Did you want to...did you think that earlier?"

"Yes, but that doesn't..."

"Yes, well now you need to think that. Or try to. Jesus, I feel like an idiot asking you this. You didn't think those kinds of things before...did you?"

"No, no, no, no. But now that you mention it...that's what I'm getting at," Sedwick said.

"Yes, okay. Well. I do want you to...please her. She wants this. She is miserable. She hasn't had anything in the last two years. That I know of. I'm in pain, and she's miserable."

Sedwick sat there and coughed. The sun poured through the window. The glass coffee table was as bright as a satellite panel.

"Well, what do you think?"

Sedwick coughed again and sniffed the air. He said it smelled stuffy. Joseph said stuffiness isn't a smell.

"Let me put it this way," Sedwick said. "If it was a color, it would be a grayish brown. Not particularly pleasant."

"I see what you're saying."

"Because, you know, I have this theory that everything can be broken down to colors. The color wheel—you know? Which is really just a series of numbers. But colors are numbers in an expressive form."

"Uh-huh. Look, Sedwick. I'm in a terrible position here. I'm willing to pay you, of course. I know this is not an easy thing I'm asking you to do."

"Pay me?"

"We decided on a hundred dollars a week. For two nights a week. That's really just for a few hours. You don't have to…you know, be romantic. It's just a function she needs fulfilled. It's just a function."

Sedwick twiddled his thumbs and blinked. "Well, I think I can try."

"The main thing is I don't want her going to some gigolo," he said. "You are single. You are the only single guy I know. Everybody's married these days. Everybody's tied up."

"Right."

"We've worked all this out, and this is the best solution."

"I'll try," Sedwick said. "I'll give it a shot."

"I know you'll find a way to succeed."

"Thanks," Sedwick said. "That's nice to hear."

A ring at the doorbell. The place is clean...clean as he could get it before three. She's wearing a beige body suit, some silk and thread conglomeration fashioned from Indian gold. The suit seems to follow each contour of her body. Her breasts, for instance, jut against the thin fabric in desperation. Sedwick does not see a panty line, or a trace of a bra. She has a matching purse in her left hand, which she squeezes ever so softly, then tosses into the air and catches with her other hand. Amira lifts the soft bag to her mouth and blows on it. Then she drops it on the floor and swings the door shut.

"God, I'm bored," she says. She sways down the hall in her heels, and flops onto Sedwick's couch. Sedwick limps after her, and sits on the cheap armchair.

"I bet," he says. He's wondering what ever possessed this woman to end up with Joseph in the first place. Not that Joseph is exactly in the red (which is the answer right there).

Sedwick lives in a tiny rancher, works an average bureaucratic job that takes little effort, although it consumes fifty-five hours a week. Joseph is the head of a major corporation.

"Well, we know why we're getting together, right?"

"I think so," Sedwick says.

"I'm glad to see you don't have any Lester Young playing or anything. No candles. No champagne. Fine. I'm just happy to be thinking about something other than…you know."

"Pretty lonely huh?"

"I thought that once—"

"I know already," Sedwick says.

"What?"

"You were going to say that you thought you'd be happy marrying a rich man like Joseph. And then the relationship went limp."

"Something like that," she says. "I guess this will be different than our usual family get-together."

"I guess so." She stands up and pulls an envelope out of a hidden pocket, and hands it to Sedwick. She tells him the check is for the next two weeks. That way he has to make good on his deal. He takes it and puts it in his back pocket.

"Fine," he says. She drops to her knees, and rests her head against his thigh.

"Oh, God," she says.

Amira pulls the top of her suit back on. The light through the window is low and soft. She ruffles his head, and walks into the kitchen. Sedwick can hear her withdraw a glass from the cupboard, and go to the refrigerator for a drink. All he has is milk and beer.

"Do you have any bottled water?"

"No," he says. "I have a faucet." Sedwick pulls his pants on, and loops his belt through the pants.

"Yeah right," she says. "What am I doing?"

"Hell if I know," he says.

"Thank you." He can hear her turn the faucet on and catch water in the glass. She walks back into the living room. She sits on the couch and drinks the water, catching her breath halfway through. Sedwick watches her look around the room.

"Your house is nice," she says. "It's fine. You don't have too much."

"I'm not rich."

"No, I mean that in a good way," she says. "What do you do for fun, other than screw other men's wives and get paid for it?"

"I like to go to strip malls."

"Oh. And why?"

"They are, you know, everything, you know, that all this stands for." He waves his arms, gesticulating east and west.

"'All this?'"

"The suburbs. Middle-class America. I'm not in denial."

"So you go to strip malls?"

"I go to strip malls to compare and contrast," he says. "I look at accessibility, design, the quality of the stores. Unification of themes. The ways the colors mesh."

"What do you mean?"

"The palettes that they use. Some are very black and white, austere. Some are orange and blue—they try to catch your attention. There is a certain combination the merchants use to draw you in."

"Well, sure, but why bother with all this. It's, you know, pretty drab," Amira says. "Isn't it?"

"You think that because you haven't tried looking into something you take for granted."

"Maybe. But I haven't tried analyzing sink basins either."

"That's another place to start," Sedwick says.

That night after dinner he drives to *The Little Shoppes* at Peach Blossom Center, the closest strip mall, and his favorite. They have little English horsy shops, and bakeries, and everything looks British and prim. Sedwick parks under one of the parking lot lamps, and rolls down the window. He sees people milling about outside the beige ice cream shop, and the beige Gap still has a few stragglers inside. The beige coffee shop is abuzz with women and men fresh from their dinners. Beige is nice and regular, he thinks. This is all so comforting.

He watches the moths ping against the lights, and he sighs contentedly. Another good day. A little different from the others, but that's okay. Everything turned out fine, he thinks. Everything will be good. The sky is clear now, and it glows to the west, even though the sun set two hours ago. It's an ugly sunset, Sedwick thinks, a dull orange. He holds his hands together and smiles, and gets himself comfy in his seat.

COLLEGE DAYS

This will not sound realistic; nevertheless, it is what occurred. First on a short list of events that drove me to sell my $300,000 rancher in Columbia, along with my successful nursery to Ellen Thimble, the equally successful architect and businesswoman, and move to a one bedroom studio apartment with a view of a gravel parking lot and two green dumpsters in Sykesville, Maryland, was that my wife, formerly Lila Weaver Humbert (now Lila Weaver) had just left me for another man. On Lila's part, it was one of those spontaneous, quasi-feminist maneuvers one can see popularized in the Hollywood dramas of the late '70s and early '80s. Yet, to use a stock phrase, I never thought it could happen to me. After eighteen good years, or so I thought, all I could claim as my own—I am speaking, metaphorically, of course, since I do own quite a few possessions, or I used to—was a pink slip (actually pink) which read, "Goodbye Gary. I'm leaving you." Since that is my name, and since I was, in fact, Lila's husband, I assumed she meant me.

Actually, in retrospect, I realized the act was quite Lila's style, as I said, once I gained a smidgen of objectivity on my situation. She was an army brat, a Daddy's girl whose mother deserted her and Sergeant Weaver one rainy winter night, or such was the story I believed to be true. It is no wonder Lila never could adjust to the dull suburban evenings that seemed to flow into one another and lose their shape inside the pittering sounds of children and devoted husbands jiggling leash-chains. At times she would go out alone to a restaurant for a drink, or to a movie. This was not unusual.

I recall my mother cautioning me: The chances are high that if you do not get along with a girl's mother, the likelihood of your marriage being a happy one with that girl are slim. Lila would watch the television—or more to the point, ignore watching it—with a frantic itch like no one else I knew; she had difficulty simply sitting still from minute to minute. I wondered if her mother had this same problem. Constantly busy ruffling the newspaper, or on the phone with somebody or other, Lila would rustle through files as if her life depended on it. Yet when I would ask her what she was doing, she would respond with, "Work, nothing." I usually returned from Humbert's before she would return from work, and her face often betrayed a sense of disappointment that I was there. Lila is a smart woman, but her emotions were still apparent. It was as if she wanted the whole house to herself.

I suppose what in actuality, Lila desired, was another place, not another person. Yet, this did not calm my biting and growing desire for her after she left me, nor did it make the situation any easier. I believe that after she left, in fact, I wanted her more than I ever have, perhaps even obsessively. Also, the situation was not alleviated by the fact that I had no inkling where, in fact, she was or who she was with. The hand-wringing father whose daughter just eloped scrambling down the grape-leafed trellis outside the bedroom window—I was that father.

So the decision to sell the house and donate all of Lila's belongings to Goodwill and the Salvation Army was one part retribution, two parts self pity. Yet pity is a defense mechanism, and after all who would or could stay in a house after its soul had just been gutted? Onwards and upwards, right? The most difficult aspect of the move was ridding myself of most of my belongings, including my plants. I decided to kill them all. Most succumbed easily to the glyphosate. I dumped plants out of pots, dumped alcohol onto the cacti, including the pears, which I absolutely adore. However, I rationalized three darlings into my life—the peace lily, the jade (which was older than my marriage), and the ficus tree—and along with a rented moving van which I filled with my necessities, I drove to the little town of Sykesville that I knew was once, in the early part of the century, a resort for Baltimoreans escaping the foul water and sweltering summers of the city. But that was the total sum of my knowledge about the place. That night I slept in the car and awoke as the morning commuters shuffled and scuffed—and no doubt gawked—past me in the morning glare.

The initial difficulties I had were of the practical sort common to any person who has ever acquainted themselves with a new place of residence, and I will not detail them here. However, what was interesting to me, initially at least, was the similarity between my apartment and the way in which a plant reacts to a transplant. Even if you transplant a blueberry bush from the seashore into the forest it will thrive and flourish on its own terms; it will come to its own awakening.

So, admittedly, I had not entirely rid myself of my past interests, nor did I intend to. I spent the first few days merely lounging in bed in various degrees of consciousness, mulling over Lila and her motivations, her justifications, her desires, her obsessions, her fantasies. To escape my funk I watered the plants. I emphasize: I wanted her, physically I mean, in a way that seemed abnormal. My body *ached*. Yet, this was a matter which actually was perhaps only of superficial interest. But not finding an explanation, I began to notice sensory details about my surroundings (which I chose for their very generic qualities, but which, in turn, seemed rather less than generic, in a generic sort of way).

To begin with, I chose a studio unit; actually, it may be called an efficiency unit. However, I was in such a fuzz during the whole apartment-search process, that when I drove into the parking lot of the Rosemont Building, I could not even remember what the room looked like, much less precisely which apartment it was. I had to knock on several doors simply to find my own unit.

The room actually was quite unique. It was an attic apartment of sorts and thus it was quite angular inside, fitted with small floor-level closets. On the right was a regular closet; only the door was cut into an angle to fit the odd frame. This was June so I opened the windows at night, and the fresh air was balmy and comfortable, as if an electric fan blew lightly and constantly over my tired body. Directly outside of the south window was an old train station, and the train whistled and chattered loudly as it passed. Did I mention the smell? It was distinctly honeysuckle, with a trace of skunkweed.

Perhaps it was the aroma that struck me, but whatever it was, I was hit by a sudden and powerful wave of collegiate nostalgia. This was an odd sensation, since I hadn't thought about college for years and years. I attended the University of Maryland and lived in a town house with a backyard filled with, among other things (namely my roommate's dog's crap), honeysuckle. I suddenly missed those simple days when the only item of concern was the next research paper, when my parents paid for everything, and it was so pleasurable to scrounge for food, especially if it was late at night and you were so hungry from marijuana (my first love of plants). Soupy macaroni and cheese the color of nuclear war. Twisted pasta with Ragú. Oh, and Campbell's soup. Pretzels, potato chips, pistachio nuts. Mmmm, fried egg sandwiches on wheat toast, crispy egg edges. Even frozen dinners, and pancakes with strawberry jelly or cheap imitation maple syrup, and runny and hot and salty and perfect peanut butter on toasted Jewish rye. Boy, oh boy.

You must understand that in times of desperate and passionate ambivalence, I am willing to consciously act in an eccentric manner (at least superficially) to achieve a type of personal healing. I will admit that I am proud of being a successful businessman, which may yet be the epitome of normalcy. Managing the several high school students I hired was a source of satisfaction for me despite the high turnover rate. Overall, it was most rewarding—this process of sculpting a young mind.

I believe I took pride in my store. Yet the problem with growers selling insect-ridden goods was a hurdle, as was the general and pervasive competition from the national chains. Of course, a greenhouse is naturally hot and messy, and wet. I went through six pairs of shoes a year, and lost fifteen pounds the first year I owned the store. The scale, whitefly, and spider mites got to the goods. And most frustrating of all, the holiday seasons really did dominate the store. The complaints during the holidays were annoying. Most questions were too specific, or too broad, and employees became quickly aggravated. Customers wrote nasty letters, telling me they would boycott for this reason, or that reason. Once a customer dropped a bottle of herbicide onto the concrete floor. I have to admit that the acrid artificial smell was never entirely eradicated from the store. This was my life.

I think, retrospectively now, that I actually longed for eccentricities in a constant effort to rebel against my surroundings. Yes, when my sister Jane almost died as a result of a horrific skiing accident, I wore Lila's straw hats around the house for a week. When our dog, Hank, died last summer— he ate *lilies of the valley* I left, accidentally, on the kitchen counter—I stopped mowing the grass for a week. I know, I'm awful. Perhaps my reactions were the result of some supernatural or superstitious segment in my mind. But what if it was some type of minor senility? Perhaps I was really peculiar, and my quirks only glowed when despair crouched to fan the flames.

At any rate, this time I decided that, instead of sprawling in the shadow of my despondency, I would open a restaurant featuring collegiate food. I would challenge myself in a new place. Yes, I thought, I will throw caution to the wind and take a step out into small time entrepreneurship. No, that was not exactly the justification. I put myself into a quiet one year retirement, and I suppose I desired something to pass my time. Yes, that had to be it, since no serious entrepreneur would begin an even quasi-conceptual (albeit retro) restaurant in a town—fifty miles south of the Mason Dixon— where the drivers are proud to display bumper stickers reading, "Save a deer, bag an activist."

Nevertheless, I flung myself full force into the enterprise. I hung up a tattered terry cloth bedspread from my youth, and my old yellowed posters from the depths of the attic. I began listening to the bubbling, yellowed, faded notes of Hendrix, CSN, and late-period Beatles. Yes, and Buffalo Springfield. I walked about with my army knapsack. I even bought a purple and yellow lava lamp, incense, and little clay painted do-whats from one of the retro-sixties-new-age-stores in Ellicott City. I stocked the refrigerator, and I formatted a menu in snazzy bubble-letters and hung an eye-catching sign on Main Street, and, of course, cleaned and re-cleaned the apartment. Then I was ready to call this new venture "College Days."

To my surprise the customers came the first day—one customer at least. But then, on my sign I made it clear, I could only seat four at a time: "An intimate Central Maryland encounter," the sign read. "Come Relive Your Youth at College Days" (incidentally, at first I misspelled "relive" as "relieve"). At any rate, my first encounter was with a Mr. Dan Colivito. He walked into my abode, normal and ordinary as Sykesville itself. He had hair parted to the left with a fine-toothed comb, lackluster blue eyes, and a normal, almost boring stocky body and face—an Everyman. Colivito's only eccentricity appeared to be the fact that he was in my apartment/restaurant requesting lunch. This was a start, though.

"You still serving lunch?" He kicked his boots against the door frame to knock off the assorted dirt and grime, wiping his feet on my smiley-face welcome mat.

"Um, yes. I sure am, sir," I said. "Come sit down. Please."

The man picked up the menu in his grainy fingers, and his eyes failed to even pop at the funky lettering. The decision process took him two minutes and thirteen and one-half seconds.

"Grilled cheese and an ice tea. Your sandwiches come with anything?"

"Usually bread," I said in jest. His face was expressionless, which told me to withdraw while I was ahead.

I watched his eyes catch view of my bed and dresser tucked behind a Japanese screen in the corner of the room, but he didn't say anything

"Your sandwiches come with anything?" he repeated for my convenience.

"Chips and fruit," I stated.

"What kind of fruit?"

"What I've got in the fridge. Let's see. Apples, oranges. And kiwi."

"Sounds like some kinda bird," he said. For a moment he leaned forward, and I thought he might just bolt. But then he sighed and said, "Apple's fine."

"What type of cheese would you like sir?" I attempted to sound official.

"Cheddar." Exotic tastes he did not have.

"Cheddar it is." He paused and scratched his chin. "Please," he tacked on for emphasis.

I supposed this was common in the restaurant business.

"We're informal here, man. Peace." I was a bit giddy. There was a long moment of silence. I think he was making sure I was not a blaring homosexual.

"What? You got a jukebox or something?" he asked.

"No. Not exactly. Do you like Hendrix?"

"Who?"

"Have you ever been to college?" I asked.

"Do what now?"

That is the way it went with Mr. Colivito. The direct questions continued. He told me about his life, yet it failed to capture my imagination. I can't say that I remember the details. But Mr. Colivito seemed to enjoy the lunch all right. He voraciously picked at his teeth with his fingernails afterwards. Only he flicked all the bits onto my carpeting, and mumbled something about a minister who might enjoy my food. A positive response if I have ever seen one.

In fact, that is the way it progressed for several weeks. A townie, or an occasional antique-hunting tourist would drop in, usually for lunch, and order from the menu. I would cook my simple collegiate meals, and they would eat them and tell me about themselves in short choppy sentences, revealing little except my own gregarious Columbia naiveté. My barrage of questions did not seem to bother them, but was only a distant distraction, like a fly banging on a windowpane.

The majority of my customers those first few weeks simply appeared to be curious. Except for Ed. He was only lost.

Over time I did begin to notice some of my customers around Sykesville, although they would not say hello to me in passing, and would not lift their eyes to meet my gaze. What should I have thought? It seemed to be an odd town not to react more vehemently to a new restaurant. So, curious myself, I decided to close my little café one afternoon and poke about the town, take in the atmosphere, try to learn about the general culture. Research your clientele, I thought. What I learned was...little. Several customers, I mean, just Jackie, had told me that they were simply glad to be able to eat at a restaurant other than Beck's or Dixie's or at the fast food joints in Eldersburg. I think they simply believed me to be nosy, and perhaps that was a summation of the entire situation. I could not help but wonder if I should purchase an African violet or two. Perhaps that would somehow entice more customers to dine in my luncheonette?

Shortly thereafter, however, I realized that I desired something more fulfilling, more revealing of the human condition. At that moment, appropriately enough, Reginald Dorsey entered.

Reginald was a minister at the Baptist church down the street. He appeared in his full dress at *College Days* one Sunday morning, requesting breakfast before his service. He proclaimed: "I ran out of food, and nobody else works on Sundays. I mean, the church folks cook up a nice sausage and pancake breakfast afterwards, but the less time I have to spend in that building the better." He said he preferred to be called Preacher Dorsey. The morning was a rainy one, as you hope every Sunday is—so you can lie in bed and read the paper without feeling guilty.

I was surprised at the benevolence of Mr. Dorsey. I always thought Baptists were more, I don't know, uptight somehow. Reginald looked the part—a high brow, thick dirty brown eyebrows, mouth with a large lower lip down-turned at the corners, a bushy and flecked mustache, shaggy hair slicked back over his balding and red-freckled head; in short he had a slight resemblance to an October weeping willow. Yet, it was Dorsey who played the vital role in what would occur next.

"Come on in," I said, possibly a bit too excitedly.

Without looking at the menu, the preacher, pastor, minister, whatever they call themselves, ordered two fried eggs and buttermilk pancakes. This was not a conundrum for me, although I risked four-week-old eggs. As I prepared his food I turned my back to him, and I suddenly felt that he would interpret my surroundings and save me from the demons that he perceived to be hovering in the dramatic shadows of my apartment. Instead he flipped off his three-dollar sneakers, revealing thirty-dollar olive-green argyle socks. "Are you retarded or something?" he asked me. Surprised, I chuckled, carefully allowing the margarine to hiss and curl in the sizzling frying pan.

"No, why do you say that?"

"You ain't got a woman or nothing. Thought you might not be allowed to breed," he droned. "From Springfield or something?"

"I don't think so," I said. Springfield, I later discovered, is a local hospital for the mentally ill.

As you might suppose, thoughts of Lila raced into my vision. I attempted to change the subject by mentioning that I had only just acquainted myself with the area, and that I was formerly the owner of a nursery to the south. He nodded, glancing about the room, and to catch his attention I asked him what types of plants they have in his church.

"Hell if I know," he said. "Carnations or gladiolas, or some such thing."

Yawning, the minister mentioned that he'd send a woman from the congregation with some peanut butter cookies. I started to withdraw myself from such an obligation on his part, but he interrupted and asked if he could use the rest room. By the time he returned to the table, I had finished preparing his food, and he was apparently no longer in the mood for conversation. He muttered something about putting his game face on. I served him, and he dined without a word, paid me, tipped me, and proceeded to lace his shoes. As he was walking out the door he said without turning around, "You ever played the lottery?"

Without waiting for me to answer, he said, "I play it once a week. Think God wants me to win; I only need one ticket. She'll be by. Her name's Angel." Then he was gone.

I wish Lila had simply done away with me. Instead she left this gloomy, muddy mess that, I must admit, I had difficulty ascertaining. Reflecting upon the last several years of our marriage, I suppose she had every right to leave me. For instance, we never approached the subject of affairs or separations, but simply plodded along like two mules towards the end of a plot. There is little doubt: My recent history is less than symphonic. Two years ago my doctor discovered that I had a severe ulcer, which left me doubled over in pain most mornings. I found myself only capable of making love to Lila if I was drunk, or if she was. And I wasn't supposed to drink. My time was almost entirely devoted to the store with little left for anything else. Lila had a career as an unmotivated processing clerk for a company named TJT. Yet, Lila was certainly adept at saving money. Lila ate little as well, and her face wilted and paled from the lack of sun. At dinner she rarely spoke about work, and longed for nothing but rest.

To speak metaphorically again, it was as if Lila were a chair I rarely sat upon. Then one day the chair walked out of the room, or simply decomposed quietly in the corner. Now that I reflect on the past, I believe she weighed 130 when we first were married, and only around 100 during our last year together. It was as if she was conserving her energy by not eating too much, since as the health officials claim—at least in the *Post*—those who are underweight survive the longest.

When Lila left me I called my best friend William, who was recently divorced, but I hung up. I could not bring myself to talk to him. Ashamed, I would sit at my kitchen table and listen to William's voice. "Hello? Hello? Hello?" William is a good-natured type of person who never suspects prank calls, which made doing it easier I suppose. I began to call daily. I would call William and listen to my friend's voice, then hang up. I think this is what occurred.

Before I moved to Sykesville I broke down in the grocery store and told a nice woman named Trisha everything. Trisha had too much eyeliner on, and she was purchasing a dying spider plant from the grocery store for Christ's sake, and I could not allow such an atrocity to be committed. I attempted to talk her out of this investment, but she was kind and led me away from the crowd of staring people, claiming that she would like to have a chat with me. She put her arm around me and even helped me carry my food to my car. "Sure," she said, "I won't buy the little plant." Trisha had two silly little golden raintree earrings that she said she bought at my store, but as I told her, we never sold earrings. She was adamant though, so who knows? Maybe I lost track. Trisha even visited me sometimes, and always waited in the lounge with the gardenias I requested, until Nurse Liedeker let her in. Trisha liked to wear bright patterned dresses, and she spoke softly to me and held my hand.

It was as if I was a house whose north face was knocked down, and I was suddenly exposed to the elements. How could she leave me for another man? If anybody in the world was faithful, I thought Lila was. Who could she possibly be interested in? What could she possibly be thinking? Regardless, these were my thoughts at the time.

I say this because when Angel arrived at my apartment, it was the last thing I expected. I remember the date was June twenty-ninth, because I had just saved an azalea my neighbor was uprooting, and I wrote the event in my plant journal. When Minister Dorsey mentioned the name *Angel*, the image that entered my head was that of an older, blonde woman with a kindly smile and a plate stacked with freshly baked cookies. When the reality arrived, it was in the form of a slinky, brown-eyed, brunette, middle-aged woman, in skintight black jeans and a tight red crew sweater with an accompanying Santa gracing her right breast. She looked tacky in a straightforward manner. Santa's cheeks appeared to be especially rosy, and I even think he may have winked at me, and her hair was pinned in a bun. In her left hand she held a brown paper bag with a plastic window so one might see the contents, the kind they have at a grocery store bakery.

"Hi there. I'm Angel."

"Hello," I said.

She handed me the bag. "These are for you." The gift was actually a package of ninety-nine cent Kmart cookies, still displaying the price sticker.

"You can have them," she said. "I always pack my lunch."

"Ahh," I said. "Yummy."

I took one cookie, broke it in half, and put the other half back in the box. "You must be a good, what?" I asked politely concerning her career. She guffawed, looked away, and failed to answer the inquiry.

"How about telling me a little about you," she said.

"Um, I'm thirty-nine years old. I am...single. I am running this little restaurant," I pointed to the kitchen.

"Nice," she said. She twirled her hair out of her bun and shuffled closer to me on the sofa. But not in a sexual manner, mind you. I recall hearing the grating sound of her pants legs scrape against each other, and I think that is when everything started to go awry for me.

"How old are you?" I inquired.

"Sixty." I couldn't believe it. The woman barely looked forty. Yes, she had wrinkles, but they were close to the surface, and her skin was still taut and shiny. Perhaps she could have dyed her hair. Her hands were still firm and blemishless.

"That's impossible." I said. "You're not sixty."

"Look," she said, withdrawing her wallet from her purse. She flipped a book of pictures into her hand. The smell of leather spurted into the air. "Here's a picture of my daughter when she was four. That was in 1950. I hadn't seen her for ages. Now she's back. She found me. We're—what's the word? Reunited."

"Congratulations," I said off-hand.

"Wasn't she cute?"

"Yeah, she sure was," I said. "What is your daughter's name?"

"Pamela or some such thing," she said. "She was born Ellen. Can't say I blame some people for changing their names. But Pamela is a dumb one."

Forgive me, but *College Days* suddenly felt intuitively wrong. I did not even think to offer Mrs. Weaver a drink. I started thinking to myself: little eccentricities, where are you? Where are you? This was just the beginning.

ABSORBER ON THE BRAIN

Billy slumped on the ledge of the loading dock, and Dad, the kid, and me sat at the picnic table snatching chili peppers out of the jar, dribbling the seeds onto our shirts like two-year-olds. My fingers felt the coolness of the pepper juice. My tongue stung, and it was good. The grass between Billy and the rest of us was cut tight.

"I found this squirrel on the sidewalk," Dad was telling the kid. "Fell off a tree, broke both legs. I took it inside, wrapped it up, went to the store and got baby formula. Nursed that thing for close to two months, until it could scurry around in the cage I bought for it." The kid's mouth was half pursed-up from the pepper, half trying not to laugh. That lunch break, we were all floating from the glue fumes. It happens.

"You have a pet squirrel?" the kid asked.

"I'll put on two or three shirts, you know, so her claws won't stab into me, and she'll wind up me like a tree," Dad said. "Sit on my shoulder. Sit in my pocket. When I walk into the store people will look at me. I give them a look. 'What? You never seen a squirrel before?'"

"Is it some kind of New Hampshire thing that you're trying to keep out there?" The kid took a long suck from his water bottle. I noticed one of his sideburns was longer than the other, and he missed a patch of hair on his neck shaving. Kid did everything real fast, not paying too much attention to anything but the final goal. His car was greasy with leaf stems sticking out of the hood. We were from San Diego.

"I don't know."

"Dad's had all kinds of pets," I said, trying to pick off the glue from my elbow. Dad's not really interested in explanations.

"Had a raccoon," Dad continued. "They're real nasty, though. Had a deer in New Hampshire. I had a skunk."

"Really?" The kid leaned forward and bit into his tomato and cheese sandwich. I could smell the mustard from where I sat. Kid said the tomatoes came fresh from his mother's garden.

"The thing was caught in a groundhog trap. His foot was dangling off the bone. I thought he might spray, but he let me take him. I took a tarp and wrapped him up, brought him into the basement. I built an outdoor cage later on. Real shy animals. He didn't come out much."

"Dad's got a soft heart," I said. He snapped another chili pepper out of the jar, joke-flashing me a mean glare.

"The skunk wouldn't spray me. That's what I liked. I let him go when I was done."

"I didn't know they had skunks in California," the kid said.

"Spotted skunks. Desert skunks. The same day I found that skunk I remember these Mexican guys were caught stealing manhole covers. They'd take them at night. Guys tried to sell them at a junkyard. But everybody knew that it'd been going on, so they were caught lickety-split." Dad raised his fingers in the air and snapped them dramatically. Loves to tell stories.

"Really?"

"The scam was on the front page," Dad said. "Because people's axles were popping off when they hit the holes."

The kid asked if we liked Mexican restaurants down there, trying to be a little host. I flagged that one.

"Oh hell yeah. Just watch out for some things. Ever heard of *chaco*? Don't serve it out here probably. It's barbecued pig intestines, sometimes stuffed. They eat that shit for cheap energy."

"That's disgusting," the kid said. Billy was slurping on his soda in his California sunglasses, looking at his feet. His hair was pulled back into one long drool.

"It is what it is," Dad said. "I saw this guy eating *chaco* with his hands right before we left. But they weren't just any hands; he had some deformity so his fingers ended at his second knuckle, you know. One in a million. But what was strange was the guy's mouth was so big it seemed to go *around* his jaw to the other side. His mouth was too big for food. The freaks out there."

"That's because California is a pile of shit," I said. That caught Billy's attention. "I would ditch it in a minute for a chance to live somewhere else back East, even here."

"California's all right," Billy mumbled. "Northern California's nice."

"Yeah, it's all right," I said. "I did take my wife up to Monterey, Big Sur, that's all right."

"That's a beautiful area," Billy said.

"But that's the exception, Billy."

"What's wrong with San Diego?" Billy said, stuffing his trash into one of those plastic grocery bags.

"Lots of things," I said.

"Name one. Name one."

"Okay. That's where you're from," I said. "That's one thing that's wrong with it." Dad shot me a look. I know, I know, fat ass Junior chases off another worker. Well, head boss Louie should find a better place to find cheap help than the skank bars where he meets his skank women. Let's keep the apples from the oranges, know what I mean?

Billy clambered over to the dumpster and chucked his trash bag into it, walked inside. Fuck him, I thought; Billy's staying home after this job. That's what Dad said anyway.

From the start nothing went right in Glen Burnie. First the sight manager gave us zoom-booms instead of scissor-lifts, then once we finally did get the lifts the battery in one was shot, and the alternator in the other didn't pop; we had to jump one with the forklift and call in the mechanics for the other one. Then the electricians had trouble with the crane since the trolley was off by two inches, and that crew almost had to shut the whole place down. The A.C. only worked on the cool rainy days to taunt us; my tools didn't make it on time; the scaffolding company overcharged and built the thing too narrow anyway (which pissed Louie off, and made it our problem); and as usual Billy didn't do a damn thing even when the temps left. And then the rest. I swear the place was built on an Indian burial ground.

I didn't think the kid was that bothered by the heights, but an hour after he drove off that one day the temp service called us and read Dad the riot act for bringing the kid up in the lifts, even the thirty-footers. Dad said, "We're from California, how should we know how you work it out here?" We did have the kid up in a fifty—once we *got* them a fucking week and a half late—spraying glue on the absorber while I put it off. Dad ragged on the kid about the queasies, and maybe that was the kid's breaking point, but the kid didn't say anything to us if it was. The whole thing was a shame too because the kid was a good sprayer, maybe the fastest one I'd ever seen.

"It doesn't have to be a painting," he'd say. Swishing the glue gun back and forth over the back of the absorber, he'd have the thing in my hands before I could turn around to get another one. I don't know, the kid maybe was just overwhelmed by the whole job. I mean, there we were in a sixty-foot tall room outside BWI where the company hired us to hang absorber so they could bounce their electromagnetic waves off it and test their satellites or stealth bombers or whatever they were going to do. The room would work like a giant microwave when we were through with the absorber.

When we first got there, the kid surveyed the whole room that was covered with metallic tape to ground the waves (he kept cocking his head and looking at himself in the tape). We spent the first day popping boxes and stacking the absorber, which is blue and black insulation with a carbon coating. Each piece costs us about twenty bucks, and the whole job was about three mil. The pointed cones facing out range from eight inches to four feet, and stick out of the wall like some kind of torture chamber. We mostly spent our time with the two footers, and the eights.

The guy Arthur from Sierra Leone was there helping for a week until we went thirty feet up on the lifts to hang the shit, and then he said he had family emergencies he had to tend to. It didn't matter much; that first week was smooth with Dad and Arthur up in one lift and me and the kid on the other, kicking absorber ass, talking about what's in Baltimore and comparing it to San Diego (which is no comparison at all). I like working with someone who can pass the time. Thank God Dad had Billy on the ground humping boxes, filling up buckets of glue from the barrels.

I don't care how many film studios he's run the cameras for, Billy's nothing but a prime example of California trailer trash. Sand-stoned surfer, lazy as a sheep on Valium, always trying to slump unloading work off onto the two temps when he could see they were taken up in the lifts. Dumb prick got his two small fingers caught in an oil drill in Texas. I also didn't like how he tried to put a jolt into the temps by shaking their hands with his gimpy hand. Billy was always out to prove himself to other people since he'd never done that for himself. I could tell Billy wasn't happy with any of it, that scowl blazing away. But what was he going to do? I was twice his size, twice his strength. I mean, I was close to being a professional weight lifter, even if the doctor said I had to stop until those hemorrhoids flared down.

Once the kid and I were taking five and he looked across the room at the electricians in their zoom-booms, with the yellow and red lights blinking. "There's something beautiful about the way those lifts move," he said. And I guess he was right. Like I said, he was one fast sprayer, even if he did get glue all over his shoes. He asked me how to get it off, and I said it's contact glue so it's not the easiest *to* get off. I said he could use nail polish remover, and that might take care of the trick. Next day he came in a pair of old painting shoes, which is the way to go. I told him my overalls only cost twenty dollars and had lasted me two years so far. And if I stuck around, I said, maybe they'd last two more. I asked the kid how old he was, and I was surprised when he said twenty-six.

When we got inside from lunch Billy already had the spot-laser pointing the shiners out—the gaps of tape in between the absorber. What shouldn't be there. He's pointing that thing all over, and I follow it because you can't always see the shiners from up close. So I'm up there on the lift. Dad yells to me that I must have found religion up there because there's a cross of shiners stretching horizontal and down. We all crack up on that one, even Billy. Dad was a more diligent and careful hanger than me, but I had speed on my side with the kid.

I came down and the kid and I loaded up the lift for the next section of the wall. As we were going up I noticed Billy marking shiners all along the far wall, which we already went over two times. He had ripped cardboard wedged into the absorber everywhere, trying to show me up. Trying to say "Junior's sloppy."

"Billy!" I yell. "We already got that wall."

"I see some shiners," he said.

No answer to that. He walked back across what he already did, ripping the cardboard back down from the absorber. Taking it out on that.

"If you can't see them from across the room, don't worry about them," I yelled.

"Fill up another bucket of glue," I said. "And we could use some more eights." The kid coughed from the propane fumes and watched Billy walk off towards the glue barrel, then peel off on the forklift towards the C-trains out front to snag more absorber. We got to our next chalk lines and the kid snuggled the respirator on, and we were off.

But when we came down the glue bucket was overflowing. Billy wasn't watching it, and glue was all over the floor. Jesus Christ, I thought. What next? When Dad caught wind he let Billy have it. Even Dad had enough at that point. Billy spent the rest of that day cleaning up his own mess, otherwise it'd be our asses that would have to pay for it.

Three days later we got that call from the temp company. We were screwed because they said we breached the contract, and they wouldn't give us shit. I thought we should call another one anyway, but Dad was against it. So then it was just the three of us.

Anyway, Dad and I defended the kid and said he'd never rat, but Billy said the kid told him that he didn't like the heights and would have to leave anyway. Billy said the kid definitely ratted. I knew better though because the kid gave us his home number, so we could call him if we ever got back into the area and needed some help. Dad appreciated that. Plus we stood up there talking about how I want to be a chef eventually, and how I'm overweight and half of it is from being married and letting myself go. But he listened. I missed that kid.

Second reason I don't think he jumped ship was he didn't get his time card signed. The next day he had to go out of his way to meet us in the commuter parking lot to get Dad's John Hancock. This was after he was already through.

"So you know anyone who wants to work?" Dad said when the kid stepped out of his car.

"No, not really," the kid said. Something about him looked droopy and disappointed. "I was just calling to see why they didn't send me the check, and here they said I couldn't even be doing what I was doing."

"I didn't know you couldn't be up on the lift," Dad said.

Billy said later that the kid was just saying that to get off, but he was one to talk since he was working the job to eventually pay for his car and take off on another vacation. The man took more vacations than the Queen of England.

"You know, once I was working for the FBI in Alexandria and the site manager saw one of the electricians dangling off a crane from his lift," my Dad said, hunching his shoulders like he does when he's telling something he thinks is funny. "You forget what you're doing up there sometimes, but the electrician probably wasn't scared. The site manager came up to me and told me, 'If you don't get him down from there, I'm going to shoot the asshole.' Well, I didn't particularly care for the electrician, real cocky, and a know-it-all-pain-in-the-ass to top it off. So I took one look at him and said, 'Fine, go ahead,' and walked off."

"I just wish the service would let me continue," the kid said.

"You could always come work for us, but that might get you in even worse trouble."

"Yeah, I don't know." He looked at his feet. Dad took the kid's time sheet and signed it, and shook the kid's hand and we were off. The kid brushed his hair with the palm of his hand, and waved to me, hand flat in the air as if to say, *stop*. Billy grinned as we drove through the security station, flashing our temporary badges back to the absorber room.

What Billy didn't expect was that Dad would make him stay on the ground anyway. Billy expected some lift time since the kid was gone, but it wasn't going to happen. Dad was jacking up the air compressor when Billy started whining to him.

"I can't go up on one of the lifts now?"

"We need you to bring in all the boxes from the C-train, remember? We have to have all that stuff in here before Monday." The company was going to seal off the room so the painters could get to the floor in the entrance room.

"I'm a skilled worker," Billy said.

"Is that right?"

"I thought of myself as one before this shit."

"Well, be skilled at doing what I tell you then, or you aren't getting paid."

"I'll get paid," Billy said. "I'll get my money."

"You'll get paid? Is that right?" As his first instinct Dad didn't get angry, unlike me. He would just say his mind calmly, then turn his back on a man and let what *he* said rattle around in a guy's head, which might be worse if the man had a conscience. Then later when the guy thought it over, that's when Dad would come back and engage. But by then it'd be too late, because the guy would've thought himself into a box. Dad clicked the air compressor on, and I couldn't hear what they said next. For all I know Dad could have apologized for me and my big mouth. Either way the rest of that day Billy whisked off in his forklift, cut boxes open and unloaded absorber, and cut the boxes down so they'd lay down flat on the concrete. He tried not to look up.

We were staying at a crappy motel two miles from the place off Route 100. Place didn't even have a kitchenette, so we were eating out of Dad's electric fryer. Since Billy slept next door, Dad and I would meet him right at the car.

After work that day Dad and I bought taco fixings, and went and got a half-case of Mickey's. It was my night to cook, so I did. After dinner I washed out the frying pan, and we drank ourselves to sleep in our underwear, finishing off with whiskey and water. We pretty much did everything together, especially hunt and fish. Some people might think that was faggy, working and living so close to your father. To me it was the best thing in the world. It was like working with another of myself, only better.

But the next morning there was a problem.

"For chrissakes," Dad said, and pounded on Billy's door, with no answer. We could hear all the commuters hum by out on the highway. Dad banged on the door again, and after I finished my cigarette, Billy opened it.

"Let's go, Billy."

"I'm not going," he said. Billy was stark naked except for his raggedy brown socks.

"Yes, the hell you are," Dad said pointing his finger into him. "I'll drag your ass in there myself if I have to. I don't care what you're wearing."

"I want to go back," Billy said.

"Back where? There is no back. You were hired to do this job."

"The kid and Arthur left," he said. "I'd like to stop."

"He was a temporary employee, Billy. Temporary. No commitment. He could leave whenever he wanted to," Dad said.

"I'd like to stop this job."

"Billy, we need your help," I said. "Okay, we *need* your help. There. Okay?"

"Fly me back to California, okay. The company should be paying for me to go home. I'm telling you I don't want to be here."

"The hell we're paying. Get your ass into work," Dad said.

"All you guys do is sit around and eat and drink. You never *do* anything, besides that and work," he said.

"What does that have to do with anything?" I said. "What do you think we're here for, Billy?" Anyway, I thought, eating is doing something.

"You sit around and fry up your meals in your little pan and then drink all night and read books. That's not a life."

"You watch television," I said. "What's the difference?"

"You talk too much," Billy said. "I quit."

Billy shut the door, and chained it before we could get a shoulder in. Then the motel guy started walking towards us with a suspicious eye. It was only six forty-five in the morning. He told us to keep it down, which didn't encourage Dad in breaking the door down. Dad tried to explain the situation, but the motel guy asked us to be on our way if we were indeed going to work, and told us to keep it down if we weren't. We pretended to get in our car, but when the motel guy walked off Dad rattled on the door again. I thought about sneaking around and getting the maid's keys. Billy didn't open it, but I could tell he was right on the other side. This time I approached too.

"Billy, I'm going to kick your fucking teeth in when you do come out," I said. "And if you do make it back to California, I'll hunt you there. It's not that damn big."

"Come on Billy," my Dad said. "I'm not giving you a raise, but we need your help. Junior and I can't do it alone. We got two weeks to put up two thousand pieces. How are we going to do that by ourselves?"

"Come on Billy," I said.

"Billy," Dad said. "Billy?" But Billy didn't budge, and by seven we were down to two. I knew Dad was nervous then; he knew we'd have to work our asses off from that point on. And it would be no guarantee that we would finish.

Before we got back to the motel, Billy skipped town. I guess he paid for the plane ticket himself. I imagined him out on Pacific Beach scoping the chicks with his three-fingered handshake, jerking off in his trailer park hoping Louie'd call him for some other gig, somewhere close enough to hear the seagulls.

I don't want to have physical issues, but I've got them. I got a splinter wedged in my cornea last year and had to have an operation. Blew part of my middle finger off with dynamite back when I was a union iron worker apprentice. Tried every drug in the book. Dad won't tolerate that now though, which is a good reason to stick around since I've gone cold turkey. As long as I get all my drinking out of the way before work kicks in is his policy. This absorber hanging pays the bills, and it's steady, and not bad pay. But it is robot work if you think about it too hard. As I told the kid, my dream is to go to chef's school, work for some Tex-Mex place, cooking real flavorful food, maybe open my own restaurant up some day. Dreams are dreams though, and I try never to forget that. That's the idea California's still got to learn.

When I got fired from my union iron worker job three years ago after I pissed on a guy's head from three stories up (they let me take my hard hat with me), Dad looked out for me. He had his problems with the bottle when he was my age. It happens to us Polacks like no others, except maybe the Irish, which is what my wife's background is (our kid's going to have a double-whammy). When I started off with Dad, he had been hanging it for twenty years already, and it was just the two of us. There are other crews, but just the two of us could do most jobs. We'd hire temps if we needed them. But then Louie started adding to a good thing, which is always worse than taking away from it, because if you take away from a good thing, you still have a good thing, only less of it. Adding to it makes it something different. But back then most of the test rooms were small. This was pre-stealth bomber. This room in Glen Burnie was one of the biggest we'd ever done, and it would take forever just the two of us.

But that's what we had to do, so that's what we did.

I worked one lift. Dad worked the other, and we finished. We didn't take breaks. We took our lunch in fifteen minutes. We worked fourteen-hour days, and believe it or not, we still finished on time. It's been worse though. Once we worked almost straight for three days, then we slept for a whole day when the job was done. We got our overtime though. No doubt.

I couldn't wait to see my beautiful wife. She was due in a month, into her cooing period. I called her the last day we were in the Baltimore area, and told her I went shopping for a *Winnie the Pooh* for my kid. I told my wife how I walked into this toy store, wearing my biker boots and absorber clothes. I asked the woman at the counter, "Where are your *Winnie the Poohs?*" She took one look at me and said, "You don't look like the *Winnie the Pooh* type." I thought, what the hell is a *Winnie the Pooh* type? My wife dug that story.

Dad and I are headed to New Hampshire next to visit my grandmother, and then we're flying back to California. I don't tell Dad this, but I think he knows that part of me would love to leave California and the father-and-son-chain-gang thing if I could. I have a son of my own coming, and Dad knows what that's like. Now I just have to wait and tell him.

Right now though, Dad and I are the two Poles holding up any job. He decided to silk-screen T-shirts for us, which we could wear under our overalls. He said they should say "Absorber Assassins," but I said they should read "Absorber Asses." My dad's made two, and no extras.

BLOODWORMS

In the beltway drizzle the Bronco slammed its brakes to red. The two cars behind the Bronco skidded, but the tractor trailer on the right stayed the course. Nicki turned against the skid to avoid the cars, but her Sentra skidded wide, spun ninety degrees, and slammed into the bed of the truck. Anita shot through the windshield. The car ricocheted towards the shoulder. Anita could smell the rain. She could hear the traffic everywhere.

The doctors said that stitching her up would take two hours. Amazingly no broken bones. Nicki never should have driven. She should never let herself take control. Nicki checked their messages. A computer voice chirped, "You may have won a free vacation to Hawaii. All you have to do is complete the survey by nine two nineteen ninety..." Nicki called their agent.

"Look, that's what I'm saying," Nicki barked into the phone. "That's exactly what I'm saying. This is a disaster for me too." The emergency room din raised the tension, compounded by the twitching in her leg. They said nothing was wrong with it. Maybe they needed to look harder.

"That's what I'll tell them," Carl Haber said. Their fourth agent may have been their worst. They quickly realized his clout was heavier than his will to put it to use.

"No, that's not what I want you to tell them. I'm telling *you* so you can be sympathetic. At least I hope you can be sympathetic." The twitching subsided. A baby wailed. An old man held his arm, moaning to himself. The Coke machine clattered. The bathroom door whooshed closed. Cell phones chimed every two minutes.

"I am sympathetic, and empathetic, and any other 'etic' you want me to be. But what should I tell them? Anita is alive but disfigured? What?"

"Plead with them. Plead with them to let me do this solo," she said. "What am I supposed to do? Her career may be kaput. Right? I'll do anything they want. Even..."

"That bit might help you."

"I got to get out of this fucking shit. What am I supposed to do? You're talking about you. You should be talking about me."

"I didn't get you in it," he said. "What do you want me to do?"

"What can you do? If I was Anita right now, it would be easier for me to manage."

The cuts were deep. Within days, thick veiny scars burrowed under her skin like bloodworms in river mud. A ski mask was a possibility, Nicki said. Who could rely on the goodwill of *Wet on Wheels* or *Broads on Beemers*? Even if the models all looked the same, they still needed faces. Anita had friends who modeled stockings, shoes, bracelets. But a part of her liked opening up a magazine and seeing herself. Her face, her shoulders, breasts, thighs, neck. Not much money in anonymity.

The possibility that Nicki could do it alone was remote. They were a pair. Two topless "horny hot-rodders" greasing each other down, heads tilted back, hair back in kiddy pigtails. Catholic schoolgirl skirts hiked to their waists. Legs spread on the trunk of a Camaro. Legs wrapped around the steering wheel. Leaning against the windshield. The mags came to *them*.

Now the tables were turned. They might have to go mainstream, out of the nudie car biz altogether. Half the cash flow. Whatever she would do, she wouldn't allow those scars to dominate her. The other way around. The other way around.

Chinese in Styrofoam. Local news in the living room. Newscaster woman (no scars) talking about a car contest. Rules: you have to maintain contact with the Toyota until all competition is eliminated. You get fifteen-minute breaks to eat and piss every four hours.

"We're getting a new car, Anita. You know it will all work out on that end."

"Hmm," Anita said. Anita rolled her ski mask under her foot. The newscaster was telling them the Toyota would be given to the last person touching the car. Sign-ups would be tomorrow at the Washington Auto Show. No perfume or books. No tape players or radios would be allowed.

"Let me guess," Nicki said. Anita felt Nicki looking right at her, but not in a self-conscious or pitying way. Her sister was looking at her the way she always does. That's the way it should be, she thought.

"I want to try it. Why not? I can't do anything but sit around anyway."

"We could sell one of the cars." Nicki said. "That might last us a while. But it's not a bad idea, Anita. You could get out of your head."

"Shit, I want to get back at something."

"*They* didn't hit you," Nicki said. "It was my fault. I'm the one you should—"

"Look, I can't blame you or anything around us. Somebody did it *to* us," Anita said. "They're somebody."

Frank Tildon, a retired Marine from Arlington, propped himself against the rear bumper, talking horses with Alan Bowden, flipping his wrist to glance at his watch. Joyce Almond, a real estate agent from Silver Spring, curled up around the front right tire. Sue Gibson, a college student, sat propped against the car door, staring at the plastic palms in the lobby. Lorraine Lorten, nurse and single mother, was trying to put her children through college. Rich Small was looking to move out of his cramped apartment. He talked to Anita about his sister who also modeled, for clothing catalogues. Socks. "I can't, you know. I just can't look at them. It's my sister's feet, you know. You know what I mean?" The convention center echoed faintly. Frank glanced at her and quickly back to Alan.

His teeth were clean. His skin was scrubbed. His pants were pressed nice and smooth. Look at me, Anita thought, look at me you fucker.

"I just look at it like 'well this is something I accomplished. I made it in here.' It's crap, but it's not me forever." Anita didn't tell him what kind of magazines. But it was implied.

"But don't you worry that someday, you know, your kids are going to see this and the kids at school will make fun of them? I mean."

"No. I can't be about worrying that all the time," Anita said. "I do what I do."

Sometimes when she went in for photo shoots, a little "gift" for the photographer was expected. She would go along. Career advancement. As Sheila put it, "You act like a whore, you will be treated worse." It's that simple. But it hadn't always been like this. Like when she was eleven, on her first date. The boy took her hand and walked her through the May Day Carnival. She could feel his pulse racing against her wrist, and he blinked. Beautiful azure eyes in the pollen air. Streamers, brownies, dart-throwing contests, dunk the principal, ping-pong tournaments, pot holders and hand-painted mugs for sale.

Her life *did* seem sordid when she drew the lines of comparison that far back. But, Anita thought, if this Marine shit-head thinks he's better than me, he hasn't looked too closely. Talking horsies! Smooth skin. Flick of the wrist. Baby-blue Ed Harris eyes. Anita didn't care if it was arbitrary or unfair: This guy shouldn't win. He was the kind of guy who bought her mags, slobbered over her, then tried to win cars. Because he could. Because he wanted to. Because he thought it was worth a shot.

They leaned against the front bumper, facing the four monitors. One woman was already disqualified for leaving the car. An accountant tried to sneak a book into the contest and was expelled. Anita was going to the wire. As she slept, foot curled around the front left tire, she held her scarred face in her hands. The scars felt thicker, more monstrous than before. They seemed to move beneath her fingers, in between the spaces where her fingers met.

The monitors allowed the contestants to make a two-minute phone call during the morning break. Anita called Nicki.

"He said you should consider plastic surgery," she said.

"No, no, no. No way. No way. I am not. I am not cutting my face up again for any amount of money they could put on the table. I'm living with this."

"I agree. Fuck him. We're getting a new agent." Anita was second in line. Five of the contestants were lined up behind her. They could have friends or spouses bring them food or drinks.

"*Hot Rods* said okay," Nicki continued. "They're going to find me another sister look-alike."

"Fine, that's what the others should have done. I'm not unique."

"Are you sure? I'm trying to look out for our best interests here," Nicki said.

"Yeah, that's good."

"You sure?"

"Yeah," Anita said.

"You okay, right?"

"Fine. I'm going to do it. I'm going to win this shit. It's the least I can do."

Two minutes. Anita thought of those punk kids that walk right across the street as you are speeding toward them; they try to control the cars by making you slow down. The cars are *The Man*, no matter who's driving. The pedestrians are

The Prols, no matter who's walking. They had a point, Anita thought.

Down to three: the Marine, the mother, and Anita. Frank wanted the car because he said he wanted to prove to himself that he could still *survive*. "This is easy compared to boot camp—or Jesus—Ranger survival shit. That can kill your ass. Now, this is easy," he said. The car would be the icing on the cake. But that's not what Anita thought. She thought this guy just wanted it because he could fuck everybody by not letting *them* get it. To get off on that idea.

Lorraine wanted the money she could get for the car. She had it all lined up. She just had to wait it out. This woman *needed* it. And when they asked Anita why she was doing it, she said why. The Marine couldn't look at her for more than five seconds. She timed him. She asked him pointless questions to see where he would look. He looked off to her ears, but not right at her. He'd look at her scars, and then off to her ears. Not at the scars. The mother's eyes never strayed. She looked at Anita eye to eye. That Marine couldn't even if he wanted to.

And she realized that she didn't really want the car itself. She didn't even want the money. That would only support everything she didn't want anymore. She would rather blow the shit up than keep it herself, she thought. She knew she didn't want it going to Frank though. She could stick it out until he left.

Day six and tired as hell. The three of them were sick of even talking to each other, and instead they sat in silence, propped against the car. They had run through everything polite society could cover: family, religion, politics, food, movies, vacations, ideals, and dreams. The whole thing was down to the wire, and nobody was ready to give an inch, least of all Anita.

But the Marine accidentally rolled out of contact with the car as he slept. He agreed with the monitors. No conflict. Four in the morning. Eliminated. Anita knew what she should do. As the sun rose full above the horizon in the east, Anita stepped away from the car. Lorraine was still asleep, wrapped around the back tire. The monitors rushed to the car to congratulate the mother. Anita walked out of the convention center, and into the dewy sunshine, and for a moment she was filled. For a moment.

FUNSHINE BLUES

It had to be the fifty that did it.

"Just leave it there," I said.

"Hell no, I ain't just leaving it," Seth said.

"It's somebody's," I said. "Somebody earned that bill."
There was a long wait when all of us could hear the water
lapping against the side of the pool and he didn't say nothing.
"We should give it to Leon," I said. Nobody else had anything
to say. Nothing funny, nothing.

"I ain't giving it to that fat mug," he said. "It ain't doing
nobody no good here."

"Just give it to Leon," I said. "Don't be an ass."

But he didn't hand it to Leon. He gave it to his hand,
and then his pocket, and that was it. He was standing there
like an idiot, dripping wet in his puke-green T-shirt and cut-
offs, and his hair was wet and glued to the side of his face. The
fifty was sopping and darker looking than I thought a bill
should be. I remember it that way.

I could smell the ink and chlorine mixing in the air from where I was sitting dangling my tootsies in the pool. I don't know, I was half drunk. I could feel the cool line of water on my ankles, and the waves were slapping the beach in the distance, and just then I remembered again it was the Fourth of July.

I guess the way it started was that we walked down the boardwalk looking at the colors splash in the sky. This was Seth, Dale, Allen, and me I'm talking about. Anyway, those fireworks reminded me of when you see oil on water in the parking lot, all kinds of different colors and shit. Allen and Seth were trying to get some girls, putting their arms around them walking, grabbing at the sides of them, or saying stuff— mostly getting shot down, flicked off, that kind of thing. Ain't none of them too smooth when it came to the females. Not even Ronnie Fischer, back in those days I'm talking about when I was right out of high school.

Anyway, that's when we saw that big black man taking pictures of the fireworks. We all started rolling when we passed the yo, 'cause see Dale said the man probably snorted too much crack, and everybody knows you smoke it even if they never would. We were drunk, and it just sounded funny to hear it I guess. I ain't racist or nothing; it was just something to say. Well, the man heard us and turned around, snapped a picture of us right away without taking his face away from the camera lens, then turned right back around real quick to the fireworks, like some kind of robot. We were surprised by that and the flash surprised us good too, so we stopped right there looking at each other. It was weird, boy. Nobody knew what to say.

"Hey slick," Dale said, "You ain't going to be able to get none of that to turn out." Man clicked another picture of the sky lighting up.

"Don't think so?" The man leaned his own body towards us but not his head. He still didn't lift his face from the camera. He clicked again into the sky, and all I could hear was the booming fireworks and this man clicking shots.

We all felt nervous then about the oddball chance fists would fly. Seth even turned to walk back around, away from the direction of the beach. Seemed like Dale was getting out of hand, like he can do. I think that's what makes him dangerous and exciting—he just says any old thing that pops in his head.

"Yo thinks he can catch fireworks with his camera," Dale said, leaning over. He started laughing mean, turning to us for support. He was laughing but his jaw was tight-looking, like he was pissed. I was just watching. Dale's shoulders looked bigger than I remember them being. But to tell you the truth I didn't see why the man couldn't get a picture to turn out.

That's when the man takes his face off the camera. It threw me off 'cause I thought it was going to be uglier or thuggy-looking or something, but his face was kinda soft, with a fuzzy mustache, and the skin was a little saggy around the ears with some peppery-looking darker spots on it maybe from the sun. Still, the way he held himself stiff it looked like the man was going to off and hit Dale across his mouth. He was wearing a uniform with a yellow stripe down the side, a dark jacket and pants, and his neck was thick-looking in the front but kinda thinner on the sides, like a big bundle of telephone wire.

But then the man smiled wide and started laughing too 'cause he saw us looking at his uniform. I remember he had big teeth, and I could see his cavity caps under the first few of them. He gave Dale a little play-punch on the shoulder, and was chuckling, and Dale gave him a little punch back and the man tugged on his uniform shirt.

"I know, I know. I'm drunk as a mug," the man said. He tilted his head to the side and scratched at his arm like it was going to help him think. "What the hell am I doing? Man, I don't even like fireworks." He was still chuckling, and some other people on the boardwalk were looking at us like we were bothering them during their Thanksgiving dinners except they weren't eating nothing. One thing I saw on one of them late-night television shows somewhere was that it's only other people make you think you're weird, and that's what makes people feel bad about themselves. I think I believe that.

"Me neither," Dale said, still scanning the man's uniform.

"My father always took me when I was little, but I never liked them. Don't know why."

"Hey, you know what?" Dale said.

"What?" the man said.

"I'm drunker than you." Dale was trying to get out of the situation.

They started laughing through their teeth, hissing like they known each other all their lives, and slapping into each other. I sighed in relief. Dale was tilting his head like he knew everything was all right, hee-hawing away.

"Look, look don't worry," the man said, flicking his uniform. "I ain't no cop."

"You're a security guard. My brother used to work that," Dale says.

"Hit the nail right on the head," the man said making an invisible punching. "Bang."

Dale stuck out his hand, and the man shook it and introduced himself as Leon. Dale introduced the bunch of us, pulling us forward one by one. That's the way Dale is. Sometimes I think Dale don't care about girls or nothing, just making friends and having a good time. Makes friends easily I guess. So we all stood there together joking and cracking up with people walking and talking around us, all of us watching the sky explode.

"Hey, what are you boys doing now?" the man asked once the show was over. We all shook our heads and Dale spoke up and said he had no idea.

"You boys ever been to *FunShine?*" Nobody had. Leon told us he worked security there and that we should follow him and sneak in behind him because it was closed and he had to watch it. And anyway, since he was wasted he said he could use the company walking back even if he was thirty or forty years old, or whatever he was, and even though we were younger. That's what he said. So we started walking because I guess that's what we all wanted to do. We didn't even know what kind of place *FunShine* was until we got there.

See, we were all buddies working at Martin's. This was Dale, Allen, Seth and me I'm talking about. Seth worked the fish counter, lopping off heads and wrapping fish, netting lobsters from the tank, that kind of thing. Dale and me worked in produce, unpacking, keeping everything fresh and wet and looking good for the customer. Allen, he worked the register, what we liked to call "working the public."

I was living out in Reisterstown with Seth, right near the dollar theater. Two dollars on weekends to watch a movie coming out on video soon, get your feet stuck to the floor by spilled Pepsi and old gum. It was the way to go. The other two of them lived across the reservoir in Carroll County. We got along real well, and hung out a lot especially if we all worked the same shift and got off at the same time, which was sometimes.

There was one tricky spot in the equation, I guess. When I had Lisa over, Seth had to go out to a movie or the mall to let me have the place, and sometimes he didn't appreciate that, grumbling and groaning and all. Once he slammed my cast iron pot into the drywall when we were talking about Lisa, and he dented it up real good. But that was all right 'cause neither of us liked cooking much. Only I got stuck with all the spackling on that dry wall come moving out time. Mostly me and Seth worked out fine though because Seth worked a lot of them night owl shifts anyway. Sometimes Lisa and me liked to be in the room right before he got off work, just to light a little fire under us. She'd get turned on by that, boy. Martin's runs twenty-four hours, even on major holidays.

Seth and me lived in this attic apartment over the Weis house. They were nice enough, as long as we didn't play the music too loud or have no orgies or nothing. Hell, the apartment was too small for that sort of thing anyway. If I laid on my bed sideways and stretched out my arms, I could touch all four walls. We did have a toilet and a shower and sink, and a tiny brown-stained refrigerator next to the bed, stocked. We also had a little orange two-burner electric hot plate that we had to plug in to the wall over the refrigerator if we wanted to cook anything. Sometimes Mr. Weis let us use their kitchen, but only on special occasions or if they weren't already eating or nothing. The way it went, Seth and me took turns sleeping on the bed.

It was Dale who was my best buddy though, 'cause in high school he looked out for me even when I was mouthing off. Dale didn't let nobody pick on me. Dale was a big tall man with a heavy bearded face and a big old mouth with huge teeth, and he kept his hair pulled back in a ponytail looking like a big old mushroom or something. It struck guys down just looking at him sometimes. Hit puberty early, and never really stopped growing. This was lucky for me since I ain't nothing but stick and bones. That's what they all say anyway. I'm the same size as Seth.

I guess I didn't want to live with Dale 'cause it'd mess everything up with us and everything, and that's what I didn't want. Anyway Dale was always broke 'cause he wouldn't take money or help from nobody, and he was always buying stuff for people just for fun. He still don't get along with his parents much, except his sister and him were okay.

The night before we left for the beach it was my turn for the bed, thank the Lord. I was just laying there, tired but the kind of tired where you get all tingly and feel good for sleep. Lisa had just left and I had a big old stupid grin on my face. I was excited Lisa had took off work for the beach like the rest of us did. She was working the register twenty hours at Fill-Er-Up, the all-you-can-eat joint. We all gave our bosses two weeks warning so the crew could be together for our weekend of fun and sun.

I was laying there telling Seth how I was real excited, and how me and Lisa get along real well.

I was saying, "I can't wait to see Lisa in that suit, boy. She told me it was real tiny and all. One of them itsy teeny-weeny jobs." The trip meant a lot to me since Lisa was shy and didn't like nobody looking at her or nothing. Lisa was living at her dad's farm since she dropped out, so she usually drove over after work if her piece of crap Ford made it that far. I'm a Chevy man myself.

Seth was listening to this, but not really listening, know what I mean? He was sitting on the chair and nodding, but his eyes were focused inside himself and his own thoughts and feelings or whatever. Then he slumped onto the floor from where he was sitting, and he started falling asleep, or pretending to. I could smell cigarettes on his clothes. He'd been out at the High's trying to get someone to buy him beer. He hated always having to ask Dale, and felt bad about it.

"I don't know though, Lisa's kinda turning into a cow," I said.

"Yeah," he said.

I was just joking with him, trying to cheer him up by telling him how Lisa was gaining some weight in her thighs, not that she was really too much. Seth didn't say nothing. I don't know, maybe it was true, or maybe it was just something to say to fill space. Lisa's arms did look flabbier, I could tell that. But that's because she drank all that beer and ate ice cream like it was going out of style. And milk. Now that I think of it, Lisa did drink whole milk like a little kitten. I didn't care, as long as she didn't gain no weight on her face. She had this cute little button nose and pointy little chin, which made her cute to me, like a chipmunk or something. But she loved that milk. I thought then that I probably talked too much about Lisa, making the nasty, or just hanging out with her. Seth must get sick of it, I thought. Not that I was trying to rub his nose in nothing, but it helped at work to think about positive things 'cause it helped everything go faster, thinking about that warm body waiting for me at the end of the tunnel.

"Hey man," I said. He grunted back a "hmm."

"Hey Seth, you get sick of hearing about girls yet?" I saw his right eyebrow wrinkle down at that.

"No man. It's the only sex I get is hearing about it." He sat up pulling his mouth back into his face and crunched against the wall. He looked pale.

The funny thing was a few weeks before I thought Seth was trying to hit on Lisa right in front of me. Knowing her, she liked it too. She was getting some milk from the refrigerator, and Seth opened it for her like it was the front door and he was being all gentlemanly. He had that little glitter in his eyes. I just pretended not to notice, but I noticed. It was the day before he slammed the pot into the wall, so I could put two and two together.

Seth stood up and got himself some water and got his sleeping bag out from the corner. I dropped the Lisa issue at that. I didn't want to rag Seth too much, especially right before sleep time. Before I fell asleep I went to the sink, brushed my teeth in the tiny bathroom, washed my hands and face, all that except flossing. I hate thinking about that little plastic string cutting into my gums.

We were all only nineteen then, except Dale. He was twenty-one. Dale had to work the night owl, so we were waiting till first thing in the morning to go. It was an even trade though 'cause Dale was getting all the beer for everyone coming.

When I came out of the bathroom, I looked at Seth.

"Yeah." He had slid into the sleeping bag at the foot of the bed. This was a furnished apartment, real nice bed.

"You think we're going to have fun this weekend?"

"I'm going to get myself some ass," he said. "That much is for damn sure."

Seth ain't much of a looker, but he's probably the smartest one of the bunch, real contemplative and all, always thinking about something. I ain't trying to be mean or nothing, but Seth was kinda short and big-boned, and he had this ugly scar on his nose from when he cut himself with gardening shears. I could never figure out how he did that. That scar was big and pink, like a big old night crawler was lying dead under the nose of his skin. I don't even know if Seth's folks know how he got the scar, and they sure as hell couldn't afford plastic surgery without no insurance.

Seth's pop worked with mine at the quarry down on Marriotsville Road. He was a man always getting himself in trouble. My dad got married again last year to a woman named Rhonda Webb. He says she's real pretty and nice, but that's not what I see from pictures: I think she wears too much shit on her face. My mom lives right down the street at the

Holland Apartments, and I eat dinner with her every Sunday if I can get myself up there to do it.

"Goodnight buddy," I said.

"Goodnight Ronnie," he said.

I fell asleep that night as happy as I ever was.

I forgot about unhooking the phone night before we left for the beach. Didn't realize it until it woke both me and Seth up that next morning. Usually it'd be work, or my mom calling to get on me about something or other. As far as I was concerned all the good things in life happened in person, and I still believe that.

This time it was Lisa and she was crying.

"I can't come, Ronnie," she said. Her voice was shaking like it does when she gets upset. "My boss just called, and I can't come."

"What do you mean you can't?" I said.

"Mary just called in sick and I'm the only one around who knows the register. I can't. I'm sorry Hon, I can't," she said. "I'm real sorry."

I was angry. I get real angry sometimes when things don't work out, and I do stupid things like hit the receiver against my chest, which is what I did that time. Knocked my own wind out of me. I guess I'm pretty dumb when it comes to things. Then I took it out on Lisa, I mean just talking, you know. And that was unfair to her, but it's what happens when you're going out with a girl. But usually I calm down and talk it out after a few minutes.

I asked Lisa for Mary's number, thinking I could convince Lisa to go through her. But when I got through I got Mary's mother, and she got on me for calling so early. Her voice sounded real professional, or like she was still at work from the day before. I forgot it was only six in the morning. I did ask Mary's mother if there was any way but Mary's mother told me that Mary flipped her car last night from drinking, and was in the hospital. Damn, I thought, damn, damn, damn.

"I'm real sorry Mrs. Hastings," I said. "I didn't know."

"Yeah," she said.

Then I felt real bad, and I had to call Lisa back up and tell her we'd have to go without her. It wasn't what I wanted, and I know it wasn't what she wanted, but I guess there are some things you can't help.

"Okay, well have a good time," she said. I could tell she wasn't happy, and I told her it'd be all right. "Okay. Have fun," she said. "You're going to be careful, right?"

"Yeah. I'll be good," I said.

I think she cried after we hung up.

Seth and me picked up Dale from Martin's and Allen from his parents. Seth's grandparents give him $100 a month to help him out, and we used that money for more beer and food. Seth was pretty generous about that sort of thing. Usually when he got the money he'd take us all out to a restaurant, or maybe out drinking down at the block in Baltimore. This time we stopped and got some cigarettes and donuts for the morning, plus bread and peanut butter, and some chips and candy for the trip. We didn't eat much that weekend. Dale had two cases we got out of his car trunk.

The week before Seth said he wanted to take that money and spend it all on girls and drinking anyway. They didn't waste no time neither 'cause as soon as we crossed the bay bridge everyone but me was half-drunk. I couldn't help thinking about Lisa. I was down, not drinking or nothing. They picked on me the whole daggone time, saying I'm whipped by her even though I wasn't. I don't know, maybe I was though, 'cause I didn't look at no other girl seriously except for Lisa. Not that looking's everything, but it's something.

Once we got to the beach we settled into this little yellow hotel room on 7th right over the boardwalk. It was on the fifth floor I think. Was some room too 'cause we could sit on the little balcony there and watch all the ladies bounce by. We musta hollered at girls that night until our voices ran out. Nobody got none though right off, just drank, and later Allen and me got sick. It was great. The hard part was sleeping though. The room was just like home, a bed and four walls. Least we had Allen around to keep it light. Allen's the jokester of the bunch. He cracked us all up, sometimes just by smiling his goofy little smile.

"Lucky we don't have no women up here 'cause it'd have to be an orgy," he said. "Ain't got room for much else." Hang around together and you all start making the same jokes.

The one that really got me rolling was when Dale looked at the sad excuse for a water faucet they got there and said, "I've had runny noses that had more water pressure than that." I think Allen's so funny 'cause he dumped so many girls, and maybe he feels guilty about it sometimes. All the others were always cheating on their girlfriends, or doing any old girl as long as she got two legs, and weren't no brown shirt. I wasn't trying to be high and mighty or nothing, but I kept thinking how I like to stick with one girl at a time.

The next day was July Fourth, and everyone and their mother was out on the boardwalk. There were a lot of families with their kids and striped strollers, and high school kids, also older college-age types drinking in their rooms with their college music blasting out the doors. That's what we were doing when we woke up around one or two in the afternoon and got to it, even though wasn't none of us thinking about going to college.

I don't think we hardly touched foot on the beach until that night when the fireworks started, and Leon entered into the picture. Our room was starting to smell stuffy and goaty. Not to mention the room was yellow, and you can only take so much of that color before you start thinking of barfing. Anyway, I had to get out into the night for a bit, and they all came running out too when they heard the popping sounds from the fireworks and thought there was a fight and somebody was getting shot. They stuffed some bottles and cans of beer in Allen's backpack, and ran out. Only once they got out there, it was just flashing colors in the sky.

I thought *FunShine* was a dumb name. It sounded like a car wash, but it was really an amusement park. That's what we found out when we got there. Leon said they do all right, but not as good as some of the others in Ocean City.

"But hey, as long as I get my bread at the end of the week," he said. "Know what I'm saying?"

I liked Leon. He was okay, especially for a yo. The way I see it is there is yos and there is niggers, and I ain't never been able to stand the ones that ain't at least yos. Then there is them yuppie blacks living in Columbia, but they're not even on the same planet. Don't get me wrong, I'm not no racist. I had some black friends in school that I'd see at parties and stuff, just can't think of their names or nothing. Anyway it was a good thing I liked Leon too 'cause we walked near a mile with the dude, just talking about fishing, beer. Leon knew all kinds of fishing stories, from living on the shore, I guess. Whether they were the truth or not who knows? At first I was real nervous being with him, even if he said he was a security guard. It was just he was so big. But after a while I felt different being around Leon. Good almost, I guess, safe. Don't ask me why.

When we got to *FunShine*, Leon fumbled with his big ring of keys until he found the right one to open the gate. Then he almost forgot the alarm code, but at the last second he got it. We scrambled in 'cause there were other people around, and we didn't want nobody to see. This was on 40th Street, right after the boardwalk. We walked past the ticket booth and none of us could see nothing. That was when Leon turned on us real quick and said that we could use anything in the park, and we could even drink beer, but that we shouldn't leave no bottles behind.

"Normally I would take your asses on the spot," he said. "But you have fun." He gave us the tour of all the cool stuff, and he told us he'd be walking around, doing his job if we needed anything else. The uncomfortable thing was Leon kept on staring at Seth's scar, like he wanted to ask Seth how he got it. I thought then that they are all pretty wise at noticing things. Seth could feel this attention too 'cause he was looking at the ground, all twitchy and nervous.

It was dark inside the park, and we could hear the water gurgling from all around like them hot springs out West are supposed to do. I could smell lots of chlorine, and even some wet, maybe mildew. The light that was in the park came from under the pools mostly, so it was like everything was under water almost, all the light glittering and flowing up. There were fake palm trees and flamingos all around too, plus

lockers and bathrooms, the kind of things you'd find at the
pool. The only family vacation I ever been to, my parents took
us to Disneyland. But *FunShine* was better 'cause it was all
ours and we didn't have to wait in line or nothing like that.
When I remember *FunShine*, I think about the dark blue sky
and water that was glittering blue everywhere that night.

So the four of us drank beer and went down all the
slides and tubes, using buckets full of water to get them wet
enough. We swam in the pools even if we didn't have our
trunks or nothing. Seth was the only one who didn't. I didn't
understand that. Leon even turned on the arcade for us to
dry off in 'cause he said he had to run them anyway. We played
air hockey and video games and I won lots 'cause I got good
hand-eye coordination. I beat Seth in the last game of air
hockey. He was starting to get in one of his pissy moods. I
don't know why he gets like that, but I can tell he was in one
'cause he didn't say nothing, and usually you can't shut him up.

Seth and Allen wanted to go too, but it was Dale's idea
to go for one more swim. So we jump in this whale-shaped
pool that was pretty shallow I guess because all of us could
walk around in it. Dale and I are just swimming, you know.

Then Allen gets in too, leaving Seth on the edge. We started ribbing him, saying, *what's the matter, man? Come on in.* He looked so serious, and against the whole idea. He looked like someone was pinching him.

Then all at once he jumped in.

We all started laughing and joking around 'cause he didn't even take his shirt off. He looked like one of them little pale kids who're afraid of a little sun. That's when he came up with the fifty in his hands, and wouldn't listen to nobody. He didn't smile or nothing. It was really surprising, because how often do you see a fifty much less find one in front of your face?

"It's a sign of something," he mumbled to himself, the bill sagging on his fingers. Nobody could understand what he said except me, 'cause I'm used to the mumbling. I told him he should just take it easy. Then maybe something hit him inside because he climbed out of the pool and just started chucking them bottles and cans everywhere, breaking the glass on the concrete and into the pool we were swimming in, all around. Nobody knew what to do.

"Jesus Christ," I said. "What the hell are you doing?" He didn't even look at me standing there dripping.

Then we saw Leon's flashlight come round all over the concrete and slides in the distance like he heard, and we knew we didn't have no time, and no choice unless we wanted to choose trouble. So we slid out from the pool wet and started going for the gate Seth or no Seth. That's when I felt glass in my feet the first step, and I cussed to myself. But I kept going somehow until we were outside of the gate, hopping on one foot, and using the side of the other. We didn't stop stumbling for two blocks, then we saw our footprints on the sidewalk. There were thin red splotches everywhere.

All of us got glass slivers stuck all inside our feet, and had to go to the hospital and everything. It hurt real bad and we had to walk on the sides of our feet to the bus stop to sit on the curb and wait for help. If Leon wasn't drunk I'm sure he would of found us; if we weren't drunk the pain would've hurt too much to ever get out of there. I mean, it started to sting, boy, real bad. The bus driver almost wouldn't let us in, but he did 'cause we said it was an emergency. Everyone inside stared at us like we were aliens or something, blood coming down onto the floor of the bus. One guy in a green and black sweater even offered to take us to his apartment to fix us all up, but we didn't trust nobody right then, especially some stranger.

Except then these two drunk girls came up to us and started joking with us, asking us what we were up, to robbing some store? We were just trying to wipe the blood off the floor of the bus with our hands and some paper towels the driver gave us, but these girls wanted something else 'cause they offered to take us back to their place to nurse us after they helped us get to the hospital. How could we turn that down? I had the one on the left, Brandi, and Allen had the other one. Dale was drunker and just passed out on the sofa.

But Seth, he was still standing there at *FunShine* holding the empty backpack, with the fifty-dollar bill in his pocket, and Leon leading him into the office and putting the phone to Seth's ear to call the cops himself. Seth didn't go nowhere, at least that's the way he told me it happened. Later I asked him why he did it, and he said he had his reasons but he wasn't going to tell them. I don't get it. I can just imagine Seth staring out into space at *FunShine* like he does before he goes asleep. Just standing there watching the pool and the light. Least Seth didn't cut his feet all up. I felt bad for him though, pretty bad.

The good thing though was Seth didn't rat on us or nothing, and we talked to him on the phone the next day, but later he was gone for a good while to the state pen, and when he came back everything was changed. I had to find a new roommate in between because I couldn't afford to pay rent myself, and none of us could afford to do much without the funds from Seth's relatives. Plus something got sour. Can't explain it. My new roommate's name was Glen, who mixed mortar for some guy working for Mr. Weis, and I guess he was good looking to women even if he was older. He had lots of them over anyway. So I got to see things from a new angle.

Lisa dumped me at the end of that summer for an older guy who I ain't never seen, and now she lives with him somewhere near Finksburg, I think. She said it just wasn't exciting anymore dealing with me and my little room, and my friends. I don't know why. I argued with her but I guess she was right, it wasn't as exciting. Maybe if I was her and she was me I'd do the same. It's funny how one person can make the difference in things.

SONS AND DAUGHTERS
OF APOSTATES

I watched the space where Harriet was headed, toward the scuffling sound behind the porch lattice. The rest of us were feeling too content and talkative to care. Harriet didn't drink unless she was upset, and she didn't seem upset.

In the dusty darkness Harriet knocked something over, and an animal burst out into the grass and stood there in the shadows in the dew, outside the glow of the porch light.

"What is it?" I said.

"It's a kitty-cat," she beamed, squeezing out of the open portal. "Look at it!"

The cat stood still out of awe or, more likely, fear. Harriet stood next to where we sat and watched the animal. Its eyes blazed in the dark, which made it seem closer than it was. Harriet and the animal just watched each other, at ease and harmonious in some way, oblivious to the human banter behind them. Oren wrapped up his story about the woman who broke a stereo component in his store, and said he brought a coconut, and went to rattle around in the kitchen for it. Harriet advanced on the cat, crawling on her knees in the dew, pulling her hair away from her face. The cat lifted its back, tail stiff, and I thought it would bolt. But then it curled around the tree trunk, and headed directly to her, seemingly friendly. Spears of grass stuck to the back of Harriet's ankles; the cat let Harriet cup her hands under its belly and hold it to her chest.

Oren came back out with the coconut. He looked like a postal worker in his all-blue slacks and shirt. His blonde hair looked white in the beam of light from the porch.

"We should just chuck it against the side of the house," he said. "What do you all think?"

Neil said yes, and I slurred some kind of agreement. Harriet turned her head from her feline reverie, cradling the cat to her.

"I don't think you should," she said. Her face looked thinner and more washed-out than I expected. "You're going to damage the house and the cat's going to take off."

"Everything will be fine," Oren said, looking to me, smiling like a truant.

"I heard the best way to do it is you heat it in the oven for five minutes, then whap it in a towel with a hammer," I said. "The meat's supposed to come off clean."

"That's too slow," Oren said. I watched the skin on his neck crease like a wet towel. He whipped around without waiting, chucked the coconut against the wood façade, popping shards all over the porch, shrubs, and cypress trees. Harriet was the only one who didn't go scrambling for the shells, laughing and whooping. I collected my share from the closest region of the porch, the steps, and offered a large fragment to Harriet; she leaned against the tree with the unaffected cat.

"I'm just so tired," she said, brushing the dirt off the coconut shell.

"You've worked hard," I said.

"I can't sleep. I don't know if it's excitement, or apprehension, or what, but I can't seem to lose consciousness. My thoughts are different."

I tried to avoid the subject by telling her we should have another one of our Harriet-Ian sleep-overs. We could play cards and watch movies and stay up late, I said. Pal around.

"I like your purity, Ian. Most guys would mean something else, I think."

"No, it's been our tradition, right? Your man has always understood."

"That's *him*," she said. We stared at each other in a pared-down curious way, but I knew *I* wondered why we had never been together. Although I did know that as important as it was for Harriet to maintain psychic distance, she probably also felt like she could approach me. But for a moment I just didn't understand the actual physics of our relationship. A couple of years ago Oren did cross that line, regretfully, for all of us.

"The cicadas sound great," I said. "I love this time of year."

"Ummhmm." Harriet lifted her weight from the tree, and turned the cat upside down in her arms. The cat was still compliant; its paws patted the air.

"Where do you see me in ten years, Ian?"

"Wherever you want to be, Harriet."

"That's it? You don't have any idea?"

"This is vacation," I said. "I haven't been thinking."

"That's not a very satisfying answer, Ian."

"I'm sorry," I said.

"I don't know," Harriet said. "I think I need to keep this cat. It feels right for me now." She leaned forward, and the backs of her thighs were powdered with mica chips and bark. The cat was white with a black belly and black paws, and looked starved, and perhaps more needy than Harriet could manage.

This oldest cluster of friends and I rented the cabin in Harpers Ferry so we could spend some concentrated time together instead of enduring the distillation process, where the group would be broken into its smaller denominations with only individual notice. The trip was my idea, since Oren and Neil were usually preoccupied with their jobs—computer software sales rep and middle school guidance counselor, respectively. Harriet, younger than the rest of us, was going off to nursing school in Texas. In the winter she would be off in Europe with her boyfriend who was living in Greece; her life was infinitely more exciting than mine.

My group of friends was, for some reason, composed of the offspring or grandchildren of former or lapsed Catholics. My grandfather's father became an atheist in college after studying Eastern religion and realizing that completely different cultures had the same message without knowing it; my mother converted to Unitarianism. Neil's parents stopped practicing religion for reasons unknown, even if they are cultural Catholics. Oren's parents, as he said, simply "lost interest" when he was younger, although he could remember going to Mass when he was very young. His father "found himself" in Nordic Methodism, then once he became bored with that, he converted to Judaism. I'd honestly wanted to actually *be* Catholic, but I simply didn't feel supported family-wise, and I wouldn't know where to start, and plus I thought conversion was too close to a sex change to be worthwhile: What would I convert *from*?

Harriet's parents were Catholic, but they both died when she was sixteen, and they had been spiritually apathetic. But Harriet refused to even talk about the C word, as she called it, although she would talk at length about the details of her parents' death, including her mother's intensive bouts of failed chemotherapy, the bone marrow transplant, and her father's freak car accident a month after the death of his wife.

Now Harriet lives with her aunt and uncle in Chevy Chase, Maryland while the rest of us live in Northern Virginia. The house itself is clutterless, perfect, and as a result, extremely icy. To make matters worse, they live directly on a street where most of the cars enter their neighborhood, so the car lights constantly troll across the back wall of their living room, adding substantially to the police-state aura. They bought thick curtains, but the light still filters through, tracing along the wall in broad swoops.

We rented the cabin from Oren's grandparents, who took a month long "golden-years" cruise to Alaska. The cabin overlooks a slow drag in the Potomac, which is swimmable.

The idea to jump in the river was Neil's, although as soon as he said it, it made complete sense to everybody, even to Harriet. We downed the rest of the wine and threw our clothes around, stumbling to search for our bathing suits.

Harriet carried the cat inside. None of us thought it was a good idea to lock it in the bathroom, though. Leaning against the sink, she stood there holding the cat to her chest.

"I'll just give it some of the hamburger and some water. She'll be just fine."

"Uncooked hamburger will give it tapeworms," Oren said. "Plus, cats don't usually eat it."

"I'll cook the hamburger then. I want this cat."

"There's going to be crap all over the floor," Oren said. "This is my responsibility, you know that? Maybe this is somebody's cat. Have you thought about that angle?"

"Yes, if they're missing a cat, they'll come around. I'll put a box with newspaper in it, until tomorrow. How much can she do in a night?"

"Plenty. She can do plenty, Harriet. Anyway, there's only one bathroom. The cat's going to squirm out when I have to take a piss."

"Just go in slowly, and watch the door so she *doesn't* come out. I mean, what's the big deal?"

"The cat's not going to be happy."

"She'll be happy," Harriet said. "She'll be happy with me."

"And you know it's a *she*, I take it."

"I know," Harriet said.

"Fine. Do what you like," Oren said. As he walked off, he pulled his blue uniform polo over his head and thumped down the hall. He ran his thumb along the wall, as if he were going to taste the residue. Harriet closed the bathroom door behind us. I sat on the edge of the tub. She placed the cat behind me in the basin, but the cat jumped out.

I was corralling the cat when I heard the metal button of Harriet's cut-offs click against the tile. She maneuvered out of her T-shirt and bra, and stood in front of me in her panties.

"This bathroom is small," I said. She blinked at me, and reached into her handbag for her bikini. She placed the bikini bottom on top of the toilet and wrangled her panties down her leg. I couldn't believe it.

"Can I hold onto your shoulder to balance myself?"

"Sure," I said. I reached out to her. I think my elbow may have grazed her pubic hair. She placed one hand on my right shoulder and scratched it with her fingernails as she lifted her legs into the bikini bottom. Harriet was behind me now, and I could feel strands of her hair on my ears. Her shampoo smelled like pineapple, and the cat curled between my feet and purred against her. Harriet pressed her forehead against the curve of my lower back and held it there, scratching both shoulders with her fingernails. I closed my eyes. I hadn't had a date in six months, much less sex.

"It's going to be fine," I said. "Man, you're the one that everyone here admires."

"I don't think so."

"Is that what they taught you to think?" I meant the military academy.

"No, that's all me. I make my own bed."

"I *am* really proud of you," I said. "Do you know that?"

"From afar maybe."

"I don't know if that's true," I said.

"It seems true to me," she said. "It's as if I've got this dark glow around me, so you know, keep it on the everyday things. Keep it simple." Part of me was angry at her for this, and I wanted to tell her that, if anything, matters were the other way around.

"It's been a long time, Harriet. We can try to change the effect of things," I said. I suddenly felt guilty for jabbing into her soft spot. "Anyway, what do you want me to do? I'm not going to cuddle with you. You have a boyfriend for that."

"Not here." I was getting the feeling that everything wasn't okay with her. We went rafting the day before and Harriet had flirted with the attendant.

"Well, he is your guy still, right?"

"I don't know what I mean. I'm getting myself worked up over nothing. I don't understand how I react to things anymore."

"You're doing fine," I said. "Like I said, I am proud of you."

"All that I did was finish," she said. "People shouldn't get so worked up about that. It's just completing the job."

"Yeah, but for what you've been through, I just think that you did great." She wrapped her arms around my chest at this point, and pressed herself into my back.

"You know," she said. Her voice was quietly offhand. "I really don't think I want fucking special treatment."

"I don't see how it can be any different. We're partially your family here."

"Don't be so dramatic," she said, pinching my nipple.

I told her I was going to get changed, so we could join the others. Harriet leaned back off of me.

"And you want me out, right?"

"I didn't say that, Harriet."

"I'll just squat here and pet the cat. You go ahead," she said. I've never dressed so quickly before. When I dropped my shorts, she turned before I could catch her eye with mine. She asked if I had a T-shirt she could borrow and I said I'd go get one from my bag. When I came back with it I said we should probably go join the others.

Neil, Oren, and I waded into the shallows, while Harriet sat on a rock by the shore and dangled her feet in. The air was dry, and from the intensity of the cicada and cricket chatter I could tell colder weather was coming.

"So who's going swimming with me?" Oren said to Harriet.

"I go swimming every day," Harriet said, meaning the YMCA. "I don't have anything to prove."

"Would anyone like to race then?" Neil had always been a good swimmer. Oren didn't seem interested, and I knew I wasn't. The water was too cold, and even though it seemed placid, I didn't trust the infamous Potomac undercurrents.

"I'm on vacation," Harriet said.

"I'll race myself then," Neil said grinning. "To the other bank and back." He huffed into the air, circled his arms in the air mockingly, and dove into the water. The three of us watched the river sprinkle up and out with each stroke, and kick. But his head stayed steady in the water. One, two, three, up and breathe. His body was a mass of motion.

Somehow, in his spectator mood, Oren decided to make peace with his enemy of the moment; he sloshed over to where Harriet sat and they spoke softly to each other, and she laughed and everything seemed fine. I heard Oren actually apologize, which was a rarity. I hoped Neil would make it without a hitch, and that would initiate a new placidity over all of us. I watched Neil touch the far bank, gasp self-mockingly and dive back in, and I knew he'd make it back.

After he swam back to us, receiving hand slaps and splashes equally, Neil said he had to go inside for a second. He came back with the watermelon, a big knife, and beer. We cut the thing open and spit the seeds and threw the rinds into the river, drinking more, and Harriet had beer. Which surprised me. At the end of August something about the watermelon felt too cold and somehow cheerless.

When we got back to the cabin, the cat wasn't in the bathroom, and we couldn't find it anywhere in the cabin. Neil and I went to sleep, but Oren went to help Harriet search for the thing. Needless to say, he felt guilty, although I think it was Neil who accidentally left the bathroom door ajar, and the screen door unlatched.

Harriet was still in bed the next morning when Oren and I decided maybe we should go out, get away from the cabin for a bit. Oren suggested a tour of the historic town, but I thought the flea market would be more lowbrow and entertaining. Oren hesitated at first, but Neil liked the idea when he woke up, and Harriet didn't care one way or another. So, after our late breakfast, we drove two miles up into the hills above the town to the old drive-in theater parking lot.

Junk everywhere. Bicycles, old televisions, books, clothes, hangers, candlesticks, everything you can imagine. The men all leered at Harriet, though she didn't notice. She wasn't wearing a bra, and her eyes looked distant and glassy. She looked beaten, and morose underneath her attempt to be a good sport. We could all feel it, and our predominant common step was a scuffle.

"You know, you probably didn't want that cat anyway," Oren said.

"Yeah, but I did," Harriet said. "That cat loved me."

"I knew a student who took in a stray Husky," Neil said. "And his family had a cat. The dog *ate* the cat. Literally. It was very traumatic for him."

"That doesn't make me feel that much better," Harriet said.

We walked past a table cluttered with toy cars, and dolls, embroidered towels, boxes of Legos, G.I. Joe figures, fake 19th century tins, records, plastic vases.

"There are plenty of cats," Oren said. "Just get one when you get there. Let's not all get hung up on it, okay?" Harriet nodded, and as we continued to rummage through the junk it seemed to sink in. She somehow made her own closure, at least momentarily. Neil and I didn't buy anything, but Oren bought a sewing kit because he said his buttons are always falling off. Harriet bought a bag filled with army men, so she could set them up on her windowsill in Texas, she said, and shoot them with rubber bands.

It was a steamy drive back in my car (no air conditioning); the highway construction didn't make it any better. Once we arrived at Harriet's aunt and uncle's, Harriet asked us if we wanted to take a last swim before we left. She didn't seem to mean that we should take her up on it. Neil didn't want to swim anymore, and he said his good-byes, but Oren and I both wanted to swim.

Harriet walked us around into the backyard. I could see her aunt and uncle talking in the kitchen inside. Her uncle was a hard-looking man who used to be a bookie, Harriet said. He spent his time taking solitary walks and reading the sports pages in the kitchen. We didn't go in.

Oren and I helped Harriet pull the cover off the pool, but the water was dense with dead insects and spiders floating on the surface. Neither Oren or I wanted to swim, but Harriet didn't seem to mind, and then suddenly she dove in. As she did laps, Oren and I fished the bugs out with nets and talked about the upcoming football season. As Harriet swam we mentioned the possibility of buying tickets to a few games.

"I don't know what to do, Ian."

"About what?"

"About her," he said, nodding towards Harriet. "I think I made a mistake, yesterday, last night I mean." His eyes burned. The sun shot into his face, and he blocked it with his hand.

"A mistake?" I watched Harriet wave through the water, her thigh muscles rippling and tan, her hair whipping through the water and insect parts, and leaves, the bottom of her feet pink and exposed.

"Yeah, you know what I mean," he said. "I can't help it. She's beautiful. I can't help feelings. Touching. It's just—"

"Jesus," I said.

Harriet touched the other side of the pool, and I thought she'd come up for air there, but she flipped, pushed off with her feet, and shot back to where she dove in.

WE'RE ALL FROM WEST VIRGINIA SOMETIME

This couple I knew lived near Martinsburg, West Virginia, which seemed odd to me since they always wanted to live in D.C., or Baltimore, or some inner pocket. But they ended up in the hills since Vicki was a minister, and Blair was a bum riding her coat tails to whatever gig she could get. They said—surprise, surprise—that they felt isolated up there and that they wouldn't mind a guest or two, and I decided that wouldn't be such a bad idea. One Friday night I told them I'm bringing my new thing with me if they didn't have something else in the works, and that the name of my new thing was Lacy. I felt like I was on some sort of crossroads with her, but I didn't know what the signs said yet. "Kelby, come on up whenever you want," Vicki said. I wondered if they really wanted to see us or if they just thought they wanted to see us. These are sentimental people we're talking about.

I picked Lacy up from her job at Blind Boy Willie's, and we stopped at a convenience store to get some grub for the drive. Lacy said she just couldn't wait to eat any longer. "Why is it that you're working at a restaurant but you're always hungry?" I said. "Eating there is the last thing I'd want to do," she said. The line was snaking through the candy aisle, so we ditched that idea, ended up speeding back to my apartment fifteen miles back for a fucking bag of chips. You know, things happened, and we ended up naked, and, would you believe, screwing. Then we realized the humidity already staled the chips I *did* have, and we had to go back to the store again for more. Should of got one of those chip clip things. So...we didn't get started for Martinsburg until eleven, eleven thirty.

Footnote: Yes, Lacy sounds like a slutty name. But, she was ten times more determined than me, which was fine because I needed someone to keep my head on straight and make me acknowledge that a relationship based just around sex is fine, and that I didn't have to be guilty for just fucking, or for liking the way things were. Not that I could help either one.

"Aren't your friends going to be pissed?" she said. "You said we would *be* there by now."

"Vicki's a minister. She has to be compassionate."

"It's going to be too late isn't it?" I was getting the feeling Lacy didn't want any part of the whole idea.

"They'll be fine. Anyway, if they get mad, that's their problem. They're *just* friends," I said. At this point we were back at the convenience store, standing in line to buy the chips. I mean, we could have used those soggy things to give each other sponge baths. The line was still long, this time because everyone and their au pairs were in line to get beer and boxes of wine before twelve hit.

"You're right," she said.

"We're going," I said.

"Let's go then. It's just West Virginia."

"What do you mean 'just'?"

"I don't know," she said. "I've never been to Martinsburg. I don't know what I'm talking about."

I said: "I was just going to *say*, 'Or...maybe you know more than I do about some things.'" I noticed that our post-coital routine was argue, make up, then it was Lacy staring out the window as if somebody ran over her cat.

Fine.

"How many times have *you* been to West Virginia?" I was cradling the sour cream and chives with both hands.

"Yeah, this must be lame to you. Like I said, you don't have to go if you don't want to go," I said. "They're my friends."

"Look, if we're going to go, let's go," she said. "But let's go then, Kelby." The other people in line sighed, and one guy glanced back at us as if we were pinpointing his emotional state exactly. I shrugged and he shrugged back. "Anyway, it's okay to judge things before you really know them," she said. "I mean it is, isn't it?"

"I'm sorry for enjoying myself and trying to please you," I said. "Maybe that's not important to you."

"I think it is. No, I know it *is*," she said.

"You don't even know what you don't know," I said. "That's what I think."

"Whatever *that* means."

"Hey, since you're the quote intellectual unquote in this relationship, why don't you grab us one of those boxes of wine so we can be by the books and everything, politeness-wise." I was really trying not to cross the line.

"I don't know. Do ministers drink?"

"Those Christians will surprise you," I said.

If there's one thing I've learned about love it's that there is only one discovery. The moment is there, and then it's gone and all you can do is remember it and try to keep it that way. That's the way it is. A minute or two doesn't seem to be enough to mangle the discovery. But it is. All it takes is one slip.

So in the car I apologized for snapping at her. Lacy scooped up my balls like a ditch digger, and said, "No problems here, cowpoke." She stared out into the dark cornfields rolling west on Route 70, and wound the window up and down.

"What's wrong?"

"I can't decide if I'm hot or if I'm not hot," she said.

"Take your time," I said. I flipped on the classical station, which felt right for the moment. Something had to calm me down.

"I wonder how Spook is doing," she said. That's her cat. "He seemed sad to see me go this afternoon. You know, he's pretty dependent on me."

"He's not the only one," I said.

"What does that mean?"

"I mean, I think I need you. I'm not sure how I feel about that."

"Are you okay?" she said.

"I'm just trying to tell you—"

"What, because we had a widdle fight?"

"Yeah," I said.

"It was juss a widdle won, wight?"

"I feel fine Lacy. I feel like beating someone up, but I'm fine."

"I hate it when you say my name," she said. She stuck her hand out the window and rolled it through the cooling air. I couldn't see a thing outside of the car.

"Lacy is your name," I said.

"It just sounds formal or something when you say it out loud."

This girl Lacy had a real icy Swedish face, and she came from a family of icy Swedish faces. But they weren't Swedish, she said; they were Swiss. I thought: What's the difference? They're all a bunch of supposedly eugenic, Nazi-sympathizing motherfuckers. Maybe Lacy was right about that judging thing.

So we got there at one-thirty in the morning, a little lost after we bungled the left hand turn off the 217 exit, but mostly half-asleep; the night sky was still orangish in the summer light. We drove up the driveway, and pulled in behind the Tercel. Yeah, we were there, behind Blair's car, the unmistakable bumper stickers all over it: outlaw tribal clitorectomies this, freedom of choice that, save the goddamn timber wolves. Hey, it was easy to find them. The two churches where Vicki preached gave them the parish house. It was a real dump; the porch had moss growing on the banister. The driveway had weeds, practically an orchard, coming out of it. When we got there the light was on, so I knew they would still let us in. Gnats and mosquitoes were squashed all over their screen door. The leg of one still ticked, one last jab into the inner light...foiled.

I asked Lacy to ring the bell. She snatched my finger and pressed it into the button.

"Team work," she said. We could hear paint chips sprinkle against the flooring as someone made their way down the steps. Two minutes later Blair came to the door, leaning over us and mussing his hair. Blair's six feet nine.

"Hey," he said. "Promptness is a great characteristic."

"Were you asleep, man?"

"It's what? What time is it?"

"It's late man," I said. "Donworry about it, donworry about it. Let us in."

"Yeah...sure. Uh-huh." Vicki crumbled down the stairs, creak-crack-crick. I made quick intros, and Vicki flicked a lighter on the coffee table, touched it to the candle garden they had there, and the room flickered into shadows. I don't think she had been sleeping. I handed her the box of wine and chips.

You can divide the world into candle-lovers and non-candle-lovers, and I'm one of the second.

"Great," Vicki said. "Wine in a box. That's classy, with a K."

"Yeah, only the best for Kelby," Lacy said.

"You want some Jamaican Rum? We've been into it all night. He has at least." Both of us said okay, and Vicki breezed into the kitchen to the left, and probably shoved the wine deep in the bowels of the fridge where they might find it during some snow storm when they couldn't make their way to the liquor store. I was surprised to see Blair drinking. I thought Blair called it off two years ago when he had to go into rehab. That was right before he met Vick. I winked at him, and he waved us to sit down on the sofa.

"So you're okay then, man?" I said.

He said he was. "I've never been too good about turning pleasure down," he said. "I guess that's about all you can say about booze."

"What do you guys want in it?" Vicki asked.

"You have punch, or any juice?"

"Got blueberry Kool-Aid."

"That's fine for me," I said, and Lacy agreed. Blair turned on the television, popped a tape in the VCR, and this computer animation stuff churned out, flashing colors all over the walls, and pretty much negating the candle effect entirely. Blair leaned into a recline, clearly drunk already. By the way, their living room had sticks hanging from the ceiling on fishing wire, and leaves glued to the walls. At any point I expected to see a rutting deer bolt through.

"Hey, what's with the deal with the nature stuff?"

"What? Oh, yeah, we're trying to keep a certain *feel* to things these days," Blair said. "It's actually refreshing. I love looking up and seeing all this living stuff around me."

"Sticks are dead, Blair."

"Well, used to be living at least," he said.

"Don't you have problems with ants, or squirrels thinking your living room is their long lost home?" Blair laughed, said he's hoping squirrels would join them. I looked to Lacy for some help, but she was entranced by the television glow.

Vicki came back with the drinks in soup mugs, and I could smell that rum from across the room. Vicki wasn't a bad looking woman, but she had a paunchy face and a hoggish little nose. The cat's pajamas is the way Blair described her, probably because she was earning the bacon *and* frying it up in a pan; but I thought she was a bit too gnomic and dumpy for my blood no matter what kinky stories he related.

Vicki squatted on the floor in front of Blair, rocking on the balls of her feet like she was about to take a crap on her nappy throw rug. The music coming out of the television sounded like someone gargling over the sound of a hair dryer.

"So the big question," I said. "Can you tell us how this West Virginia thing is going?"

"Very fine," Blair said. "It's nice."

"Very fine for you. Good, good. What are *you* adding to the situation though?" I said to him.

"Oh, he's a big help," Vick said, seemingly appreciating the friendly jab. "He's thinking of going back to school."

"That's right," Blair said.

"This is a guy who took eight years to get his undergrad degree. He's taking pottery classes?"

"Yeah," Vick said.

"Blair— the great all American ceramist. Ceramist? Is that what they're called?"

"Potter, potter," Lacy said. "It doesn't matter anyway." She pulled her hair back and held it there with her hand. I'm not sure if she did it to expose her neck for me, or to say *I'm not trying to be sexy here, I'm just trying to be a good date and hang out with your friends.* Maybe I did love her.

"He does help me with my sermons," Vicki said. "He still organizes the youth group meetings, right, honey?" She patted his leg briskly.

"Yes ma'am," Blair said.

"Oh fuck you," she said.

"Yes ma'am." Blair leans down and gives her a rolling-eyed kiss on the neck.

"Okay, okay," I said. "Try to keep it vertical."

"You don't know the half of it," Vicki said.

"Really?" Lacy sat up.

"Well, yes. But yes, um, things are very decent here."

"Decent?" I said. "Does 'decent' really cut it?"

"Let's put it to you this way," Blair said, watching the swirling electronic shapes on the walls. "Martinsburg's not really the slicker life, but after we stick it out here, we can go back. There's lots of places we can go from here. I mean, restraining our mouths is most of the battle."

"Yeah, there's so much here we'd like to change, it's almost overwhelming," Vicki said. "So in that way it's easier to deal with than something closer to what we'd identify with, like Baltimore."

"It's a lost cause?" I asked. I just imagined all those political organizations weeping collectively over the loss of Blair and Vicki Williamson.

"Lost isn't the word for it," Blair said, kicking his feet up. "You know, this guy from our congregation gave us a barrel of feed corn last week for giving a strong sermon on Abraham. What the hell am I going to do with this stuff though, raise hogs?" We were all sucking on our drinks.

"That might be enlightening for you," I said.

Blair and Vicki related the ins and outs of their two congregations, which were composed of about thirty people total, each centering around little churches with ramshackle pews, and borderline Appalachian world views.

"But hey, you get a free house, right?"

"Free house," Blair said. "We're all from West Virginia sometime."

"What the hell does that mean?" Lacy rolled her eyes, and bit her cup.

"It's the state motto," Blair said. "My version of the motto at least. Bumper stickers are rolling off the assembly line as we speak."

"So are you saying we all have hillbilly blood sometime, is that the interpretation?" I asked.

"Something like that," he said.

"I don't get it. How does a guy from, I don't know, Thailand, let's say, how does a guy like that have hillbilly blood? That is what you're saying right?"

"Metaphorically speaking, is what I'm saying. And anyway he wouldn't have *American* hillbilly blood. Guy'd have the Thailandese equivalent."

"I think it's Thai," I said.

"Yeah, right. We're not as sophisticated as we think we are," he said.

"You *are* drunk." I snorted the rest of the rum down, and the mood felt suddenly loosey-goosey, just what I was hoping for on a Friday.

I asked Vicki when do we get the tour of the place, but she said later, in the morning, when we could see things. Lacy asked Vicki what else is new, which seemed over-familiar. Vicki said nothing, nothing really. Ho-hum. These aren't the type of people who were about to ask us about *our* lives.

"So you're bored out here then?" I asked. They looked at each other askew, and Vicki's eyes widened as if she was trying to convey something to Blair.

"Well, we might as well rip open the present now," she said. Vicki rocked back and forth, flicking her fingers against her palms. "You both seem suitably happy and you've come all the way out here."

"What do you mean?"

"We have a surprise announcement for you. Umm, well, we've decided to have an open relationship."

"What do you mean 'open?'" I asked.

"We mean open, like open. What do you mean what do we mean?"

"I mean, how open are we talking about?" I asked. "What, do you announce a brothel after the services?"

"We haven't decided yet," Vicki said. "We're looking for some excitement, I guess. I don't know, it's pretty boring out here so far."

"So...okay," I said. "Have you been on one of your little fuck-fests yet, or what?" I felt mortified by this idea. I could barely finish a glass of wine, much less hop into group sex.

"No, it's still under construction," Blair said. "It's still in the theory stages." He reached to turn the television up, as if he didn't want to even hear my response.

"So what do you think?" Vicki said.

"You *are* a minister right?" I said.

"I'm fine with it ethically, if that's what you mean. Methodism is the denomination of the heart."

"I don't know how much the heart has to do with any of it," I said.

"Well it does," she said. "Because we've come to this realization, and it's that we just can't get everything out of each other. Nobody can get everything out of one person. We need—"

"What?" I said.

"We need to play off other people, I think. We think." Blair nodded at me and scratched his eyebrow with his thumb.

I told her that I didn't understand this. They just got married; they were in love by any definition I could come to terms with—why complicate their lives with something extra?

"Vicki, I think it's a great idea," Lacy said. Yeah, she also thought snorting coke twice a day (and I don't mean the rival to Pepsi) was a 'great idea.'

"You think that is a great idea?" I said.

"I've always been curious to try things, with more…something, exposure…more people around," Lacy said. "I don't see anything wrong with that."

"Right, that's what I'm saying," Vicki said. "I mean you do get a little something different from everybody."

"It doesn't have to be the clap though," I said. "Jesus. Maybe you are all more polygamous than I am. I just don't see it."

"I do think people can be categorized that way," Blair said.

"I feel inferior then," I said. "How about that?"

"Get off it, Kelby," Lacy said. "Nobody is truly devoted. Why do you think people get married? To fend that shit—"

"Well, I don't know about—" Blair said.

I said: "You know, at this point I have no idea what—"

"Right," Vick said.

"No," I said. "I am really a one-woman man."

"Well, good for you," Lacy said. "That makes you a saint to be reckoned with doesn't it?" Vick's eyes sparkled in the TV glow. Lacy chuckled, and downed the rest of her drink. I could see her eyes with the mug in between them, but her nose and mouth were covered.

"Okay, well, maybe we should get some more drinks," Vicki said, loping to the kitchen. She asked Blair for a hand, and he came back with a basket filled with corn. Vick brought the drinks back into the room, and handed one to Lacy, who immediately sucked half of hers down. "Since we are in West Virginia," Vicki said, "we should have a shucking contest." She counted out twelve ears to each of us. I looked at Lacy, but she didn't look back.

"Okay, okay," she said. "When I say go, everybody shuck. Whoever gets all their ears freed first wins."

"Is this really some kind of tradition?" I said.

"Just concentrate on the corn," she said. "On your ready. Get set. Go!"

"What will we win?" I said, peeling the first ear.

"You'll just have to wait and see," she said.

So despite his inebriated state, Blair won the contest—
he's got the biggest hands. But I came in a close second. Vick
said two of mine didn't count because I still had too much silk
stuck to the top of my ears. I said, "I don't get it. How do you
know what is too much, and what is not enough?" My answer
was Vick is the judge, and I am just a measly contestant. At any
rate we gathered all the silk and corn sheaths together and
queued into the kitchen to feed them in the garbage disposal
on my suggestion. It would be like throwing the stalks to the
lions, I said, which it was. We cheered as the disposal ground
each sheath into the drain. Then Vick cleared off the table, and
Blair turned off the lights again.

Lacy and I sat across from each other at the table, and
Blair sat next to me. Vick unscrewed the overhead bulb and
put a red bulb in it, and turned it back on, which underlined
their apparent goal. She asked if anyone wanted to *eat* corn
now, and I took her up on that.

"It's feed corn," she said. "But it's still corn."

"Let's give it a shot," I said. She grabbed an ear,
wrapped it in a paper towel, turned the faucet over it, and

popped it in the microwave. A yellowish-orange pinch pot sat on top of the microwave.

"Is that one of your recent creations?" I asked Blair.

"Yeah!" He seemed genuinely excited, and popped up to snag it.

"He's quite a potter," Vicki said, and sat down next to Lacy. Blair handed me the pot and sat back down. The thing was bulbous, and bumpy as if boils pocked the exterior walls of the pot. The yellow glaze was the shade of dried piss. It was maybe the ugliest thing I've ever seen, and I thought that love could be the only reason why Vicki would actually say she liked it.

"This is horrible. It's hideous, Blair." Nobody laughed, though I wasn't trying to be savage. "You are the worst potter I've ever seen," I said.

"Oh," he said. And I immediately regretted this. "Well, I'm just a, you know, beginner, you know..."

"Whew," I said. "Now *that* was judgmental." The four of us sat in relative silence after that. When the microwave dinged, I got up myself to get the corn. The light and steam poured out into the room. Vicki and Blair stared at me like I just skewered their pet dog.

"The butter's in the refrigerator," Vicki said flatly. I got up, buttered it, and sprinkled salt and pepper on it, and returned to the table. The three of them watched me chew into the ear. Lacy's look wasn't a look. It was a glare. Vicki turned to watch her stare at me.

"What?"

"Oh nothing," Lacy said. I said the corn wasn't bad. It *was* tough, but I wasn't about to admit that. I just then noticed a box on the counter with utensils sticking out of it, and glasses in newspaper.

"What's all that stuff?" I asked.

"Just a box on the table," Vicki said. "Blair's parents gave us some old kitchen stuff." I finished my corn, and picked my teeth with my fingers. Vicki stumbled to get me a toothpick, and I felt suddenly tired. They finished their drinks. Blair asked me if I wanted to go for a walk.

"Sure," I said. "We should do something." That box made me think how temporary things felt, and I bent down to tie my shoes tighter as if that would help my defenses against whatever was coming. The ladies said they would hold down the fort.

Blair and I scuffed along the shoulder of Barbary Road. The cicadas and crickets were deafening, not a car on the road. My watch read four. The white line was cracked and blistered, and we walked for maybe half a mile without saying anything.

"Lacy's nice," he said.

"Uh-huh."

"Kind of pretty."

"Mmmm," I said. We kept walking in silence.

"Hey man," I finally said. "I'm sorry. I didn't mean to go against what you're doing, you know, with the pottery stuff."

"Yeah. It's harder to find things to do out here, and I'm trying to find something. Maybe I need to keep looking," he said.

"Don't listen to me, okay. Forget it. You're just starting off."

"Okay."

"What I don't understand though," I said, "is why everything revolves around doing something else besides what you came out here to do."

"I came out here to find out what I wanted to do."

"No, that's not it. You're married."

"Yes," he said. "That's what I wanted."

"You came out here to be with your wife, and God, because that's what her life is. Like it or not the big guy's paying your bills."

"Yeah, um, maybe it's too much, or not enough I don't—"

"I'll tell you what," I said. "It doesn't surprise me that you want to have an open marriage. Whatever you guys want. Maybe it's better that way. But what is surprising to me is that Vicki wants that, and I don't know how that happened."

"She convinced me."

"She convinced you."

"Right," he said. "I'm telling you, something here has changed her. She said before you guys came that we should seduce you and Lacy, and switch off. She wants you, man. Can't you feel the tension?"

"I don't think—"

"Yeah, she's way, way over there, and I'm just trying to keep up with her. The whole drinking thing. I mean come on."

"Man, I'm—"

"I don't know if she needs me anymore," he said, brushing his face with the back of his hand. "I don't think we really love each other." We walked over a bridge, stopping halfway. The sound of water hit us like a wave of television static. The black water under us seemed smoother than it should have been in the dark. Blair spit into it.

"Is that why you guys are doing this?" I said after a few minutes.

"I'm not sure. For her, I think that's part of the reason."

"I doubt it," I said. "I seriously doubt it."

As we walked back towards his house the sky seemed to be lightening into a paler black, and I could start to see the outlines of things. I could see the roof of the parish house as we scrambled up the driveway, and I could hear some classical waltz playing on the stereo inside. Blair kicked the stems of the weeds in his driveway. I asked him if he was going to do anything about them, and he said maybe. I was thinking Lacy and I would finally get the tour of the place they live in—I'd been there all night and I'd only seen two rooms. Maybe they weren't proud of what they had, maybe that was it.

We stepped inside, and scraped into the kitchen. In the red light vapor Lacy and Vick danced together, shifting foot to foot slowly. Vicki's hair was over Lacy's shoulders, and vice versa. They were breast to breast, feet to feet, swaying to the ump-bah-ump-bah, eyes closed. Lacy rolled her head to the side and Vicki nuzzled her mouth into the exposure. I looked up at Blair, and in the reflection of his right iris I could see the web of saliva as Vicki's mouth opened into Lacy's neck.

THE TENDER

I was down in the basement. I pour in the old milk, five quarts. Heat it 30. Add the whey. Let it stand for fifteen, coagulate the milk with the Rennet tablets, stir in. Then I'm out to read that guy Mach who thought Einstein was mostly wrong.

After two hours I go back, pour out the whey, cut the mass into two-inch cubes, go back and read some more in my room if I feel like it, then I check up on the heterozygous Saanen kid Henry doesn't know about. Then drain again, and cut again, hang the sack and let the whey drip out.

Next day I salt it, lay it in olive oil, add the thyme, rosemary, peppercorns, juniper berries, garlic and pepperoni bits, and we have Henry's chevron on order to sell six a pound to Martin's deli counter up in Eldersburg where all them yuppies are moving. Or I guess Henry does whatever he wants with it.

I'm 58. My name's Wendell. I'm what you might call a goat tender, and cheese making's part of the duty for my brother Henry. He's the damn owner.

It's that next day that she comes over, when I was down there finishing up the cheese. Sharon Barth was her name. She comes to talk to Phil, who works with me, and she finds him right up outside the closed hatch door going to the buck shed. I just listened out of view, wondering what the hell's going on.

"I just wanna come over and thank you for everything, and wish your boss well and all," she says. I don't understand what she means. My brother's never sick.

"Okay," Phil says. "That'll do."

"Where's your little friend?"

"Mara? She works with us."

"Yeah, her," the woman says.

"She's off in the doe shed. You know, she helps out too."

"She was so sweet yesterday. I don't know what was wrong with me yesterday," the woman says. "Whew, I was in a mood." It was then I completely stop what I'm doing. The woman's voice sounded so... something. I pictured her as short with muddy hair, graying a little up on the crown. A woman who's been through and through.

"Yeah, well, I've been there," Phil says. In my mind I could see myself in Phil's place, talking to this woman. I give her a big old bear hug, and we squeeze soft. Smelling skin and hair. Touching. She's inside my arms and shoulders, but I ain't that big. Razor-sharp is how most people see me. Pared-down and icy they think, with my buzz hair compact in Bauman's gel.

"What's this?" Phil says. I try not to make much noise. I can hear some ruffling outside.

"This is for your boss, and you too if you want. It's German slaw."

"My grandma was German," he says. "This have that good potato vinegar in it?" More crinkling. "Yes indeed," he says.

"You make sure he gets it for me?" I didn't know how Phil knew this woman, and I felt like I wanted to. I thought Phil was a lummox.

"Sure can, sure," Phil said.

"Make sure to tell him I hope he feels better," she says.

"Gotcha. I guess he does."

"Good, good."

Then that's it.

When I didn't hear nothing, I went out and took the half-and-half kid and walk him out to pasture. It was cool out and the air pressure was jacked down. Them stratocumulus clouds were a kind of brace for something. Me and the kid had to watch out for the swampy parts so he didn't get stuck, or eat the clover and bloat up in the rumen. These mountain animals in a swamp—all Henry's crazy idea.

But this kid was a trooper, and he bounces right along, swishing past the parts I bump him from. I pat him on the head, and feel his breath on my hand. Didn't have no name for him, but I decided he'd be the one to take out with me when I'm scouting for feed—pick some brambles for the bucks' treat. I like to pick one to help me let my mind go. Mostly I like to think about how some things tick. Ain't like my brother Henry who's got it all backwards and thinks feeling is thinking. Some people surprised we're related at all.

My brother Henry looks like a mountain man, with his big frizzed beard and glasses, and big drowsy eyes. Everything's big about him except height. I'm taller. He wears suits everyday. Real formal. Except sometimes he wears baseball hats with them to block out the glare if he's out tending with me. But usually it was Mara and that new guy

Phil who helped. Henry was too busy with his other properties usually. He owns lotsa buildings. I'm just me.

So I was wrong, the lady wasn't gone.

I come back and put the kid in the pen with the others, and when I'm out she's standing there puffier than I imagined. Craggy face with thin, friendly lips, and hair snipped short in a kind of bob nicer than what she's wearing—jeans and a yellow button-downer with beet stains on the left side. The buttons are up to the top. Her belt buckle looked like a man's, with a polished steel hawk on it in full flight. Got clay-smeared canvas sneakers on, no brand. Her ears didn't look pierced, and her neck had slack to it, and I sense her right on.

"Are you Wendell?"

"Yes ma'am," I say.

"I wanted to wish you well. My name's Sharon." She was the kind of person I like to be around, the kind that gives quicker than gets. I nodded to her. She took my hand and rattled it in hers. Meaty.

"What for?"

"I was talking to Mara and she said you might be out back here."

"I'm usually out here." I didn't see what business she had with me. She crossed her arms, and pinned her one hand under the lumps there, looking like she was amused at my take on life.

"Here's the thing. My son's got this bone disease, see." I sighed and crossed my arms.

"Sorry to hear that."

"No. And the thing is I hear goat's milk is real good for that kind of thing. I was sorta wondering if I could buy some off of you."

"Yeah," I say. "We can do that." I told her, why don't you just take some free? So I take her back to the basement, and to the coolers. Unlatch it open, get a good gallon for her. She takes out money.

"No it's on me," I say, and hand her the gallon. "On me."

"You sure about that?"

I pour her a glass from another half-full gallon and ask her to sit down on a metal foldout chair in the corner.

"What about the slaw?" I say. She looked away, around the room at things.

"I think it's good slaw," she said.

I turned on the back fluorescents, and sat down myself on the white roller chair near the cooler. We talk and drink milk out of them hard plastic cups. She tells me about the disease, which makes her son's hip disintegrate inside, and makes his bones brittle and easily broken. I forget the name of it. Her son broke his leg three times now. She said the milk should help him, if she can get him to drink it. He's seventeen and a heavy boy, but he's got his problems—itching and wheezing, vomiting, bronchitis. Number one: he's allergic to cow's milk. It's not the milk, she said, it's the immunoglobulins. The gut wall closes so the protein can't be absorbed by the bloodstream. Picked up all them details from the doctors telling her over and over. I told her the goat's milk may help, might. She says he might take it.

I tell her all about working on the farm, and knowing Henry. Somehow she had this idea that Henry was sick though and he wasn't. But I drop that, don't want to cross her or nothing. Don't want to add one more thing on top. I told her he'll be back tomorrow morning, and I give her his phone number at home for good.

"It's always nice talking to you all," she says. "I feel like nobody else experiences the same things."

"I know how that is."

"It's better to be normal," she says. "But I guess nobody's really got it all normal."

"I want to just be like most people," I said. "Not all, just most."

"Me too," she says. "Ain't everybody like that?"

"That's true," I say.

She finishes off her milk, and takes the jug I gave her, and says she's got to get back and cook for her sons and husband. It's some sort of birthday party for her man, and her sister's watching the kid roast on a spit as we speak. I walk her out to the car with her cup in my hand, and watch her back out into the road. The gravel crunkles under her tires, and the sun angle drops a shadow of her in her green Olds, moving off. I walk inside. Sharon left a skin of unfinished milk at the bottom of the cup, and a bead at the top where her lips touched.

What I should have done next was call Henry and see how he was doing, but I didn't think it out. Instead I played gin rummy with Mara, Henry's daughter who lives on the farm just like me. Mara's got this way with men that takes them by surprise. I look at the way her and Phil carry on.

She's behind the wheel—she controls and he don't even know it.

She's got this green pair of sweat pants on, and black shorts over top. White tube top, with a white T-shirt underneath. I can't help thinking about some things, and I guess only a hypocrite would deny it. We played for a good hour and a half, and Phil is in and out fixing himself dinner, not paying us no mind. Mara's drinking a beer. Phil's drinking a beer. I'm drinking tea, black. Mara goes for another beer, and a third later, and she still beats me. She snaps the cards down when she goes out, and lifts her chin just a bit, when she's tallying up the score. Real vixen. I let her win 520-450.

Then I went to my room. Mara dropped out of college, running from a boy. I forget when her birthday is. But then I feel sorry for her. I'm no humanitarian, but sometimes you can't help it.

Then I got to sleep reading some book I got from the library: *Anaximander and the Origins of Greek Cosmology.* Maybe that college experience got me interested in it.

Everyone knows about Anaximander of Miletus. Studied with that guy Thales. Wrote everything is boundless and ain't nobody knows how to translate it. Believed the universe is symmetrical, discovered astronomy. Drew a world map around 600 B.C. All those Milesians stole from the Babylonians, and they stole from the Sumerians, and them Sumerians stole from God knows who. I don't know.

But nobody knows about Anaximander's brother, Prymolindes. I think he partially invented the parthenios aulos. It's the highest pitched of them. That thing was the most important wind instrument of ancient Greece, or that's what I read in one of them books.

My brother Henry thinks he's smarter than me. But he's huff and puff, all generals, no specifics. I'm the one who's got the details down. I'm the one who works with things. Maybe Henry thinks everything is boundless too, but he's wrong. Too negative for me.

When I was asleep it rained.

"That's unacceptable, Wendell," Henry says next day. I don't say nothing.

We're in the tool shed out behind the house, looking for a trowel for one of his simple tenants. The rain slanted harder with the wind, and speared into the ground, and against the shed. We're both dank just from walking down from the house, and trying not to shiver in the dusty air back there. Try to stay bold, I think. He's in his black suit with gray pin stripes, drinking steaming water out the old green ceramic mug glued back together on the handle.

"Wendell, you just do anything you feel," he says. "You're a long way from being where you should."

I had just told him about Sharon and the gallon of milk I gave her for her troubles, and he didn't take it too well. He's rumbling through the tools. Tools and things are clattering around, and he's pulling and yanking at hoes and hedge clippers and chicken wire. I know he's going to say organizing is something I need to do. Waiting for the other shoe to drop.

"You like slaw," I say. "Did you try hers?"

"I'm sure she was very nice," he says. He was even suggesting...

"I see where you're coming from," I say. He comes up with a small shovel.

"I'm not going to feel sorry for accusing you of anything." He takes a poke through the rakes and brooms, says he knows a trowel is back there. He's pumping up a sweat. It smelled like rust and mulch in there.

"You should put this on the list too," he says. There it was.

"I don't see why—"

"It doesn't matter what you see or see through. The issues are different if you're trying to help me, which you are. I'm glad for that."

"I'd like to—"

"Plus, I'm paying you, remember. I am."

"That ain't the point, Henry. The damn—"

"I'm trying to filtrate this through Wendell, and make sense of it, because it makes no shit-assed sense to me," he said. "We don't give away what we can sell." I hate when Henry talks like this. Like I'm just some dumb teenager. It's one thing written in a physics book straight; it's something else when Henry's talking.

Then he blew it wide open by bringing up Sylvia, who I was supposed to marry but didn't. I told him not to even...He said he'd bring up whatever he felt was...I said he should pull back...So I thump him hard in the chest with both hands, stumbling right out the tool shed. Snagged my arm on a nail-hanger on the back of the door. I must of closed the door in on myself because the scratch was down near my pit.

Couple seconds later I open it back up, saying sorry didn't mean to…and he stands there bunched up in his wet suit and slurping his hot water with both hands around the bottom. I'm holding my cut arm, the rain slappety-slapping against the shed roof. He tells me he's not paying me for that day, and to go inside and dry off and stay inside for the day, goddamnit. Walks away. Fine. I don't know why he's the way he is with me. He's different with everyone else.

It's true. I came two days from being married with a family myself. Over thirty years back Sylvia was thirty-one, and I was twenty-five. She'd been married before, but her husband was killed in Korea. They had a little boy, Carl, who was eight. We met up at Forest Diner once when I was looking for a good stack of griddlecakes. Our orders got mixed up and we had to trade; well, we didn't *have* to. So we talked on about the new stores coming up on 40, farmers selling their land out. How the merchants down on Main Street were none too happy. We both sat up at the counter, and the woman behind it wore strong strawberry perfume, and had her hair pinned up with a blue and pink Disney pen running through it.

Sylvia was tall and stocky, meat on her bones. She had dark, wiry hair and small eyes close in to her nose. She was a fine woman, and I think she loved me because I'm not the kind of man to go out much, and I was ready to be hers.

But two days before the bells struck she called me, and I was excited to hear her. Told her so. But she told me she was calling from Indiana. She said she was on her way to Idaho, making a change of scenery. More space to roam. Left in the night when she said she was going out with her girlfriends. Sylvia couldn't manage things being near to what they were. Plus she thought she might be sick of Maryland weather—all the rain. A year later my father died, and Henry got the farm. I got the cars. My love life since then has been not much.

I sat in my room, and read Mach's principle. This is what it says: "An object at rest or moving at constant velocity with respect to the distant stars feels no forces acting on it. Conversely, an object accelerating with respect to the distant stars feels forces acting on it."

Then Phil and I eat what we dig up in the refrigerator while Mara's out milking the does. We found corned beef and Swiss cheese and some old potato buns that we toasted out the staleness from. We put mustard on them, and eat them sandwiches with Bosc pears and pretzels. I drank tap water in a glass.

Phil told me about his wife Greta, who lives up in Finksburg. He tells me she and him are on the skids, and he expects divorce might come from it on her end. I ask him what Greta is like. He says he loves her but knows he can't be what she wants him to really be. I listen to him sound like an oaf. He says he can't really try, and she expects too much. He told me he never wanted her to need anything from him in the first place. He drums his knuckles against his head when he says this. Somehow this makes me feel better. I think about asking Phil what he thinks about that woman Sharon, but I decide not to.

I told Phil we should finish the fence later on if the rain slows. He needs to nail together some extra plywood boxes for the kids, and make sure to mark off the kid pasture, and make sure to check on that doe with mastitis that he was tending. We also had to really pick up the pace on trimming the hooves to avoid killing their joints, I said. Phil asks why we can't let them out in the rain, and I tell him it's because they will bleat. Phil was way off from learning the basics of goat farming, but he was trying. Henry was only hurting himself, I thought.

After lunch I take a nap, and don't dream.

I wake up when Mara comes knocking on my door. She asks what happened with me and Henry, and I told her.

"Somebody's gotta be on him for something *mejor*," she says. "He's been grumpy. Don't think about it."

I ask her if she ever liked science when she was in college. She says she was more a language type. Says she never liked the hardness of the numbers.

"But it ain't hard," I say. "It's just thought hard."

"Same difference," she says.

"No it ain't either," I say. It's all right there in front of you with math. It's right there, I say. I tell her how I liked science when I went to school for a bit.

"Henry's here for you," she said. "That's what I came in to tell you. He's here."

I yawn, and tell her to do whatever she feels like. I'm just laying here. Five minutes later he's in my room trying hard but saying the same old things—responsibility, kindly discipline, soft-heartedness, and patience. It's raining hard still. I wanted to tell him he's got the ground to stand on to say them things, but I just asked him to leave instead.

When I hear Henry's shiny new VW pull out towards Route 32, I get out of bed. I put on my coat, and walk down out to the buck shed to brush down the Toggenburgs at least. I go to the stanchion and swab it with soap and water. I check on the milk refrigerator, see if it's humming as it should. I take a tub of milk to the basement, and put it in that refrigerator for the chevron four days off. Go down to the does and do the routine check—water, feed, see if any emergencies are on the way. Nope.

It was still pouring, and I felt nice just listening to sounds of water on everything, even if I wasn't getting no pay.

I take the same hermaphrodite kid, and start walking him out to pasture, rain or no rain. By the time it's a year old it would be dead, horned to death, or imploded from some sickness or another. Or Henry'd order him skinned and sold for ground, if he found out. But he wouldn't.

When we was leaving the stall the kid watched me, tail upright. I thought he's a pretty good Saanen by the looks, except for that female part. Seemed alert. I put a leash on him this time. Goats will walk in circles to eat the same certain thing so a leash is a good trainer. This no-name kid loves it anyway. We're strolling along like we've known each other a long time. He eats weeds, and pops along with me to the maple shoots and sprigs of Trees-of-heaven he loves.

I walked him about ten acres out to where Henry and I used to grow pumpkins and acorn squash before that, and I watched the kid step over the old gnarly stems. When he was bent over into a chew, I paused, and swung my leg hard as I could and cracked him under the jaw with the top of my boot. His head clapped back, neck cracked. He was fluttering in the brush and I stomped his skull into the soil, and covered him with nearby thickets and brush. Henry wouldn't even walk that far back. Poor guy.

I plod along back by the roadside perimeter with an old big band song running through my head, and I go down to the stream. I can't remember the name of the song, but it had a big trumpety sound like most of them.

I sit on a rock and watch the rain spray through the tree limbs, down into the stream water. I thought even if I had Sharon's phone number, I probably wouldn't do nothing about it. I knew that much about myself. Used to think I'd die by the age of 30, and that would be a good life. But then I was older and I knew things. At that point I wanted to sink deeper into the feelings around me, and do my best.